Fusion Core Book 1

TENSION

Edited by: ProofsbyPolly

For all content inquiries, please check out my website:

TENSION

5

For my readers,

Thank you for holding space for broken characters who still fight to find beauty in the wreckage.

PROLOGUE

Mateo

Florida heat still clings to my skin, thick with sweat, champagne, and cheap perfume.

The trophy's somewhere on the dresser, crooked and gleaming beneath the flickering hotel light. The girl I barely remember is gone now, her scent lingering in the sheets like a footnote to a night I'll forget by morning. If I make it to morning.

My hands shake as I crush another pill beneath the bottom of my glass, swirl it into the amber liquor, and down it without thinking. It burns sweet and sharp, and my veins hum instantly, welcoming the rush like an old friend.

I should be flying right now. We won. I danced like fire tonight, my steps searing into the dance floor. The crowd was on their feet. My partner couldn't stop smiling. I was the golden boy again, the charming bastard who commands the floor and owns the after-party.

I am good at this.

I am good at this.

The music from the after-party club still echoes in my head, low and pulsing like my heartbeat. I want to go back. I want another drink. Another body against mine. Another pill. The night's too alive *to stop now.*

But my legs feel weird.

I laugh as I sit alone on the edge of the hotel bed with a hand pressed to my chest. My heartbeat's too fast. Or maybe too slow. It's hard to tell. Everything is soft around the edges now, melting into a comfortable haze that I don't want to leave.

I crawl to the bathroom, dragging my body like it's someone else's, and slump against the tub. The tiles are cold. My vision tilts. My mouth tastes like metal.

And then the wave comes. That moment when the high peaks and plummets at the same time. Euphoria sharpens into panic. No, regret.

I took too much.

No, I chose too much.

I thought I could handle it, like I always do, but this time feels different. My limbs are lead, my fingers twitching uselessly against the floor, and my lungs forget how to breathe.

And still, I'm thinking about the next pill. The next time. The next night, because I don't want to stop. Not really.

But I don't want to die.

Not like this. Not on a bathroom floor in a hotel off the I-95 with no one left who actually gives a damn.

I try to move. To crawl. To scream.

Nothing happens.

The room darkens around me, slow and steady, like the closing of a curtain.

And all I can think, right before it all disappears, is that I was supposed to be someone.

Chapter One

Mateo

My breath gets trapped in my throat as I bolt upward on my bed, my body trembling and soaked with sweat. Swallowing down the phantom metal taste in my mouth, I suck in a breath and let my chest expand with the much-needed oxygen.

It's always the same nightmare, an agonizing torture I've been forced to relive nearly every night for the past year. My brush with death, and now my sentence in purgatory. Not quite dead, but not quite living either.

I'm paying for it now, giving up a piece of my soul every day as penance for what I had let myself become, how far I succumbed to the call of the forbidden. I've always been attracted to things I shouldn't have, things that aren't good for me, but my lesson has been learned and I'm trying to get back what I took for granted.

After spending six months in New York, studying Business Economics at NYU like I was told to do, I finally broke and searched for dance studios in my area. My career has deviated from competing on a dance floor to one day spearheading our family's large photography company, and just thinking of it threatens to send me into a spiral. My parents forbade me to ever dance again, with reason, but I haven't gone a single day in the last year without thinking about it. *Longing for it.*

I've held off this long for them, wanting their approval and trust, but most of all, their forgiveness.

From the age of four, I've been wearing custom shoes and hand-stitched shirts and vests, all while gliding along a polished hardwood floor for a table of judges. It's not just in my blood, it's seared into my soul. How do you let something go after nearly nineteen years? The short answer is: You don't.

Pushing the blankets off my damp body, I get out of bed and head for the railing of my second-level bedroom. My loft is an open concept with no interior walls, the twenty-foot height split by a raised sleeping area accessed by a set of metal stairs. My hands grasp the cool railing as I stare straight ahead at the window, showcasing the first snowfall since I've been here.

New York is vastly different from Los Angeles this time of the year, and as far away as I could be from my family without leaving the country. My father, Emilio Sanchez, will never forgive me for what I did, and I'll forever be the son who found solace in pills and cocaine. So much so I nearly died for them. No matter how much I've changed, that's how he'll judge me, even though my longing for them died the moment I was robbed of my future because of them.

Stretching my arms over my head and shaking out my hands, I try to chase away the lingering effects of my nightmare as my body aches with pains I'll never fully be rid of. They remind me every day of the life I let slip away, of the release I so desperately need back. I hiss out a breath as my feet hit the cold metal of the stairs and make my way down toward the only room in this place with a door. My bathroom.

I despised this apartment at first. The industrial feel of

it and the lack of interior walls made me feel so inconsequential in the large space, but now, after months of solidarity inside of its walls, I love it. The two parallel walls are red brick, giving the place a rustic vibe, leading to the single window on the adjacent wall, one large enough to fill the entire space with sunlight or starlight. Floor-to-ceiling panes reveal a New York landscape, and being on the top floor, I get a beautiful view of the skyline and not the buildings beside mine. My father may hate me for what I've done, but my mother will always have a tender spot in her heart for me. When he demanded I be sent across the country, away from my friends and the life I worked so hard for, my mother made sure I had a beautiful place to live in. She may not have had a say about my punishment, but she eased the sting of it by picking this apartment.

At first, being away from home and my family was agony. I've never lived on my own, nor have I been alone with my own thoughts for long, extended periods of time. I was too used to filling those spaces with the noise of parties or the blissful silence of drugs. Now, I've come to like sitting in silence and self-reflection.

Leaning over the large vanity counter, I turn on the facet and splash my heated face with cold water. Looking up, I watch in the mirror as each drop of water drips from my jaw, the beads taking the remnants of my nightmare with them. My forced exhale clouds the mirror, but my light brown eyes shine through with a sadness I could never mask. I fear I'll always feel like my soul is cleaved in half, the other piece floating somewhere in Florida. The place where I swallowed my last fatal pill at the American Dancesport Festival.

Brushing back my unruly black hair, I grab the towel hanging from the bar and dry off my face. My skin has grown too ashen, my body too lean, and my face gaunt. All because I've been shut away from the world, left without a purpose, as my fractured soul drifts through each day, waiting for death to provide a reprieve.

I throw the towel onto the counter with a sigh, my morbid thoughts doing nothing for the depression that's encompassed me. Even though I've brought shame on the Sanchez family, my mother insists I go to meetings weekly, but I can't take any prescribed medicine to chase away the clouds hanging over my head. Liliana Sanchez, my mother and internationally acclaimed prima ballerina, says I have to learn to heal myself to prove I no longer want a chemical high. I'm struggling to make it through the day, but I agree with her. I've proven to be weak when it comes to drugs, especially those obtained through a prescription. All it took was one small back injury, providing a prescription to my addiction.

My bare feet pad along the heated floor of my loft as I head toward the kitchen, needing a drink to soothe my parched throat. The light from inside the stainless steel fridge makes me squint as I reach in and grab a bottle of water, the cool plastic like a balm over my palm. I unscrew the cap and turn to face the window, tipping the bottle back and drinking half of it in one go.

The snow falls harder, blocking out the light of the moon and creating shadows along my light hardwood floors. Placing the bottle on the dark granite countertop, I make my way to the tan leather couch. Curling up on the cold cushions, I grab the red fleece throw blanket from the back and drape it over my body. There's no way I'll fall back asleep tonight, and even though I'll pay for it in the morning, I don't bother to head back to bed. I'll only toss and turn until the sun rises and my day begins. It'll be an even longer day because I have a Narcotics Anonymous meeting after school as well.

I'm trying to follow all the rules, trying my best to prove that my recovery will stick, but it's gotten me nowhere. My parents are still adamant I don't dance, still strict about knowing my daily routines, and even though they're on the other side of the country, I'm watched like a hawk. I have a driver to take me from home to school, to meetings, to appointments, then straight back home. I have a cleaning lady who comes into my loft twice a week, not to just clean, but to search through every drawer and cabinet, reporting back to my father. Even the doorman downstairs calls him a few times a week to tell him how I'm looking and acting.

I miss dancing, I miss the feel of my feet as they kiss the ballroom floor, and I miss the sweat of pushing my body to painful limits. Despite it being a year since I've danced, I can still close my eyes and imagine the steps for the Foxtrot, Jive, and Viennese Waltz. My hips also remember the sway of the Rumba, Samba, and Cha-cha.

My earlier search for dance studios near me yielded two, but only one has former world champions as owners. Greyson Ford is an exceptional dancer in his own right, but Vaeda Lewis was well-known during my time competing in the Youth and Under 21 divisions. She and her dance partner, Gerardo Martinez, were like royalty in the circuit. As soon as I saw her name, my stomach flipped and my hands grew damp. This was the one, the studio I needed to join. *Fusion Core Dance Studio*. Just the name sends a shiver down my spine, a feeling of fate coming over me. I want so badly to dance, and if I can be instructed by some of the best, I know I could make a comeback.

My hands shook as I filled out the form online, my heart pounding out a rhythm of fear. If my parents found out I applied to join an advanced dancing class with the potential to compete again, they would drag me back home and lock me in a room for the rest of my life.

Now, I would just have to figure out a way around my family.

Slipping into the back of the Range Rover, my eyes meet Roger's in the rearview mirror. "Hello, Roger," I murmur as I put on my seat belt.

"Good morning, Mateo," he replies, his eyes still scanning my face. "Everything okay?" He no doubt sees the exhaustion in my features, the bags cushioning my eyes, and the change in my body from when I first came here to now.

"Yes," I reply, keeping my answer short. I like Roger; he's a good man who cares about me like a second father, but his loyalty will always be to my parents.

"I can bring you Theresa's chicken soup if you're not feeling well." His hazel eyes focus back on the road as he pulls away from the curb, the traffic already bumper-to-bumper at 7:30 in the morning. His wife, Theresa, is a chef here in New York and owns a restaurant. Her food is to die for.

"I'm not sick, but if you're offering Theresa's food, I won't say no." I grin at him as he laughs, the sound reverberating inside the SUV.

"She and Sara have been asking for you. You should come over for dinner sometime soon." I bow my head at his suggestion, my chest tightening. It's not that I don't enjoy his family's company, I just don't have it in me to be social. Sara is just turning nineteen, and even though we are only four years apart in age, I feel so much older than her. There's no other explanation, I'm dead inside. It's the reason why I found relief at the bottom of a pill bottle; it made me *feel* something.

There was a time when dance wasn't enough, when winning trophies and thousands of dollars held no appeal, and when the chemical high gave me the euphoric chase, I was hunting. I'm an addict, it's clear I always have been, and it's not for drugs. It's for the adrenaline and excitement in pretty much anything. Once dancing became routine and my days mindless, I sought out more.

There will always be a risk, a constant threat, that I will succumb again, but I fight it with every fiber of my being. Like these past few months as each day grows more and more bleak. I've been filling my time with more NA meetings and school, but nothing will ever beat the rush of dancing.

Silence falls over the vehicle as I rest my forehead against the window, the flurries lightly descending from the sky as the snow tapers off, leaving behind a thin layer that'll melt away by this afternoon.

"I miss dancing," I confess when the silence becomes deafening. "I don't know what to do with myself." I surprise myself with the admission, but I realize I need to say it out loud.

His exhale sounds around me as he stops at a red light. "Your parents are worried about you and dancing, Mateo. I can't even imagine what they went through when they found out what happened. If Sara had been through the same…" he trails off and clears his throat. "Find yourself another passion. Put that energy into your schooling."

"I'm majoring in Economics, Roger," I huff and lift my head from the window to meet his eyes in the rearview mirror. "No amount of passion will make it interesting."

"I'm sorry, Mateo." He needn't apologize, none of this is his fault, and there's nothing he could do to change the situation.

Fifteen minutes later, he pulls up to NYU and turns in the seat to watch me grab my bag and remove my seat belt. "Thank you, Roger." I try to give him a sincere smile, but from the look on his face, I don't think I succeeded.

"I'll be back here at three and we'll head to your meeting." Shrugging my bag over my shoulder, I get out of the SUV and head toward the main building, my bag lighter today than most days.

Once I'm inside the doors, I turn to watch as Roger pulls away from the parking lot, then turns back out into traffic. Open auditions for the advanced Latin and Ballroom classes at Fusion Core are at 10am, giving me two hours to get back over near my apartment in time to make it. I hate deceiving him, especially knowing he'll get hell too if I'm caught, but it's a risk I'm willing—no, needing to take.

Thankfully Roger didn't notice my thin sweatpants and less-filled backpack. I only packed my dance shoes and a few water bottles, knowing I'd be walking back most of the way until the traffic clears up enough to hop on the transit.

The icy breeze stings my face as I walk back outside, dragging my scarf across my mouth and zipping up my jacket. Everything will be worth it if I get picked for this class. Then, when I cross that bridge, I'll figure out how to attend them.

Chapter Two

Mateo

The studio is located two blocks from my apartment, the building nearly identical to the one I live in. With thirty minutes to spare and ice blocks for feet, I rush inside and sit on the stairs to change my shoes. Anxiety has kept me from planning a routine, so I decided to rely on my muscle memory for today instead.

It's a risk, but these are classes, not a competition.

Fusion Core is on the main floor, and I follow the signs until I find a corridor with three girls and one guy standing against the wall, a nervous energy stifling the narrow space. These classes aren't like most. If you apply for the advanced classes, you have to audition and they only have a limited number of spots open.

Four spots are what they're offering, and as I look around, I feel confident I'll snag one. I'm an exceptional dancer, there's no point in being modest, and I have an impressive résumé—as long as I leave out the part where I became addicted to Oxy and cocaine.

"Hi," the girl standing closest to me says as she holds out her hand. "My name is Yvonne."

My heart pounds as I slip my hand into hers, knowing she must feel how clammy it is. "Mateo," I mumble, hoping she doesn't recognize the name.

By no means do I think I'm famous, that's not what's worrying me. It's not knowing if she was in my age-class and perhaps competed in the same circuit as I did at one time, having insider information about the destructive aftermath of my spiral. Not that I would remember her name, having been high out of my mind most of the time. I barely remembered my own.

"I love that name," she husks out as relief coats over me.

"Thank you," I say a little louder, my secret still hidden.

"What dance are you doing?" She leans against the wall beside me as the others turn to listen in on our conversation.

"Not sure." I bite my lip as my eyes flick over the others before returning to her. "You?"

"Samba." She nods, a small smile working around her mouth. "It's my strongest dance."

"Samba is beautiful," I reply as the door opens and an older gentleman stands in front of us. Greyson Ford.

"Welcome to Fusion. We have four spots to fill today and that's all. Choose your dance wisely and have your song choice ready. There will also be a short interview with me and the co-owner, and the dance will be performed after that. Are you guys ready?" His gray hair is coiffed back over his head and his blue eyes twinkle with excitement as he looks at each of us. "My name is Greyson."

We all murmur our hellos, and I pray I'm only imagining things when his eyes land on me and stay there a fraction longer than the others. It's nerves. It's been a year since I've had these shoes on my feet, and even though I want this desperately, I'm hoping to remain under the radar for as long as I can. My family would not take the news calmly, and convincing them I'm fine wouldn't be enough.

We file inside the studio as I take a deep breath. The wooden floors shine to perfection, and three of the four walls are covered with mirrors, while the fourth has the door we came in through and another beside it. The anxiety coursing through me has me second-guessing this for about ten seconds. What if they know about my situation? My overdose and exit from the competitive circuit were never made public, but rumors did circulate.

Greyson asks us to line up against the wall as he motions for the only other guy to follow him through another door for his interview.

"I'm so nervous." I turn toward the voice as two girls stand together, both with their arms crossed over their chests. They turn to look at me, giving me tentative smiles. "I'm Kari." The first holds out her hand, her light blonde hair gathered into a bun on top of her head. "And this is Fran." She motions to a tall, willowy girl, her black hair in a French braid and her face filled with anxiety.

"Vaeda Lewis is the best dancer in the circuit," Yvonne cuts in as she leans over to speak to them from my other side. "She'll be a hard one to impress."

"She's the reason why I'm here," Kari says, her teeth chewing into her bottom lip. "I need this class."

I try to zone them out as I begin a routine in my head. Coming here unprepared may be my downfall, but I won't go out without a fight. When an idea hits me, my heart speeds up as a smile curves along my lips. It'll be a risk, but everything about me being here is risky. Just as I'm thinking through the playlist on my phone and the perfect song to use, the door opens and the guy steps out. His skin is a few shades paler than when he went in and his brown eyes are filled with fear.

"Kari George. You're next," Greyson calls out.

Kari heads toward Greyson as my eyes follow the guy who takes her place beside me.

"Well?" Yvonne breaks the silence, blowing a tendril of light brown hair out of her face. "How was it?"

"I almost threw up," he confesses as he blows out a breath. "Lewis is intense." My heart sinks into my stomach as I contemplate leaving.

"I'm Yvonne." She reaches around me to hold out her hand. "How long have you been dancing?"

"Adam." He takes her hand for a limp shake, then drops it. "Ten years next week," he murmurs. "Vaeda made it sound like it was nothing, especially when I've never competed."

Shit.

They're going to ask me about competing. I shake out my hands as I try to calm my insides, and for the first time in a long time, I crave something to take off the edge, to numb my heightened anxiety. My heart pounds with the revelation as I shake out my hands once more and breathe. I want this so much that I'm willing to overlook my bout of weakness.

The door opens again just as I'm finishing counting down from ten, and Kari walks out, looking a little down, but nothing compared to Adam.

"Yvonne Cardenas,"—Greyson snaps his fingers—"you're next."

Yvonne gives me a wink as she passes, her confidence shining while the rest of us struggle to keep our feet on the floor.

"Are you okay?" Fran asks as Kari falls against the wall beside her. "How bad was it?"

"Not bad, but they were asking me what studios I

danced in before and if this was something I was serious about. They felt my dancing experience was lacking and told me I'd have to prove them wrong with my performance." She shakes her head, her bun moving precariously. That's her first mistake, not having her hair secured. It makes her look unprofessional, and it'll be a problem when she dances.

I run my hand over my gelled-back hair, my fingers moving until they stop at the nape of my neck. This is how I wear my hair most days, something I've kept up since my dancing days. I hate having my hair loose around my face unless I'm at home.

"Vaeda has a way with words, making you feel so small," Adam growls, his short, curly hair moving as he turns to look at Kari. "I wouldn't want an instructor like that."

"Most are like that," I say quietly as they turn their heads toward me. "In a class meant to mold competitors, they also aim to toughen your skin. A good instructor will guide and teach you each dance, but a great instructor will tear apart everything you thought you were good at, only to rebuild you into something indestructible."

"Have you competed?" Fran asks as the door opens again, saving me from answering.

Yvonne emerges with her mouth in a grim line and the sparkle that was in her light brown eyes before is noticeably missing. "She's a bitch," she snaps as she retakes her spot beside me.

"Franchesca Taylor," Greyson calls out. "Let's go."

I'm last. An ominous feeling comes over me as the others begin to trash-talk Vaeda Lewis. It feels like I was purposely saved for the end, and it does nothing to calm my beating heart.

"Mateo!" Yvonne's hiss draws me out of my thoughts as I turn to look at her, her chin jutting toward Greyson standing in the open doorway. His eyebrow is raised as I start forward, my feet on autopilot as my stomach sours with unease.

Greyson motions for me to go ahead of him, my shoes clicking against the polished floors, sending echoes around our heads. I'd pay more attention to how heavy my steps are if my pounding heart wasn't overpowering the sounds instead. This is my last chance to turn on my heel and escape, to continue studying business and leave dancing in my past, but my will is stronger than any fear I possess.

A table appears in front of me, two chairs positioned beside each other and facing where I entered. Greyson quickly sits in the vacant seat, but my eyes are on the woman sitting in the other. Her posture is perfect, her porcelain skin shimmering, and not an auburn strand of hair out of place. Vaeda Lewis looks regal as her chin lifts a fraction higher, giving her an air of arrogance as she somehow makes me feel looked down on, even though she's seated and I'm standing. Suddenly, I feel so small, my towering 6'3" stature doing nothing to ease the discomfort.

"Mateo Sanchez," she reads from a page on the table in front of her, her full lips barely moving as the husky lilt of her voice invades every one of my senses. I don't just hear her, I feel every syllable as the sounds course through me. "Could this be the same Mateo Sanchez who competed in the World Championship division?"

And there it is, my worst nightmare coming to life. I nearly laugh out loud at the naivety of my coming here, at my thinking I could escape the past. How can you run from the past when it's chasing your future?

"The same," I murmur as I stand a little straighter. There's no sense letting the shame I live with each day seep from every pore. I'm here to start over, and even though I've hit rock bottom, I have the claws to drag myself back out.

"What brings you here to New York and our humble

studio?" Greyson cuts in as Vaeda gives him a scolding look, her dark brown eyes shooting arcs of electricity his way.

"You have a beautiful studio," I begin as Greyson nods and Vaeda rolls her eyes from him and back to me, her stern expression making me swallow down any other compliments. "I'm hoping to start over and once again fall in love with dancing."

The room becomes quiet as Greyson shifts in his seat and Vaeda continues to stare at me, her eyes narrowing before she says, "A redemption, Mr. Sanchez. That's what you're looking for, and you want our studio to provide it." She gives me a cruel smile, the motion barely meeting her cold eyes as she watches me with a calculating stare.

"I mean no disrespect when I say your studio can't save me from what I've done, only I can do that, but yes, this is a step in saving myself, Ms. Lewis."

Her jaw tenses with my proclamation as Greyson dips his head, a ghost of a smile coating his lips. "Correct me if I'm wrong, but your final competition was in Florida over a year ago. September 15th was the date of the American Dancesport Festival, the international qualifying competition, right, Grey?" She turns to Greyson as he schools his features and nods, his eyes still focused on me. "That was the last anyone had heard about the young prodigy, Mateo Sanchez." She spits out my name as though it's sitting poison on her tongue. "Nearly thirteen months ago," she clarifies as I remain silent, my stomach tightening as acid works its way up my throat. "What happened?"

"I needed a break," I explain as I skate around the truth. "My mind and my body were suffering, and I was an empty shell who forgot my purpose."

A sarcastic scoff echoes around the room as Vaeda's frozen face finally crumbles into a sneer, the expression not subtracting from the stunning beauty of each feature. "There were rumors of drugs, sex, and complete debauchery." Her palms flatten to the tabletop as Greyson turns to watch her, his eyes widening at her disdain. "Inappropriate relations with other competitors, rumors of illicit behavior amongst coaches, and all-nighters spent in the seediest nightclubs of the city."

Some of the things she's stating were just rumors. I didn't have any affairs with coaches that I could remember, and inappropriate relations are something that happens all the time in our world. She should know, it's how she met her husband. I bow my head, taking each accusation like a blow to my soul and letting them find their mark as it withers even more. "Rumors are out of my control." I lift my head to find her frigid stare once more. "But I can appreciate your need to protect the reputation of your studio. I apologize if my presence today has tarnished it in any way. Forgive me for coming."

With my hand to my chest, I let my sincerity shine from my eyes before turning around and walking steadily toward the door I came in from. As soon as my hand meets the cold metal of the door handle, I hear Greyson's voice as he whispers Vaeda's name harshly. I open the door without a backward glance and step back into the studio, closing it behind me softly. It was worth the chance, but it's clear not enough time has passed for forgiveness.

With a nod to the others, I leave the studio and head back down the hallway toward the building's entrance. Time is a fickle thing, and even though time will erase my actions, it will also steal from me the future I long for.

Just as I'm stepping out onto the cold streets, the sound of my name being called gives me pause. I turn to find Greyson jogging toward me, his silk dress pants flowing with each hurried step. "Don't walk away," he pants as he stops in front of me. "You are a talented dancer, one many still speak of, and you can redeem yourself."

"Thank you," I mutter as a cold breeze brushes by

my face, making me grit my teeth against the onslaught. "I appreciate you giving me a chance."

"I'm not just giving you a chance, Mateo." He smiles, his eyes shining with mischief. "I'm giving you a spot."

"What?" I let go of the door as his hand presses to the glass, preventing it from closing fully.

"Classes start in two days. Be here at six o'clock in the evening."

"But Vaeda—"

"She is not the sole owner of this studio," he states as he stands a little straighter. "We each were to choose two people, and you are one of my choices. Don't make me regret it." He finally steps back as I watch the door shut, the glass pane reflecting my shock back at me. It's a few minutes later when the frost on my cheeks snaps me out of my trance.

I didn't even dance.

Chapter Three

Vaeda

"You're a goddamn fool, Greyson," I snap as I close the studio doors for the night. "We're trying to keep this place open, not invite more scandal."

"You can't deny the talent that man has," he retorts as I roll my eyes and stride back into the studio. "We could put ourselves on the map with him."

"Or he could burn it all to the ground with no one else to blame but ourselves!" I bellow as I turn on him, making him stumble back a few steps. "He's a drug addict, hedonist, and there's no amount of money his family can pay to make any of it disappear! We might as well douse this place in gasoline and light the match now."

"Everyone deserves a second chance, Vae." Greyson walks around me through the interview room, opening the door to our joint office. I follow behind him, my heels hitting the hardwood floor with purpose. "He looked clean and repentant."

I scoff loudly as he sits at his desk, his arms crossing over his chest as he awaits my barrage of complaints. He doesn't understand how much of my legacy is tied to this building. The blood, sweat, and tears I've endured over my career, only to have it end in an inferno of flames because he wants to play God and hand out forgiveness. "Please rescind his invitation."

"What if you could have one more dance? One more competition? Would you grasp it with both hands, or would you turn your back?" He leans forward, his face eager for my response.

My heart slams up into my throat as instant longing coats my insides. I would give anything to be on a competitive dance floor again. "I didn't squander my future, Grey, I was robbed of it." I turn from him and fall into my chair, the motion lacking my usual grace. Achilles tendonitis cut my career short, and even though I can still dance, I'm limited to a studio instead of the rigorous training for competitions.

"We've all made choices without considering the consequences, especially as young adults. I believe he deserves a second chance, and think about how our studio would soar. The buzz would be journalists' ambrosia, and we will once again be on the map." The energy of his excitement hits me square in the chest, but the moment it comes in contact with me, it fizzles and dies.

Greyson Ford III was a world champion on the dance floor many times over. His old-money name did him no favors when his family disowned him for his sexual orientation. He didn't wallow for a second. Instead, he took a suitcase of his belongings and left his castle in England to become a worldwide known dancer, throwing his success in his family's faces. Greyson is the epitome of turning lemons into lemonade.

"You've picked him and Yvonne, and although she was a remarkable dancer, you have no idea if they will even be compatible." It's the last complaint I have, hoping his rigid need for perfection on the dance floor will shine through.

"If they are not, I will replace her." His flippant response has me straightening in my chair as I stare at him, my anger rising once again.

"You would kick an aspiring dancer with impeccable technique out of the program for a junkie?" I snarl, my words punctuated with my ire.

"Former junkie, Vae," he corrects me as he turns in his chair to look me in the eyes. "It's astonishing you're admitting to her impeccable technique when all you did was criticize her for the entire interview and dance number."

"Yeah, well, you know we were taught to never believe we are the best." I wave him off as he chuckles, the sound bringing a smirk to my mouth. "We've worked so hard for this place, and I'd hate to see that kid ruin it completely."

"He's a man, Vae." He gets a twinkle in his eyes as I roll mine. "An attractive one at that."

"You never could resist a pretty face," I grumble as he gets up out of his chair to come toward me, his arms reaching out to pull me into his chest.

"I promise not to let him fuck this up. His face will give us the notoriety this place needs to bring in the money. Vae, we need the money," he stresses as I shove him off me and brush his lingering scent off my blouse. "Think of what it could mean for us to enter the competitive circuit again."

"Trust me, Greyson III, I know how much we need the money." I feel myself give in as I rest my chin on my hand. "He's your responsibility, and whatever happens, you will be the one at risk."

Despite my groan, he gathers me in for another hug, his squeal of excitement skating along every nerve. Mateo Sanchez better be reformed, or else I'll fucking ruin him for good this time.

"Gerardo!" I call out as I step into our penthouse, dropping the keys into the dish by the door. "I'm home!"

Following the sounds of music, I enter through the kitchen to find him swaying at the stove while he stirs a spoon in a large pot. My heart clenches as he raises his other hand, flicking it out in a perfect flamenco motion.

When my career ended abruptly six years ago, at the age of twenty-seven, so did Gerardo's, but he's never held that against me. He made the decision to quit, and a year later, we were married in a lavish wedding in Barcelona.

We were always best friends, from the age of fifteen, but we only became lovers after my injury. Sometimes I wonder if he married me because he felt pity, or if he truly did have romantic feelings for me the entire time.

"Amor," I singsong as his hips do one final swirl before he turns at the sound of my voice, his luscious mouth curving upward. "It smells divine in here."

"I'm making soup," he says as he drops his hand and sets the spoon on the counter. "You weren't well this morning, and I wanted to make you something warm."

Gerardo makes me feel like I am the most important thing in his world, and I know I hit the jackpot the day we became dancing partners. He's always been by my side, ready to support me in everything I endeavor, but it isn't passion that binds us, it's understanding. Gerardo knows me better than anyone else ever has, and we've built a life on that foundation. One of trust and unwavering loyalty. As I sit on a barstool, watching him stir the pot with his characteristic flair, I'm reminded of how lucky I am to have someone who accepts me as I am.

"How was the studio?" he asks, sliding a steaming bowl of soup across the counter toward me. His tone is light, but the subtle crease in his brows tells me he's worried.

"Greyson is taking risks again," I admit, picking up my spoon and letting the rich aroma fill my senses. "He invited Mateo Sanchez to join the program."

Gerardo's movements pause for a fraction of a second before he recovers, grabbing the ladle to serve himself. "*The* Mateo Sanchez? The one with the uh... colorful history?"

"The very same." I sigh, swirling my spoon in the broth. "Grey thinks he can turn him into our studio's saving grace."

"And you don't?"

"It's not that simple." I meet Gerardo's soothing, rich-brown gaze. "I can't afford to let my guard down and accept a *former* junkie, not with everything we've worked for hanging by a thread." The studio is struggling, and we've failed to recruit champion-material dancers to put us back on the map.

He leans on the counter, his expression soft. "Vaeda, you've always had an eye for potential. If you didn't see something in him, you'd have fought harder to keep him out." He's hit the mark.

When Greyson chased Mateo down to offer him a spot, I could've followed, fought it, but I didn't. I remember Mateo Sanchez, and I can never deny his talent. It was a shock to see him standing here in New York, in our studio, searching for his comeback story, and as much as I hated that he was using us to do it, we were also using him for ours.

I smile faintly, appreciating Gerardo's faith in me even when I'm not sure I deserve it. "Maybe, or maybe I'm just too tired to fight Greyson when he gets this determined." There's been some tension between Grey and me lately, and it boils down to the monthly rent, electricity, and expenses piling up. It's the lack of interest in ballroom dancing these days, as kids would rather learn thirty-second-long TikTok dances instead, which means we're becoming obsolete.

"Either way," Gerardo says, lifting his bowl and gesturing for me to join him at the small table by the window. "You'll make it work. You always do."

I follow him to the table, the bowl of soup warming my hands as I release the stress I'm feeling with a sigh. Sitting across from him, I feel a rare moment of peace settle over me. Gerardo has a way of settling the fire inside of me, of dousing my flames in cooling water and bringing me back from the edge of a complete meltdown.

"There's something clawing inside my stomach,"—I grip the silk material of my blouse in my fist—"and it's hard to ignore." I release my blouse and pick up the spoon, bringing the soup up to my mouth and taking a long inhale. I've always followed my intuition, and even though I know Mateo could catapult us back into the scene, I have a feeling the decision to keep him will change the trajectory of my life.

"Taking a chance on anyone is a risk, and unfortunately, Mateo Sanchez is a larger risk than most. That's why you're feeling this. I'm sure Greyson has considered all the threats, and if he's still confident, I say give it a go. Mateo did have a stunning future ahead of him at one time." He shrugs and slurps his soup, a habit that's always bothered me, but I've chosen to ignore it.

"He ruined that future for himself," I retort and drop the spoon back into the bowl with a *clang*. "How do I know he won't do it again? And with my name connected to it?"

"You don't, *amor*." Gerardo shakes his head and gives me a sympathetic sigh. Or maybe it's pity. "But imagine if he brings you glory… with your name connected to it?"

MATEO

The fluorescent lights overhead buzz faintly as I sit in the cold plastic chair, my hands folded tightly in my lap. The room smells of stale coffee and disinfectant, and everyone looks overburdened with guilt for mistakes they made that can never be erased. My Narcotics Anonymous meeting begins as it always does. Marissa, our leader, a middle-aged woman with kind eyes and a soft voice, calls for introductions.

"Welcome, everyone," Marissa says, her smile reassuring as everyone sits down. Her presence is like a steady pendulum, grounding us when all we want to do is disappear. "Let's go around and share something about how the week has gone. Mateo, would you like to start?"

I stiffen under her gaze, heat creeping up my neck as all eyes turn to me. My mouth feels dry, and my pulse quickens. After a moment, I manage a tight nod. "Hi, I'm Mateo, and I'm an addict."

The chorus of "Hi, Mateo" follows, the sounds both comforting and intimidating. I glance down at my hands as my fingers fidget with the hem of my sleeve.

"This week was… challenging," I admit, my admission lifting a weight off my chest. Holding in fears, doubts, and guilt only feeds the poison gripping your soul. "I'm trying to rebuild something I lost when I overdosed last year. I was a ballroom dancer and competed internationally when it happened. My future was bright, but I celebrated my many wins with drugs, and now I'm here. It's been hard because every step feels like a reminder of how I almost threw it all away."

Marissa nods encouragingly. "But you're taking those steps, Mateo. That's what matters."

Her words feel hollow, but I nod anyway, the pressure in my chest easing slightly as the attention shifts to the next person. I listen as others share their struggles and victories from the past week. A missed temptation here, a celebrated milestone there. Their words wash over me, some striking chords of empathy, others fading into the background noise of my own thoughts.

As the meeting continues, I focus on the stories of finding strength after faltering. There's a rawness in the honesty shared here that I both respect and fear. One man, whose name we learn is Dan, speaks about relapsing after three years of being clean. His voice cracks as he admits to feeling like he's back at square one. I catch myself clenching my fists, the fear of falling into the same trap making my stomach churn.

When the meeting ends, my muscles are tense, my jaw aching from being clenched for so long. I stand from my chair and nod to a few others who are sticking around to talk a little more. As much as these meetings help me, I never stay beyond the hour I'm required. It's as though the stories told inside these walls still hover over us, their whispers a constant reminder of our failures. So I head for the exit and thank Marissa on my way out, her hand brushing mine in a gesture of support.

The cold winter air outside bites at my face, a welcome contrast to the stifling warmth of the meeting room, and I wrap my jacket a little tighter around me. Winter in New York is such a drastic change from the California weather I'm used to, and instead of making me homesick, it feels like a cleansing restart.

I find Roger waiting by the curb, his hulking frame leaning against his black Range Rover. He's been a great companion since I've arrived, and knowing he's an old family friend of my father's makes me feel less alone. Before me, Roger worked security detail for events and high-profile people. Then my father filled him in on the failures of his only son and begged him to take this job after he exiled me.

He straightens when he sees me, pulling open the

door with a practiced motion. "That was a good crowd this afternoon," he remarks as I climb into the back seat. "How was the meeting?"

"Fine," I reply curtly, pulling the seat belt across my chest. The word feels inadequate, but I don't have the energy to elaborate. Roger nods as he closes the door. He never forces me to divulge everything, and his patience is appreciated, even though I know my father grills him for information every day.

I relax into the seat as the city lights cast fleeting shadows across the interior of the SUV, then press my forehead against the cool glass of the window, my breath fogging up the surface as we weave through traffic. My mind drifts to the studio and its polished floors, the mirrored walls, and the echo of my shoes against the wood. I can't stop thinking about it.

"You know," Roger drawls after a stretch of silence, his voice tentative. "You're braver than you think, Mateo. A lot of people wouldn't have the guts to face each day after what you've been through."

I glance at him through the rearview mirror, caught off guard by his words. "Thanks, Roger," I murmur, unsure of how to respond. It's the first time he's ever said anything about my overdose, and for a moment, it chips away at the wall I've built between us.

When we pull up in front of my building, Roger turns to look at me. "Get some rest tonight, Mateo. You look like you need it."

I force a small smile. "Thanks, Roger. Good night."

The elevator ride to my loft feels endless, the buzz of the machinery matching the thrum of anxiety in my veins. By the time I step inside, the quiet of my apartment reminds me that I am utterly alone. My parents are across the country and still trying to work through my betrayal, and my sister is on another continent, keeping her promise of never speaking to me again. It hurts to even think of her, so I work hard not to. I toss my bag onto the couch and head straight to the closet where I keep my dance shoes.

Sliding my feet into the familiar leather, I feel a jolt of electricity rush through me. The cloud of despair begins to lift as I step onto the hardwood floor of my large living room, the space giving me a reprieve from my loneliness.

I start a song on my phone, the rhythmic beats of a Cha-Cha filling the loft. My muscles remember the steps before my mind can catch up, my body moving with the beat. The sway of my hips, the snap of my arms, the seductive power in every movement. It's the greatest high, and I wonder why I ever searched for more.

The large, ornate mirror I bought when I moved in is propped against the wall, reflecting my form, and for a moment, I see a glimpse of the dancer I used to be. The one who could captivate a room with just a glance, who could command the floor like it was an extension of his body, but the illusion is fleeting, replaced by the gaunt shadow of the man I've become.

I push harder, sweat beading on my forehead as I lose myself in the rhythm. The music shifts to a Viennese Waltz, and I transition seamlessly, my movements softer now, more fluid. The elegance of the dance wars with the turmoil inside me, but it's a solace I desperately need.

As the song fades, I pause, catching my breath. The silence in the room feels welcoming now, wrapping around me like a heavy blanket. I walk to the window, the city lights below twinkling like a distant beacon. It's always there, deep inside me, the need to find an easy high. Leaning my forehead against the glass, I close my eyes and let the memories wash over me. The competitions, the crowds, the overwhelming rush of adrenaline as I performed... They all feel like a lifetime ago.

Before I can dwell too long in the past, I push off

of the window and head into the kitchen, grabbing a towel to wipe the sweat from my face. I'm not ready to stop, not yet. The next song on the playlist is a Samba, its lively rhythm jolting me back to the present. I slip back into position, my feet gliding effortlessly across the floor as I chase the transient feeling of freedom.

Time blurs as I dance, each song pulling me deeper into the movements, into the person I used to be. It's only when my legs give out and I collapse onto the couch that I realize how late it is. My chest rises and falls in heavy bursts, my body spent but my mind clearer than it's been in a long time.

Staring up at the ceiling, I think about the studio, about what Greyson and Vaeda must see when they look at me. A project? A risk? Either way, I'm hoping to prove that I'm a dancer worth believing in.

For now, I'll settle for surviving the night. I'll lace up my shoes again tomorrow and take one more step forward. Even if I don't believe in myself yet, I can't bear the thought of proving everyone else right by giving up.

Chapter Four

Vaeda

The morning sunlight streams through the large windows of the studio, throwing long streaks of light across the polished floor. I move through my stretches in front of the mirrored wall, my reflection a farce. The image is similar to the dancer I used to be, but it's only an apparition. My movements feel stiff today, every pull and stretch tugging at the old injury in my achilles. A pang of frustration surges through me as I try to deepen the stretch, only for the sharp twinge to remind me that my body no longer bends to my will the way it once did.

"Damn it," I mutter under my breath, dropping my hands to my knees as I take a deep breath. The dull ache isn't new, but it's a cruel reminder of the career I was forced to abandon. I push up and shake out my legs, focusing on loosening up before my next class arrives.

This morning, I woke up to a cold, empty bed. Gerardo left early for his shift as an editor for the local newspaper and didn't bother to wake me with an 'I love you' or a kiss. It's been that way for the last few years, and even though I know we're slipping away from each other, I can't seem to find the need to fix it. Our marriage isn't as important to us as it once was, but that's normal when a couple has been together for as long as we have. Right?

The sound of the studio's front door opening pulls my attention, and I straighten my posture, rolling my shoulders back. Despite the lingering tightness in my heel, I force myself to exude confidence and poise. The couples file in, some preparing for their wedding and others wanting to learn a ballroom dance before they're too old to attempt it, their chatter filling the room with an energy that's both invigorating and bittersweet. They're here for the joy of movement, the connection that dance brings, and I'm here to guide them, even if I can't fully feel that joy myself anymore.

"Good morning, everyone!" I call out, clapping my hands together. My voice carries through the space, and the group quiets down, turning their attention toward me. "Welcome back to beginner's Waltz class. Let's line up and start with some basic framework."

The couples shuffle into place, their postures ranging from eager and upright to hesitant and unsure. I weave through the lines, adjusting a shoulder here, tilting a chin there.

"Remember," I say, pausing near a younger couple who are giggling nervously. "Grace starts with the frame. Your connection with your partner begins here." I gently adjust the man's hand on his partner's back, nodding in approval as they fall into a smoother hold. "Now, let's talk about the rise and fall," I continue, stepping to the front of the room. My heels click softly against the floor as I demonstrate, my movements fluid despite the undercurrent of discomfort. "In the Waltz, it's all about seamless transitions. You rise on the one, glide through the two and three. Let's try it together."

I hit play on the sound system and the music cues up, the soft, lilting melody of a classic Waltz filling the studio. I count aloud as the couples move, stepping in time to the rhythm. Some falter, their feet tangled in hesitant missteps, while others glide with an ease that comes from practice.

"Good! Keep your shoulders down," I guide them, nodding toward an older gentleman whose focus is etched into every line of his face. "Yes, that's it. Beautiful frame."

I move among the dancers, offering encouragement and corrections, my focus sharpening as I immerse myself in their progress. For a moment, the ache in my heel fades into the background, replaced by the satisfaction of seeing my students improve.

"Excuse me, Ms. Lewis?"

I turn to see a middle-aged woman with dark brunette hair tied back in a neat bun. Her partner stands beside her, fidgeting with his tie. "Yes?"

"We're struggling with the spin. I keep losing balance," she admits, her voice tinged with embarrassment.

"That's all right," I assure her with a warm smile. "Let me show you." Taking her place beside her partner, I guide him through the spin, emphasizing the subtle weight shift needed to keep the balance.

"It's about trusting each other," I explain, stepping back to observe as they try again. "Your partner supports your momentum, and you follow through. Yes, that's it! Much better."

As I move away, I stop by a couple who seem to be struggling with footwork. The woman's toes have been stepped on twice, and she's grimacing while trying to keep her composure.

"Let's break it down," I suggest, stepping between them. I demonstrate the steps slowly, exaggerating the glide and pivot. "The Waltz is like a conversation. You listen to your partner as much as you speak with your movements. Try to feel the rhythm, not fight it."

They nod, trying again with renewed focus. Their improvement is small but visible, and I clap lightly in encouragement. "There you go. Keep practicing, and it'll become second nature."

The hour slips by in a blur of music and movement. By the time the class winds down, the couples are flushed and smiling, their initial hesitations replaced by a newfound confidence.

"Wonderful work today, everyone," I say as I gather them near the front of the studio. "The Waltz is a dance of elegance and connection, and you're all well on your way to mastering it. Keep practicing, and we'll build on this next week."

Applause ripples through the room, and I watch as they file out, their conversations buzzing with excitement. Some will use the shower rooms we had installed as a perk of a membership, and others will head home to soak in their own tubs.

The studio falls silent again, the serenity of it lost as reality tumbles back in. I lean against the mirrored wall, pressing a hand to my Achilles as the dull throb returns.

"You okay?" Greyson's voice startles me, and I glance up to see him standing in the doorway, a coffee cup in hand.

"Fine," I reply, straightening. "Just a little stiff today."

He walks over, his eyes narrowing as he looks at my heel. "You've been pushing it again, haven't you?"

"I'm fine, Grey," I insist, brushing past him to gather my things. "It's nothing I can't handle."

"You don't have to prove anything, Vae," he huffs, his tone soft but firm. "Not to me, not to anyone."

His words hit a nerve, and I pause, clutching the strap of my bag. "It's not about proving anything. It's about not giving up."

He doesn't respond, but his silence isn't filled with

frustration. We have an understanding that only comes from years of friendship.

"I'll see you tonight," I say, glancing at the clock. "The Advanced Class is on the schedule, and I want to watch how they do."

Greyson smiles faintly. "Just don't scare Mateo off with your perfectionism."

"No promises," I reply with a smirk, heading for the door.

Instead of heading home for a few hours' break, I make my way to a small bistro down the block. The air is filled with the smell of fresh bread and roasted garlic as I step inside. It's one of my favorite spots, a place where the noise of the city fades and the pulse of quiet conversation takes over.

"Table for one?" the hostess asks, and I nod. She leads me to my usual cozy corner table near the window, where I can watch the world go by.

I order a simple meal of spinach and goat cheese salad with a side of tomato bisque and let myself relax for the first time today. As I eat, I replay the morning's class in my mind, analyzing each interaction and wondering how I can help my students improve even further.

By the time I've finished, the tension in my shoulders has eased. I pay the bill and step back into the brisk air, feeling more centered. Mateo's class is only an hour away, and I want to be ready to see if Greyson's gamble on him will pay off.

Slipping into the lingerie boutique a few shops down from the bistro, I figure I could pass the last hour by finding something to spice up my night with Gerardo later. Maybe I should put forth more effort, and even though the passion has been lacking lately, our love is still as strong as ever.

I'm sure he would love to see me in something red and lacy, his favorite color. It's been a while since we've spent a romantic night together. I've been exhausted working every day to make sure the studio stays afloat, and Gerardo has been working odd hours. Writing is his second love, dancing being the first. Admittedly, romance is the furthest thing from our minds when we walk through the door each night.

My fingers slip over the delicate silks as I make my way around the small displays, the smell of lavender and vanilla slipping through my nostrils.

"Can I help you?" Turning, I find the smiling face of a beautiful girl, her brown hair shining and her lithe body at ease as she watches me. I've been a dancer for nearly my entire life, and because of it, a person's athleticism is the first thing I notice.

"I'm looking for something to surprise my husband with. He loves the color red." I lift a bra and panty set, the bright red screaming debauchery.

"Oh, put that back." She gives me a mischievous smirk. "I've got just what you're looking for."

I follow her to the back of the store, and when the rear wall display opens up in front of me, I nearly choke on my intake of air. When I said I wanted something sexy, I didn't realize that it could mean something completely different to another person. Yet, when I reach up and touch the smooth material, I feel myself grinning widely, my cheeks lifting with the motion.

Maybe this is exactly what we need.

MATEO

The phone buzzes on the nightstand, and I groggily reach for it, the screen's brightness making me squint. Roger's name flashes across the screen. With a groan, I swipe to answer, trying to sound convincing despite the guilt of my plan rushing through me.

"Hey, Roger," I croak, adding a sniffle for effect. "I'm feeling under the weather today. I don't think I'll make it to class."

"Understood," Roger replies, his tone professional but laced with concern. "Do you need anything? I can bring over some soup or medicine."

"No, no, I'll be fine," I insist. "I'll just take the weekend to rest."

Roger hesitates before responding. "Alright, Mateo. Rest up and let me know if you need anything. I'll see you on Monday."

I hang up and drop the phone onto the bed, staring at the ceiling. Skipping another day of school isn't ideal, but I need the day to prepare for tonight's class. My thoughts are interrupted by the shrill ringtone piercing the silence again. I glance at the screen and feel my stomach drop. *My father.* Honestly, I'm impressed with just how quick Roger was in telling him I'm taking the day off.

I answer, bracing myself. "Hi, Dad."

"Mateo." His voice is sharp, already full of distrust. "Roger tells me you're not feeling well. What's going on?"

"It's just a cold," I answer him, keeping my tone light. "Probably nothing, but I thought it'd be better to stay home and rest."

There's a pause, and I can almost hear him calculating whether to believe me. "You're not… slipping, are you?"

The accusation stings, but I swallow my frustration. "No, Dad. I'm clean. I've been going to my meetings. This is just a cold."

"Good," he says curtly, though the doubt lingers in his voice. "Because if I hear otherwise—"

"You won't," I interrupt, trying to keep the conversation from spiraling. "I'll be fine. I'll call you tomorrow, okay?"

"Alright," he relents. "Rest, Mateo."

Then the line goes dead, and I exhale deeply, the tension in my shoulders refusing to dissipate. I can't dwell on it. Tonight's class is too important. I drag myself out of bed, heading to the kitchen to make a light breakfast. The mundane act of cooking steadies me, grounding my thoughts as I prepare for the evening ahead.

Leaving my building is easy enough because it's around the same time as my NA meetings. Sure, if by chance my father calls the main desk to ask if they've seen me, I could be caught. It's a risk I'm willing to take though. If all else fails, I could tell him I decided to go for a last-minute meeting without bothering Roger for a ride.

By the time I arrive at the studio, the nerves are back, twisting in my gut like a coiled spring as the worry of my family finding out fades. The familiar scent of polished wood and slight traces of rosin fill the air as I step inside. The other dancers are already milling around, stretching and chatting in low voices.

"Mateo!" Yvonne's cheerful voice cuts through the throng of conversation. She waves me over, her smile bright and inviting. "Glad you made it."

"Hey," I reply, trying to match her enthusiasm. She's dressed in a sleek, black leotard and tights, her hair pulled back into a neat bun. Her confidence is infectious, and I feel a little less out of place.

I sit on the bench and pull my shoes from my backpack, the feel of them supple to my fingertips. These are the shoes I wore during my final competition, the one I won and celebrated by swallowing enough pills to end my life. I force the thoughts away, determined to create new memories with them, hoping they replace the old.

Greyson claps his hands, commanding attention as he steps into the center of the room. "Alright, everyone, let's get started. Congratulations to Yvonne, Kari, Adam, and Mateo for making the cut. You are the first group in our advanced program. Now comes the real work." There's a ripple of excitement and nervous laughter among us. Greyson's gaze sweeps over the group before settling on me for a brief moment. "Tonight, we'll focus on partnering technique," he continues. "Yvonne, you'll be paired with Mateo. Adam, you're with Kari. Let's see what you've got."

Yvonne shoots me a playful grin as we move to an open section of the floor. "Looks like we're partners."

"Looks like it," I hum, my nerves easing slightly as her energy pulls me in.

The music starts, a slow waltz with a rich melody. We fall into frame, her hand light on my shoulder as I guide us into the first steps. Her movements are fluid, matching my lead with ease.

"Not bad, Mateo," she teases, her voice low but playful. "I was worried you'd be stepping on my toes."

"Thanks for the vote of confidence," I quip, focusing on keeping our steps smooth.

"Oh, don't get me wrong," she continues, a mischievous glint in her eyes. "You're good. I just didn't expect you to be this good." I can't decipher if her teasing is because she looked up who I am or her attempt at flirting.

Without replying, I instead concentrate on the rhythm and our synchronization. She's right; this feels good. Better than I'd anticipated. My body remembers the steps, the mechanics of the dance, but it's more than that. It's the connection, the unspoken communication between partners, that makes it come alive.

Greyson circles the room, offering corrections and feedback. When he reaches us, he watches silently for a moment before nodding. "Good connection. Mateo, keep your frame strong on the turns. Yvonne, don't rush ahead. Let him lead."

"Yes, sir," she responds with a mock salute, earning a chuckle from Greyson as he moves on.

From the corner of my eye, I notice Vaeda standing near the mirrors, her arms crossed, and her sharp gaze fixed on the pairs. She approaches us as the music transitions into a faster tempo, her presence commanding without a word.

"Yvonne, your energy is great, but your transitions are too sharp. Smooth them out. Mateo," she says, her tone calm but clipped. "Your frame is improving, but your footwork is lagging slightly on the turns. You need to trust your lead more."

"Yes, ma'am." I nod, adjusting my stance as the music starts again.

Vaeda steps back, watching us closely. Her instructions are clear, cutting through the noise of the room. I can feel her presence as we dance, her critique pushing me to focus harder.

"Good," she praises after a few minutes, her expression softening just slightly. "There's potential here. Keep refining."

Yvonne flashes me a grin as we continue, the faster Foxtrot tempo forcing us to concentrate. By the end of the session, my muscles ache, but it's a satisfying burn. Dancing is giving me back my purpose, and I have only Greyson and Vaeda to thank for giving me a chance.

"You've got potential, Mateo," Yvonne mocks Vaeda's earlier sentiment with a roll of her eyes as we gather our things. "I think we'll make a great team despite everything."

"Thanks," I mutter, forcing myself to hold back an answering eye roll. If Yvonne knows who I am, then her comment is her way of rubbing salt in my open wound of the past. It's hard not to give in to the urge to question her, to tear open her words and force her to her knees in apology. That was the old Mateo though, the one who expected everyone to bow down. This Mateo is grateful for another chance at life, for another chance at greatness. I won't let anything come between me and my success.

Not even the remnants of my tattered ego.

As the others trickle out, I notice Vaeda lingering by the edge of the studio, scribbling into a small notebook. Summoning a bit of courage, I approach her, wiping sweat from my brow with a towel.

"Ms. Lewis?" I begin, my voice a little uncertain.

She glances up, her sharp brown eyes catching mine. "Mateo." She lifts her chin, her tone hiding the undercurrent of curiosity. "Good work tonight."

"Thank you," I reply, shifting on my feet. "Your feedback really helped. I haven't danced in a studio setting for a while, so it means a lot."

Vaeda closes her notebook, crossing her arms as she studies me. "It's obvious you have talent, Mateo, but talent isn't enough. Consistency, discipline, and trust in your partner will make or break you in this program. I don't need to remind you to remain sober, do I?"

I shake my head, her words striking a chord. "No. My

sobriety won't be an issue. I'll work harder to prove myself."

Her gaze narrows slightly, and for a moment, I think I see something like understanding flicker across her face. "See that you do. Greyson believes in you, and I'm willing to give you the chance to prove yourself. Don't waste it."

"I won't," I vow firmly.

Vaeda nods, her expression unreadable. "Good. Have a good night, Mateo."

"Good night, Ms. Lewis." I absorb her dismissal, watching as she turns and heads toward the office. There's something about her presence, commanding and chilled, that lingers even after she's gone.

My body shivers with the cold air as I grab my coat from the hook and step out of my shoes. After tucking them into my bag, I sling it over my shoulder and head out of the studio. The hallway is quiet as I make my way to the exit, the burn of Vaeda's words still moving through me.

Vaeda Lewis may already have her opinion formed of me, but I'll work hard to prove her wrong. There will come a day when she looks at me with pride, and just the thought of her eyes lit up with delight when she gazes at me makes my heart rate pick up.

CHAPTER FIVE

The ride home is uneventful as Roger quietly maneuvers through the Monday midafternoon traffic while I stare out the window. My mind is preoccupied with the upcoming night, and my stomach churns with both anticipation and nerves. When we pull up to my building, Roger glances at me through the rearview mirror.

"Feeling better, Mateo?" he asks, his concern evident.

"Yeah," I reply, offering a faint smile. "Thanks, Roger."

"Let me know if you need anything," he says as I step out of the SUV.

Upstairs, I drop my schoolbag by the door and head up to my room to change. The crisp shirt and tailored pants I've been wearing all day are swapped out for comfortable sweatpants and a loose hoodie. As I lace up my sneakers, my thoughts drift to the elaborate plan I've pieced together over the past weekend.

It started with a late-night search. I found the original building plans for my apartment complex buried in a city archive online. That's when I discovered it: a fire escape leading from the roof to the street, bypassing the front desk entirely. The idea sparked something rebellious inside me, a flicker of ingenuity from my more questionable days.

The lock on the rooftop access door was easy to pick. I'd surprised myself with how quickly the old skills came back. It isn't something I'm proud of, but it is useful now. I stuck some heavy-duty tape over the mechanism to keep the lock open, ensuring I could come and go without attracting suspicion.

I pull my hood up and sling my dance bag over my shoulder. Heading to the living room, I grab my phone and check the time. The building is quiet as I step into the hallway, the muffled drone of someone's TV the only sound.

Taking the stairs two at a time, I climb to the roof. The door creaks faintly as I push it open, the cool evening air brushing against my face. The city sprawls below me, a mosaic of lights and shadows. I make my way to the fire escape, the metal groaning softly under my weight as I descend. The thrill of slipping out unnoticed sends a rush of adrenaline through me, but I quickly push it aside, focusing on the task ahead. I'm not wanting to get caught up in this feeling, this euphoric high.

Once on the street, I blend into the flow of pedestrians, heading toward the studio. The walk is brisk and invigorating, the rhythm of my steps syncing with the beat of my thoughts. By the time I reach the studio, the nerves have settled into a simmering excitement.

The place is already buzzing with energy when I arrive. Music drifts through the air, and the sound of footsteps echoes from the practice room. I slip inside, greeted by the familiar scent of polished wood and the weak tang of sweat.

Greyson is in the main room, adjusting the sound system, and he nods at me as I enter. "Right on time, Mateo. Get warmed up. We'll be starting in fifteen minutes."

I head to the side, dropping my bag and slipping on my dance shoes. The snug fit feels comforting, reminding me of when I first became a dancer. Around me, the other dancers are doing the same, their movements a mix of eagerness and casual familiarity.

Yvonne waves at me from across the room, her ponytail swaying as she chats animatedly with Kari. Adam is off to one side, practicing a series of turns with a focused expression. The camaraderie in the room is palpable, but there's an undercurrent of competition, a subtle tension that keeps everyone on their toes.

As the session begins, Vaeda enters the room. Her presence shifts the energy immediately. She's dressed in sleek black leggings and a fitted top, her hair pulled back into a sharp bun. Her gaze sweeps over the group, assessing with a practiced eye.

"Alright, everyone," Greyson says, clapping his hands. "Tonight, we'll be focusing on rhythm and musicality. Vaeda will be leading the instruction, so listen carefully."

Vaeda steps forward, her posture commanding but fluid. "We'll start with a basic Cha-Cha sequence," she announces. "Partners, find your spots on the floor. Show me what you got."

I pair up with Yvonne, and we move to our section. The music starts, a lively Latin beat filling the room. I count under my breath as we step into a basic routine, my focus split between leading Yvonne and staying on tempo.

"Good frame," Vaeda states as she passes us, her keen eyes flicking over our form. "Mateo, let your shoulders relax. Yvonne, watch your timing on the chaîné turns."

We adjust immediately, the corrections snapping into place like puzzle pieces. Vaeda's feedback is to the point and accurate, even if the delivery isn't laced with kindness. It's clear she expects perfection, and that pushes me harder. I crave her approval like the rush of a chemical high.

As we move through the sequence, she circles back to us, her expression still guarded. "Better," she murmurs, though her tone carries an edge. "But don't let this be a fluke. One good session doesn't erase a reputation. Consistency matters, Mateo."

Her words hit like a cold splash of water, and I nod, biting back any retort. She's not wrong, even if the words sting. "Understood," I manage, keeping my voice steady.

"Good," she replies curtly, her attention already shifting to Adam and Kari as Yvonne's expression is filled with confusion. I'll be lucky if she doesn't question me at the end of the night. She may be my partner, and eventually should become a close friend, but I'm not ready to tell her everything yet. I don't trust her, but maybe that will change as we continue to work together, then I can judge how trustworthy she is.

The music continues, and I force myself to focus. The connection with Yvonne strengthens, our movements becoming more cohesive as we navigate the sequence. We finish off with a dramatic pose, Yvonne's smile shining brilliantly. The end of the session brings the feeling of accomplishment. I'm learning my partner, my body is being challenged, and my past recedes a little farther from my future.

The hour-and-a-half class rushes by, and the others begin to pack up as I linger near the mirrors, stretching out my calves. Vaeda approaches again, her mood serious but less severe this time. "You handled yourself well tonight," she admits, though her tone is still cool.

"Thank you," I reply, meeting her gaze. "Your feedback really helped."

She studies me for a moment, her expression unreadable. "We'll see if it sticks. Talent isn't enough, Mateo. It never is. Show me discipline, and maybe I'll start to believe you're serious about this."

The skepticism in her words hangs in the air, and I nod. "I will. I want to prove myself."

Vaeda's lips press into a thin line, and for a brief moment, I think I see something like reluctant approval flicker across her face. "Good. Don't waste my time," she warns before turning and walking away.

Her words echo inside my mind as I gather my things, her biting tone cutting through the post-class fatigue. She doesn't trust me yet, that much is clear, but there's a challenge in her distrust, one that fuels me. I am an addict chasing my next fix after all, and Vaeda's approval has gripped my fixation.

As I'm zipping up my bag, Yvonne strolls over, her smile easy and inviting. "Good class today." Her warm smile does little to erase the sting of Vaeda's icy demeanor. "What did she mean by your reputation earlier?" She nods toward Vaeda, her eyes drifting over my shoulder.

There it is. I knew she would ask, and yet, I don't have an answer for her. I don't want to lie, but I'm not telling her anything either. "It's a long story." I shrug as her eyes flick back to mine, that look of confusion settling over her features once again.

The weight of her scrutiny makes my skin prickle. She's trying to figure it all out. She doesn't have a clue about who I once was, but she knows there's something I'm hiding. The idea of having to explain my sobriety one day looms large in my mind, a hurdle I'm not sure I'm ready to face.

I wonder if she'll push for more, and my heart races as I wait. "A few of us are heading out for drinks. You should come," she states instead, slinging her jacket over one shoulder as I exhale with relief.

I hesitate, my chest tightening. "Thanks, but I think I'll pass. I'm pretty wiped out."

Yvonne tilts her head, her grin turning teasing. "Worried

you won't keep up? Come on, just one drink." Alcohol was never my true problem, but it did open the gate to abusing my prescription.

"I'll take a rain check." I stay firm with a polite smile, trying to keep my tone light. "Next time, maybe."

She shrugs, her eyes sparkling. "Suit yourself. Don't work too hard."

As she walks away, joining Kari and Adam near the door, I catch a glimpse of Vaeda from the corner of my eye. She's standing near the office, her gaze locked on me. Her expression is masked, but there's a distinct energy shifting around her, as if she's sizing me up even now.

The walk back to my building is quiet, the sounds of the night helping to steady the whirlwind of thoughts in my head. I scale the fire escape quickly, the rhythm of my steps matching the beat of the Cha-Cha still echoing in my mind. Tonight, I feel the edges of something I haven't felt in a long time. Control. A small victory, maybe, but enough to keep me moving forward.

VAEDA

The cool night air brushes against my face as I step out of the studio, tightening my coat around me. I've always found solace in the quiet after a class, but tonight, the lingering image of Yvonne flirting with Mateo twists in my mind like a thorn.

Yvonne, with her easy confidence and playful demeanor, had no hesitation in inviting Mateo out for drinks. The way she leaned toward him, smiling like he was her next conquest, made my teeth clench. Not because I care, well not like that, but because it's reckless. She doesn't know anything about him, about the demons he's fighting.

My steps echo against the sidewalk as I make my way home. I've seen many women like Yvonne flirt before; it's harmless and part of their charm, but Mateo is fragile, whether he wants to admit it or not. There's something in his posture, in the way he carefully avoids meeting my eyes too long, that screams he's holding on by a thread. Yvonne's casual advances could unravel that thread, and I won't let her risk it for the sake of a fleeting crush.

The studio wasn't without its usual challenges tonight either. Mateo stumbled slightly during the second run of the Cha-Cha sequence, his foot slipping off rhythm. Yvonne laughed it off, brushing his arm and offering encouragement, but the exchange grated on me. Encouragement isn't what Mateo needs; he needs discipline. He needs structure, not soft smiles and flirtatious glances.

I'll have to speak to her in the next class. Nothing dramatic, just a quiet word to pull her aside and remind her to keep things professional, and if she presses, maybe I'll mention Mateo's history. Not the details, it's not my story to tell, but enough to make her think twice. The last thing he needs is distractions or complications. Grey may see him as our star dancer, but I still see a risk.

By the time I reach the penthouse, my irritation has settled into a simmering frustration. Gerardo greets me at the door, his broad smile like a cooling balm over my mood for a moment. Until I remember my discarded lingerie bag in the corner of our closet. I wanted to wear it for him the same night I brought it home, but he was late getting in and groaned with exhaustion as he dragged himself into the shower.

The frustration I felt that night returns twofold as I step inside, forcing a smile to my lips. He's dressed casually, his hands dusted with flour, the scent of fresh bread wafting from the kitchen. My stomach growls with hunger as I swallow down the ire growing inside me.

"You're home late," he says, leaning in to kiss my cheek. His touch is warm, familiar, but tonight it feels more grating than comforting.

"Long class," I reply, slipping off my shoes and hanging my coat by the door.

"How did it go?" he asks as he heads back to the kitchen. "Are they improving?"

"They're fine," I force out the pleasantries, following him. The words come out sharper than I intend, but I don't correct myself. I'm too wound up to soften my edges.

He glances over his shoulder, sensing more than I let on. "Who's causing trouble now?" he teases, his tone light but curious.

I sigh, leaning against the doorframe of the kitchen. "Yvonne," I admit. "She asked Mateo out after class. It's unprofessional." When his features flick with confusion, I take a deep breath to stave off the anger and remind myself he doesn't know everyone in my classes. "Yvonne is in the Advanced Class and partners with Mateo."

Gerardo pauses mid-knead, tilting his head toward me. "She asked him out? Like on a date?" His grin only fans the flames burning inside me as I rub at my temple.

I nod, crossing my arms. "She's too flirty and reckless. Mateo doesn't need that kind of attention. He's complicated."

Gerardo's lips twitch into a small smile as he resumes his work. "She's young. Let her have her fun."

"It's not just fun," I insist, stepping into the kitchen. "For one, it's unprofessional, and two, Mateo isn't like the others. He doesn't need distractions with his checkered past."

Gerardo picks up the dough and slaps it down on the counter with a thud. "Or maybe he does," he suggests mildly. "Just because he had a slipup in the past doesn't mean he needs to be micromanaged now, Vaeda."

The calm in his tone fuels my frustration. "You don't understand," I snap. "I've seen people going through what he is before. He's not ready. If Yvonne pushes too hard—"

"And if he surprises you?" Gerardo interrupts, his voice still maddeningly even. "If he's stronger than you think?"

I press my lips together, unwilling to give in. "I don't trust him. He's not here because he wants to be. He's here because he needs something. An escape or a distraction. That's dangerous."

"Maybe or maybe not," Gerardo concedes with a shrug. "But you're not always right, Vaeda."

I narrow my eyes, his casual dismissal like a stone in my shoe. "This isn't about being right. This is about protecting the studio."

"And by doing that, you're alienating Mateo?" Gerardo counters, his tone calm but pointed. "Maybe you should think about that before you push too hard. *You* don't want to be the reason he relapses."

He studies me for a moment longer, then puts the new loaf into the oven and leaves the kitchen, his usual warmth replaced by quiet detachment. I know I've pushed too hard, but I can't shake the feeling that I'm right. Mateo's future at the studio, his future period, is too precarious to leave to chance.

Left alone in the quiet, I lean against the counter, my hands gripping the cool marble surface. The night stretches outside my floor-to-ceiling windows, the surrounding buildings alight with life. The frustration bubbles up and I push it back down, concentrating on the ambient noise of the city below, muted as though the world itself is holding its breath.

I glance toward the living room, the glow of the city lights filtering through the tall windows. Gerardo's touch is everywhere in plants I never remember to water, books stacked haphazardly on the coffee table, and a throw blanket draped over the couch. The warmth of his personality stands in sharp contrast to my need for order. It's a balance we've always had, but tonight it feels like a divide.

With guilt burning its way from my stomach up into my throat, I head toward our bedroom with the intent of making up with him. We don't find ourselves at odds often, and when we are, it's the worst feeling in the world. He's always been there for me, no matter what, and doesn't deserve the attitude I bring home after a hard day at work.

I make my way down the hallway toward our bedroom when I notice the door to his office is ajar, casting soft, golden light onto the tiled floor. Inside, I hear muffled voices and music, and curiosity gets the better of me. With a slight push, the door opens a little wider, and I find the TV on, the image on the screen taking my breath away.

It's me and Gerardo during our final competition, a month before our lives changed forever. He's spinning me across the floor during a Paso Doble, his strong steps full of passion and testosterone as my full red skirt flares out around my hips. We look regal, and in all honesty, at the time, we were. We dominated the competitive circuit, and the sight of us in our glory twists the knife in my chest deeper.

It's a punch to the gut to see him being nostalgic for the life we once had. In my mind, he was content being married to me and living a life away from the pressure of competing and keeping that number one spot. Clearly I was wrong.

Gerardo lifts a crystal tumbler of whiskey to his mouth, his back to me, while he sits on the couch and watches us on the screen. The guilt I was feeling a few moments before becomes a boulder-size weight on my chest as I back out of the room and head to our room, my hand slapping over my mouth to hold in the sob that's working its way up my throat.

As soon as I'm in our bedroom, I uncover my mouth and let the cries break free. It's rare for me to lose control like this, to give in to the buried pool of despair and set the tidal wave free. I scramble into our closet and shut the door as I crawl into the corner and drag my knees up to my chest, rocking back and forth as tears stream down my cheeks and drip from my jaw.

It's my fault we no longer have champion titles, and it's me who stripped Gerardo of the chance to have more. He made the choice to leave with me, but it's because of me he even had to.

My eyes skip to the bag beside me as a fresh sob slips from my mouth. The lingerie bag will probably never be opened, and that beautiful red outfit will never kiss my body like I bought it for.

Everything feels like it's crumbling around me as my control slips, and I curl into a ball and force myself to feel before I shut it all down for good.

CHAPTER SIX

Vaeda

The studio is quiet when I unlock the front doors early Saturday morning, the polished floors reflecting the muted glow of the overhead lights. This time of day is my favorite, the stillness before the chaos of classes and rehearsals. It gives me a chance to center myself, to remind myself why I've poured so much into this place.

I set my bag on the bench by the mirrors and slip off my coat, pulling my hair into a tight bun. My reflection stares back at me, my expression nonchalant and calm. Today, I'll need all the calm I can muster because I need to make it through an entire class with Yvonne and Mateo without losing my mind. My eyes are still a little pink and my skin looks a bit sallow, but I feel renewed after my few hours alone wallowing in depression the night before.

Gerardo came to bed late, his breath thick with whiskey and his steps sloppy. It's been a while since we've fallen into bed together and let sleep overtake us. Lately, I'm either crashing before him or he's fast asleep before I even step out of the shower, so this display I witnessed last night as I pretended to sleep was new.

How often does Gerardo drink? And how often does

he do it while watching us dance?

I'm midway through a series of stretches when the sound of the front door opening catches my attention. Glancing at the clock, I frown. It's too early for the others to be arriving. I straighten and turn just as Mateo steps into the studio, his dance bag slung over his shoulder.

"You're early," I say as I study him. He's dressed in another pair of sweatpants, which are tied low on his waist, and a thick sweater, the hood up over his head. He walked here. I can tell by the pink staining his cheeks from the chilly weather.

He looks slightly taken aback by my presence, but he recovers quickly. "I thought I'd get some extra practice in before class," he replies, dropping his bag near the wall. "Greyson told me it would be alright."

I nod, watching as he takes off his sweater and changes into his dance shoes. His shoulders are stiff, his body looking coiled and ready to strike, or maybe I'm just seeing things. Instead of being annoyed with him taking time away from my solitude, I see an opportunity to forget my troubles.

"The space is yours," I offer, stepping to the side to observe. "What were you going to work on today?"

Mateo straightens, a flicker of hesitation crossing his face before he moves to the center of the floor. "I've always been strong in the Latin dances," he begins as he stretches, bringing his fingers to his toes and making his tank top rise on his back. "So I thought a little extra time on ballroom was needed." He begins with a basic Waltz sequence, his frame solid but his steps slightly stiff. I cross my arms, watching closely as he transitions into a spin that's just a beat too slow.

"Stop," I demand, my voice cutting through the music. He halts mid-step, turning to face me.

"Your spins are sluggish," I point out, walking toward

him. "You're hesitating, holding back. Why?"

Mateo shrugs, his gaze darting to the floor. "Just warming up."

"Warming up doesn't mean holding back," I counter. "If you're going to practice, practice like it's a performance. Otherwise, you're just reinforcing bad habits."

He nods, his jaw tightening as he adjusts his stance, then starts again, this time with more intent. The improvement is immediate, but there's still a stiffness in his shoulders that I can't ignore. I wasn't imagining things earlier.

"Relax your shoulders," I advise, stepping closer. "You're carrying too much tension. Let the movement flow from your center."

Mateo exhales sharply, rolling his shoulders before trying again. This time, his movements are smoother, more fluid. I nod in approval but don't offer praise. He's good, but good isn't enough. Not here.

"Better," I concede finally. "But you still have work to do."

He steps back, wiping the sweat from his brow with the back of his hand. "Thanks," he mutters, though there's a flicker of irritation in his tone and frustration shining from his eyes, the sight making me bite back a grin. Good. He should be frustrated. It'll push him.

"Can I ask you something?" Mateo says after a moment, avoiding my eyes in the mirror.

I raise an eyebrow but nod. "Go ahead."

"Your injury," he begins, his gaze meeting mine briefly before shifting away. "Does it still bother you?"

The question catches me off guard, though I mask it quickly. "Why do you ask?"

He hesitates, his hands fidgeting at his sides. "I… I noticed you don't move as much as Greyson during class. I figured it might have something to do with your injury."

For a moment, I consider brushing him off, but something in his expression stops me. He's genuinely curious, not prying for gossip.

"It does," I admit, keeping my tone neutral. "Achilles tendonitis. It's manageable, but it ended my competitive career."

Mateo scratches at his chin slowly, absorbing the information. "That must have been hard."

His sympathy grates on me, though I know it's well-intentioned. "It was," I state simply. "But life goes on."

He doesn't press further, sensing the boundary in the way I cross my arms over my chest. Instead, he shifts his weight, his focus returning to the floor. "Do you think I'll ever compete again?" he asks, the vulnerability in his voice surprising me.

"That depends on you," I respond, my voice sounding robotic and lacking empathy. My emotional well has run dry, and unfortunately, he's receiving the brunt of it. "Talent isn't enough. You know that. It takes discipline, consistency, and a willingness to push past your limits."

He nods, though his expression remains thoughtful. "Thanks for the feedback," he murmurs, moving back to his bag.

"Mateo," I call after him. He pauses, looking over his shoulder. "You have potential. Don't waste it."

A flicker of determination lights his eyes, and he nods again before turning back to his things to grab his bottle of water. I watch him for a moment longer, then return to my own stretches. There's a spark in him, but sparks can burn out just as easily as they ignite. Only time will tell if that spark will transpire into an inferno for Mateo Sanchez.

The quiet is short-lived. A few minutes later, the sound of the studio door opening once more reaches my ears. I glance up to see Yvonne entering, her energy a stark contrast to the calm of the morning. She flashes Mateo a bright smile as she drops her bag beside his, and it sets my jaw to stone.

"Morning," she chirps, bending down to swap her sneakers for dance shoes.

"Morning," Mateo replies, his tone easy but reserved. I don't know why that reassures me, but it does. Maybe he's not as interested in her as she is in him. That could also work against them when it's time to compete. Judges love healthy sexual tension between partners. They want the dance moves to mimic the sensuality of being together between the sheets.

I watch as they move to the center of the room, side by side, stretching in unison. Yvonne chatters away, her voice light and cheerful. Mateo listens, nodding occasionally, his posture more relaxed than before. The ease between them grates on me, though I can't pinpoint why.

My gaze narrows as Yvonne places a hand on Mateo's arm to demonstrate a stretch, leaning in a little too close. He doesn't seem to notice, or maybe he does and doesn't care, but I feel the irritation rising, hot and unwelcome. My teeth crack as I watch her reach out and brush his thick black hair from his forehead and laugh when he shakes it back into place.

Her flirtation is in his face and she's making it known that she wants him, while Mateo is holding himself back, not falling into the path of unprofessionalism. I think that's what I've been worried about lately. If he gives in to Yvonne and has what she thinks is a harmless night out and a harmless one drink, will he spiral and take us all with him? Is he worth that risk?

Her loud giggle has my eyes flicking back to their reflection in the mirror, and this time, Mateo is watching me. His eyes are like pools of honey shining bright from his face as he smiles tentatively at me before turning back to listen to whatever Yvonne is saying.

Why does this bother me? It's none of my business. Yvonne's behavior, Mateo's reaction… none of it should matter, and yet, the sight of them together gnaws at me. I shake my head, forcing myself to focus on my stretches.

The irritation lingers though, a low warning in the back of my mind. *It's not jealousy,* I tell myself. *It's a concern.* Yvonne's flirty nature is harmless most of the time, but Mateo doesn't need distractions. He needs structure and encouragement, not someone hovering too close and making him forget why he's here.

I'll talk to her soon, I decide. Quietly and privately. She needs to understand the stakes… for Mateo and for the studio. For now, I let the moment pass, keeping my gaze on my own reflection in the mirror, willing myself to stay composed.

MATEO

The studio is buzzing with energy today; the vibe filled with excitement and intrigue. When I first arrived there, I found just Vaeda. I could sense her quiet sadness and immediately thought it was her ankle. I can sympathize with losing everything you worked so hard to have, but in her case, it was stolen. Not lost like mine. Now that Greyson and the others are here, the atmosphere has shifted, and we can all see the twinkle shining in Greyson's eyes. He has something big to tell us.

Greyson stands at the front of the room, his posture immaculate, his hands clasped behind his back. The murmurs among the dancers are quiet as he steps forward, his piercing blue gaze sweeping over the group.

"Good morning, everyone," he begins, his voice commanding yet warm. "Today's class will focus on refining your skills, but first, I want to share some exciting news."

I glance around, catching Yvonne's curious expression and Adam's slight frown of concentration. Even Vaeda, standing near the mirrors with her usual guarded demeanor, seems more attentive than usual.

"In six months," Greyson continues, "there is a prestigious ballroom competition in Paris. The International Dance Open invites competitors from around the world, and it is one of the most celebrated events for dancers at every level, including intermediate. This is an opportunity not only to compete on a global stage but to represent Fusion Core Dance Studio."

A ripple of excitement moves through the room. Paris. The thought alone sends a jolt of adrenaline through me. To compete again, to stand on a stage with the world watching. It's exhilarating and terrifying all at once.

Greyson holds up a hand to quiet the murmurs. "Before you start packing your bags," he says with a sly smile, "I want to make something clear. Not everyone will be going. Over the next four weeks, Vaeda and I will be watching closely to determine which couple has the potential to shine on that stage. Only one pair will represent us in Paris."

Yvonne leans toward me, her voice low. "Looks like it's time to bring our A game."

I nod, my throat tight. The stakes are higher now. Every step, every turn, every glance will be scrutinized. There's no room for error.

"We'll begin today by focusing on the Viennese Waltz," Greyson announces. "It's a dance of love and elegance, and it will quickly show us who can handle the pressure." He gestures to Vaeda, who steps forward with her usual poise.

"Find your partners," Vaeda instructs, her tone brokering no nonsense. "Take your positions on the floor."

I want to curse out loud for revealing to Vaeda that my ballroom is rusty. She'll be scrutinizing me more now, and it adds a disadvantage to my and Yvonne's partnership.

Adam and Kari move together like magnets, their stances fluid and attuned. Yvonne and I move to our spot, falling into frame with practiced ease. Her hand rests lightly on my shoulder, her touch steady. The music begins, the haunting melody filling the studio as we glide into motion.

Greyson and Vaeda circle the room, their eyes sharp and unforgiving. Every so often, one of them stops to offer corrections, their voices cutting through the music like percussion instruments.

"Extend your arms, Adam," Vaeda calls. "Kari, match his energy. Your movements need to be cohesive."

"Yvonne," Greyson says as he passes us, "watch your turns. They're too abrupt. Let them flow naturally."

Yvonne adjusts immediately, her movements softening. I focus on maintaining our rhythm, letting the music guide me. The dance feels smoother now, more connected, but I can still feel Vaeda's eyes on me, her gaze heavy with expectation.

As the song ends, Greyson claps his hands. "Good," he praises. "Take a moment to catch your breath, then we'll run it again."

I step back, rolling my shoulders as Yvonne grabs a water bottle from her bag. "You're doing great," she gushes, flashing me a grin.

"Thanks," I reply, though my thoughts are elsewhere. The idea of competing in Paris looms large in my mind. It's more than just a competition; it's a chance to prove myself, to reclaim a piece of the life I thought I'd lost.

Vaeda approaches as I'm adjusting my posture, her expression unreadable. "Your frame is improving," she observes, her voice low enough that only I can hear. "But your footwork is still inconsistent. You're letting the music lead you instead of taking control."

I nod, her words cutting through the haze of my thoughts. "I'll work on it."

"See that you do," she responds, her gaze lingering for a moment before she moves on.

The second run-through is tighter, the group's collective energy heightened by the stakes. Every movement feels charged, every misstep amplified. By the time the class ends, my insides are trembling with exertion and desperation. I want this so bad.

As I gather my things, Yvonne nudges me. "Paris," she rasps, her eyes shining. "Can you imagine?"

"I'm trying not to," I admit with a grin. "It's a long way off."

"Not really," she hums, slinging her bag over her shoulder. "Time flies when you're having fun, and I am having so much fun with you, Mateo." She's definitely flirting, and it only serves to lock up my throat, making speaking impossible. I nod and give her a small smile.

She follows Kari and Adam out of the building, leaving me relieved when she doesn't invite me out again. I would love to live that free, to step into a bar without the urge to buy an entire bottle of vodka and use it to chase down a handful of pills.

I linger in the room, taking my time to wipe the sweat from my forehead and neck while telling myself it's preventing a flu as I walk home, but truly, it's the enigma of a woman who has captured my curiosity.

Vaeda stands at the mirrors as she moves into her dance frame and begins to glide along the floor. She's grace personified, and it's hard to blink in case I miss something. Even Greyson steps out of his office to watch her, a smirk lifting his mouth as his gaze meets mine.

He comes to stand beside me as I haul on my hoodie and beanie. "She's too hard on herself, and it'll only get worse as this competition comes closer. She craves perfection, and since her injury, she can't see it in her reflection any longer. If she's hard on you, it's because she sees the potential for perfection." We watch her spin, her shoulders maintaining the posture as her neck elongates like an elegant swan. "I want to see your redemption, Mateo. I'm hoping you'll be joining us in Paris."

His words stick with me as I leave the studio. The evening air is cool against my skin, the setting sun launching long shadows on the pavement. Paris. The possibility feels both exhilarating and distant, like a dream just out of reach, but as I make my way home, a quiet determination settles over me.

Four weeks. That's all the time I have to prove I belong

on that stage, and I won't waste it.

Hours later, I'm sprawled on my couch, my muscles aching from the evening's class. The TV is on, but I'm barely paying attention to the muted images flickering across the screen. My mind keeps circling back to Greyson's announcement, the weight of his expectations, and the allure of Paris.

The sound of my phone ringing cuts through my thoughts, and I glance at the screen to see my mother's name. With a sigh, I sit up and answer.

"Hi, Mami," I say, trying to sound cheerful despite my exhaustion.

"Mateo, mi amor." Her warm voice fills the line. "How are you?"

"I'm fine," I reply, leaning back against the couch. "Just tired from school."

"Are you keeping up with your classes?" she asks, her tone gentle but probing. "How are you finding economics?"

"It's… fine," I remark, hesitating. "I mean, it's a little boring, to be honest."

"Boring?" she repeats, concern creeping into her voice. "Mateo, you know how important this is for your future. Your father and I…" she trails off, but I know where she's going.

"I know," I interrupt gently. "I'm doing the work, Mami, but it's not something I'm passionate about. You know that."

There's a pause on the other end of the line. When she speaks again, her voice is softer. "What would make you happy, Mateo?"

I pause, the words catching in my throat. Finally, I

admit, "I've been thinking about… finding a dance class."

"A dance class?" she echoes, surprised. "Mateo, your father…"

"I–I know," I stammer quickly. "But I've been staying out of trouble. I've been doing everything you and Dad asked. I just… I need something to look forward to, something that makes me feel alive again."

She's quiet for a long moment, and I can picture her biting her lip, weighing my words.

"You don't know what we went through when you had your overdose. You will never understand what that did to me and to your father. Even your sister was devastated. We never want that to happen again." Just the mention of my sister, Grace, has my throat sealing with emotion.

I miss her, and even though she's still harboring some anger toward me, she's still one of my most favorite people in the world.

"How is Grace?" I inquire, hoping for some new information.

"She's enjoying school in Paris. I'm proud of her. Her instructors say she has the makings of a bright future as a prima ballerina." Pride rushes from her mouth and saturates her words as they stab into my chest.

I'm proud of my sister too, and I also have selfish reasons for wanting to go to Paris. Grace is there, which means I could convince her to talk to me again if I have the chance to see her face-to-face.

"I wish I could turn back time, Mami," I whisper as pain inches its way upward from my chest. "I just need a second chance."

"I'll think it over," she relents, her voice filled with hesitation. "But, Mateo, you have to promise me you'll stay focused. No distractions, no slipping back."

"I promise," I breathe out, the relief in my voice evident. "Thank you, Mami."

"Take care of yourself, mi amor," she urges, her voice warm again. "We'll talk soon."

"Good night, Mami," I say before ending the call.

As I set my phone down, a mixture of hope and apprehension swirls inside my chest. It's a small step, but with it comes a swell of excitement.

Chapter Seven

The buzzing of my phone jolts me awake. I blink groggily, disoriented for a moment, before realizing it's my ringtone. Grabbing the phone off the nightstand, I squint at the screen, the number unfamiliar.

"Hello?" I mumble, my voice still thick with sleep.

"Mateo!" The voice on the other end is chipper, way too energetic for this hour. It takes me a moment to place it.

"Yvonne?" I ask, sitting up straighter. "How did you get my number?"

"I begged Greyson," she admits, laughing lightly. "And he caved. Don't be mad. I'm calling with good news."

"What kind of good news?" I grumble, still trying to wake up.

"We have the studio to ourselves today," she announces, her enthusiasm bubbling through the line. "No interruptions, no distractions. Just us working on our Rumba."

I rub my hand over my face, my mind racing. I'm supposed to be home today, it's Sunday, keeping up appearances for my dad's "perfect son" routine. Groceries and packages are scheduled to arrive, and the doorman will definitely report any unusual activity to him, but the idea of uninterrupted time in the studio is too good to pass up.

"That's… great," I say carefully, trying to hide my hesitation.

"So you'll come?" she presses.

"I can come for a few hours," I relent after a pause, already forming my excuse. "But I have a study group later, so I can't stay long."

The lie rolls off my tongue and it gives me pause. I used to lie as well as I told the truth, blurring the lines until I couldn't tell the difference. In some ways, it scares me to be falling into the same bad habits I once carried in the past, but I tell myself that it's necessary. I either tell a harmless lie or I tell her the truth, baring the ghosts that still haunt me.

"Perfect!" she exclaims. "I'll see you there in an hour."

"Yeah, see you then," I reply, hanging up. I set the phone down and stare at the ceiling for a moment, the implications of my decision settling over me. If I want to compete in Paris, I have to take risks. This is one of them.

The studio feels different when it's empty, and it's when I like it the most. The usual buzz of chatter and movement is replaced by a calm stillness, the kind that amplifies every sound and every breath. Yvonne is already there when I arrive, stretching by the mirrors. She grins when she sees me.

"Took you long enough," she teases. "Ready to get started?"

I nod, setting my bag down and slipping on my dance shoes. The familiar feel of the floor beneath my feet helps settle the nerves of sneaking out and the greater risk of being caught today. Yvonne cues up a playlist, and the sultry rhythm of a Rumba track fills the space.

"Let's go from the top," she says, moving into position. I place my hand on her back, our movements tentative at first as we find the beat together. The music swells, and we begin to flow through the steps.

The Rumba is a dance of tension and release, of push and pull. Every step demands passion, every movement an unspoken conversation between partners. Yvonne's body moves fluidly, her arms extending gracefully as she turns. I match her steps, my focus deepening as the music intensifies.

"Stronger connection," a voice calls out, startling us both. I glance toward the mirrors and see Greyson leaning against the wall, his sharp eyes dissecting every move. Vaeda stands beside him, her arms crossed and her expression unreadable.

"You're too focused on the steps," Greyson continues. "The Rumba isn't about technique alone. It's about emotion and storytelling. Show me your chemistry."

Yvonne and I exchange a glance, her cheeks flushing. We start again, this time letting the music guide us more freely. I concentrate on the tension in her movements, the way her body leans into mine before pulling away. My hand on her back steadies her, grounding us both as we move through the sequence.

I need to be here in the moment with Yvonne, but my gaze keeps flickering toward Vaeda. I can't help it. Her dark eyes are fixed on us, and even from across the room, I feel the heat of her stare. There's something about the way she watches so intensely that makes my pulse quicken.

"Better," Greyson says, nodding. "Now, refine the footwork. Vaeda?"

Vaeda steps forward, her gaze locking on mine like a tether, and the air suddenly feels heavier. "Your weight transfer is too abrupt," she observes, her tone cool. "You need to let the movement travel through your entire body, not just your feet. Watch."

She steps into the center of the room, and my vision seems to narrow on her as the music fills the space around us. Her movements are smooth and deliberate, her body an effortless extension of the rhythm. There's a sensuality to the way she moves, the way her hands and hips speak the language of the dance. I watch intently, too intently, as heat coils low in my stomach.

When we try again, it's better, though not as seamless as hers. I can still feel her gaze on me, keen and knowing, and when I meet her eyes, there's a flicker of a challenge, or maybe that's what I'm hoping for. Perhaps Vaeda is envisioning herself in my arms, my hands drifting dangerously close to the swell of her ass. It leaves me feeling excited, my breath coming out in short puffs. It feels like I'm chasing my new high.

"You're getting there," she mutters, her tone neutral, but her words carry a hint of approval. "Keep working on it."

We run through the sequence again and again, each repetition bringing small improvements. The music crescendos, and Yvonne and I hit the final pose, her body arching gracefully as I hold her steady. Even as I hold Yvonne, my eyes betray me, sliding once more to Vaeda. Her arms are crossed, her expression guarded, but there's a crack in her armor, the briefest flicker of interest that's brewing between us. It's forbidden, probably fleeting, but utterly undeniable, like a shot directly to my vein.

"Much better," Greyson exclaims, clapping his hands once we straighten. "Take five, and then we'll do it again."

As I step back, wiping the sweat from my brow, I catch Vaeda watching me. Her gaze is piercing, as though daring me to look away first. My chest tightens as a thousand unspoken words catch in the space between us, my high climbing with it.

Determined to prove myself to her, to everyone, I nod before turning back to Yvonne. The competition in Paris isn't just a dream, it's a goal, and I'll do whatever it takes to get there. Even if it means ignoring the pull I feel every time Vaeda's eyes meet mine.

The music starts again, the Rumba's seductive rhythm flowing through the studio like a current. Yvonne steps into position with a confident smile, her hand slipping into mine. I steady my breathing, grounding myself in the steps we've practiced countless times.

This time, we aim for more emotion and chemistry. I focus on the tension between our bodies, the lean, the pull, and the subtle give in her movements as she follows my lead. Yet even as we flow through the same sequence, something feels off. My mind isn't fully in the dance. It's with Vaeda.

She stands by the mirrors, her arms crossed, and her laser gaze fixed on us, analyzing every movement. I can't help but notice the way her auburn hair catches the light, strands of copper and gold glimmering with every subtle shift of her head. Her dark brown eyes are intense, their heated stare pressing against my skin.

"Stop," she snaps suddenly, her voice cutting through the music like a blade. Yvonne and I both freeze mid-step, startled.

Vaeda steps forward, closing the distance between us with a confidence that makes my stomach tighten. "You're still too stiff," she says, her gaze locking on mine. "You need to feel the connection, not just mimic it."

Then she pauses and tilts her head slightly, a challenge glinting in her eyes. "I'll show you."

Yvonne steps back without a word, her expression carefully neutral, and suddenly Vaeda is in front of me. She places one hand lightly on my shoulder, the other slipping into my palm. Her touch is firm yet soft, and the subtle scent of her perfume, musky and floral, wraps around me, intoxicating and impossible to ignore, and my high catapults.

"Ready?" she asks, though her tone makes it clear she expects nothing less.

I nod, my throat dry, and we step into the music.

Dancing with Vaeda is nothing like dancing with Yvonne. Vaeda's movements are fluid, effortless, as though the music itself flows through her veins. Every shift of her weight is perfectly balanced, and when she presses into me, there's a magnetism that leaves me breathless.

"Your frame," she mutters, her voice low but insistent. She lifts my arm slightly, adjusting the angle of my hand on her back. Her fingertips brush against mine, sending a spark through my skin. "Better," she murmurs, her eyes flicking up to meet mine.

I try to focus on the steps, on the tension and release of the Rumba, but it's impossible. Her presence is overwhelming. The soft curve of her freckled nose, the way her auburn hair glows under the fluorescents, the faint sheen of sweat along her temple that catches the light. Every detail of her feels magnified, as if we are the only two who exist on Earth.

"Don't just lead," she directs, her voice pulling me back. "Listen. Respond."

Her words echo in my mind as we move, and I start to let go of the choreography, letting the music guide me instead. Vaeda's body leans into mine, her movements a perfect conversation of music and feeling. I feel the shift in her weight before it happens, the subtle push and pull that connects us.

"Now you're getting it," she says, her breath warm against my cheek as we turn.

But I'm not sure I am. My heart is pounding too hard, my concentration splintering under her proximity. Those adorable freckles along her nose, the way her dark eyes seem to see straight through me. It's too much. Every step feels charged, every glance a spark waiting to ignite, and I'm on the edge of a second overdose.

When the music crescendos, she pulls away sharply, leaving me holding nothing but the air between us. For a moment, the absence of her touch feels almost unbearable.

Vaeda steps back, her expression as unreadable as ever, though there's a flicker of approval in her eyes, or maybe it's curiosity.

"Not bad," she states, her voice clipped. "But you're still holding back. Work on that."

I nod, swallowing hard, but my throat feels tight. As she turns away, her perfume lingers in the space between us, a haunting reminder of how easily she unraveled me.

Yvonne steps forward again, her smile a little strained, and we move back into position, but as the music starts up once more, my mind keeps slipping. Not to the competition, not to the steps, but to Vaeda. To her chocolate gaze, her warm skin, the unspoken tether that hangs between us like the echo of a forbidden melody, and to the anticipation of my next hit.

VAEDA

The music fades, leaving the studio in a charged silence broken only by the rhythmic pounding of my heart. I step away from Mateo, letting the space between us grow, but the echo of his touch remains on my skin like a brand. My chest feels tight, and I force myself to focus on adjusting my hair, tucking loose strands of auburn away from my face.

It was just a dance, I tell myself. *Nothing more.*

But I can't deny how my body betrayed me in those moments, how every step felt electric, every glance too charged. His hand on my back, firm yet hesitant, sent a warmth coursing through me that I had no business feeling. His honey eyes, so intent on mine, made me feel like the only person in the room.

And I hated it.

Hated how magnetic he was, how easily I was drawn to the raw determination in his gaze. It wasn't just his technique, though that had been better, more connected, and more alive. No, it was something else entirely. It's similar to what I used to feel with Gerardo when we danced, but I felt it deeper in my core.

I cross my arms, stepping closer to the mirrors to create more distance from him. From the corner of my eye, I see Yvonne laughing softly at something Mateo said. She leans into him with the easy familiarity of a partner, and I feel a flicker of relief. They're the same age, in sync, and the perfect pairing. I'm just his teacher, and yet...

I glance at my reflection, catching sight of the freckles across my nose and cheeks. They've always been there, a remnant of my youth, but today they feel like a mocking reminder of the years between us. Mateo is young, full of untapped potential, while I have a husband waiting at home. A husband who trusts me.

The weight of guilt settles inside my chest like a boulder, and I shift uncomfortably, as though moving could dislodge it. What am I doing? This isn't about Mateo; it's about the competition. About helping him succeed. *That's all it is.*

As much as I try to rationalize, I can't forget the way his gaze lingered, or the way his body moved with mine. It wasn't just a dance. It couldn't have been, not with the way my pulse raced and my breath hitched every time our eyes met.

No.

I turn sharply, facing the mirrors as if confronting myself. This isn't about him. It's about the Rumba, about the story we're supposed to tell through movement. Mateo needed to feel the connection, the push and pull that defines the dance. That's what I was showing him. Nothing more. *So why does it feel like more?*

I force myself to think of Greyson's critiques and of the competition in Paris. Of the pressure to see Mateo and Yvonne succeed. This isn't about me. It can't be. Mateo's future depends on my guidance, not my… feelings.

I press my lips together, trying to push down the confusion and unease swirling inside my chest. When I danced with Mateo, it was different because of his rawness, his focus, and the intensity he brings. It's my job to shape that into something tangible. To refine him and make him shine. To make Fusion Core succeed.

Anything else is a distraction.

I glance toward the clock on the wall, realizing how late it's getting. Gerardo will be home by now, probably preparing dinner or reading on the couch. He's been patient through all of this, through my late nights and extra rehearsals. He trusts me, believes in me.

The thought of him waiting makes the guilt heavier. I shake my head, inhaling deeply to steady myself. Whatever

I thought I felt during that dance wasn't real. It couldn't have been. I care about Fusion Core's success, that's all. Anything else is a figment of my imagination, a fleeting moment of weakness that I'll bury and never let see the light of day.

"Ready to go again?" Greyson's voice cuts through my thoughts, pulling me back to the present.

I nod briskly, not trusting myself to speak, then stand beside Greyson as Yvonne takes her place at Mateo's side. They move into position as I fold my arms and watch, schooling my expression into bored nonchalance. Professional and detached.

But as the music starts again and Mateo's gaze locks briefly with mine, I feel the faintest tremor inside my chest.

No.

It's nothing.

It can't be.

Later that evening, I step into the penthouse, the familiar scent of freshly baked bread wafting from the kitchen. The warm, homey aroma tugs at something deep inside me, reminding me of the life I've built here, the life I chose. Gerardo stands at the counter, arranging a tray of cheeses and olives with his usual meticulousness.

He looks up as I enter, a warm smile spreading across his face. "Welcome home, amor," he says, setting the tray down and wiping his hands on a dish towel. "Long day?"

"You could say that," I reply, slipping off my coat and hanging it over a chair. My voice sounds even to my own ears, but inside, there's a tangle of thoughts I can't seem to unravel.

His eyes flick to my jacket and I know it bothers him, but he won't say anything. He'll just hang it by the door later when I get ready for bed. My bad habits are something he's overlooked, and I'm too lazy to change. "Perfect timing," he continues, his tone cheerful. "I wanted to talk to you about something."

I raise an eyebrow, already wary. "What is it?"

This is how we've been acting for the past few days, overly cheerful and skating around the fact that he drank himself into a stupor over our old competition videos as I sobbed in our closet.

"Your birthday," he singsongs, his smile widening like a child revealing a secret. "I'm planning a surprise party for you next weekend."

I groan, pinching the bridge of my nose. "Gerardo, it's not a surprise if you tell me about it, and you know how I feel about surprises."

"Which is exactly why I'm telling you about it," he counters, his eyes twinkling with mischief. "You deserve to celebrate, Vaeda. Thirty-three is a milestone."

Every word he says is meant to make me feel cherished, yet it only enhances the discomfort I've been carrying since I left the studio. I force myself to nod, even as my mind betrays me, flashing back to the warmth of Mateo's hand on my back and how his amber eyes held mine just a second too long. I shake the thought away, but it lingers, unwelcome and stubborn. There are ten years stretching a gaping hole between us.

"Every year is a milestone," I mutter, hoping the comment sounds lighthearted. Gerardo's enthusiasm is hard to resist, even when it's directed at something as unnecessary as a party.

"Trust me," he stresses, stepping closer and placing his hands on my shoulders. His touch is comforting and familiar. "It'll be perfect. Just let me handle everything."

I nod again, grateful for the support he offers, but the

guilt only grows heavier. He's always been this way: loving, patient, and unshakable in his devotion to me. Yet no amount of his kindness can erase the memory of the studio today. The way Mateo's fingers had pressed against mine, his grip firm. The subtle smell of his sweat and cologne mixed with the music as we moved together.

It wasn't just a dance, my mind whispers, and I immediately shut it down. It was just a dance. That's all it was.

"Fine," I concede, relenting. "But keep it small. And no ridiculous themes."

"Of course," Gerardo vows, his grin widening. "Small and tasteful, just like you."

His words are playful, affectionate, and they should comfort me, but I feel a strange hollowness instead. I force a slight smile, letting him think he's won.

As Gerardo moves back to the kitchen, humming softly to himself, I sink onto the couch and stare out at the city lights beyond the windowpanes. My mind is a battlefield, fighting to stay in the here and now with my husband, where I belong.

Only I can't seem to stop replaying the way Mateo looked at me when I corrected his steps. The way his touch felt so strong, deliberate, and yet deferential. The way his gaze lingered when I stepped back, as if he didn't want to let me go.

"Vaeda?" Gerardo's voice pulls me back, and I look up to see him holding out a glass of wine, his expression warm and expectant.

I take it with a small smile, muttering a quiet, "Thank you," but my chest feels tight. Gerardo deserves all of me, and yet tonight, my thoughts are fractured, caught somewhere they shouldn't be.

This isn't about Mateo, I tell myself again. It's about the competition. It's about pushing him to be better, about helping the studio land on the map. My connection to him is professional and nothing more.

So why does it feel like a lie?

"Here's to you," Gerardo says, raising his glass in a toast.

"To me," I echo softly, clinking my glass against his, but as the wine slides down my throat, the remorse remains a quiet, relentless ache.

Chapter Eight

The morning sun casts soft reflections onto the mirrors as I sit cross-legged at the edge of the floor, clipboard in hand, while Greyson paces in front of the mirrors like a restless lion. The air is filled with the scent of wood polish, and the faint whir of the heating system serves as a background to our conversation.

"Mateo and Yvonne have undeniable chemistry," Greyson says, his voice brimming with certainty. "Their movements are romantic, precise, and dynamic. They're exactly what we need to make an impact in Paris."

I shake my head, jotting notes on the clipboard. "Yvonne is strong, but Mateo still lacks polish. He's improving, but he's inconsistent. Kari and Adam are reliable and steady. They're a safer choice."

Greyson halts mid-stride and turns to face me, his hands on his hips. "Safe isn't going to win us a spot on the international stage, Vae. You know that."

I glance up at him, my pen hovering over the paper. "But they're dependable. They've been training more as a team. That counts for something."

"Dependable is a good word for a plumber, not a competitive dancer," he snarks, resuming his pacing. "Mateo has school and meetings to attend to, and still, he's accelerated past Adam and Kari, in my opinion. We need a spark, something that makes the judges sit up and take notice."

Before I can retort, the studio door opens and Kari and Adam walk in. Their faces light up when they see us, and they head straight for the center of the room, their energy buoyant. Kari's blonde hair is tied in a sleek bun, and Adam's posture is straight, his steps confident.

"Morning," Adam greets, his smile wide and eager.

"Good timing," I say, rising to my feet. "We were just discussing you two. Let's see how you're progressing. Show us the routine you've been working on."

Kari nods eagerly, her exuberance shining through, and Adam matches her enthusiasm with a determined expression. They move into position, their bodies aligning with practiced ease. Greyson and I step back, giving them the floor.

The music starts, a lively Cha-Cha rhythm filling the studio. Their movements are clean, their timing impeccable. Adam's frame is solid, his footwork true, and Kari's lines are graceful, her extensions beautiful. Yet, as I watch them glide through the routine, a nagging feeling settles over me. It's all there on the surface, the technique, the synchronization, the polish, but there's no fire. No spark that elevates the performance from good to unforgettable.

When they finish, I clap lightly, nodding as they catch their breath. "Good," I begin, keeping my tone measured. "Your synchronization is strong, and your lines are clean, but there's something missing."

Kari tilts her head, her expression questioning. "What do you mean?"

I step forward, gesturing toward the space they had

just danced through. "You're executing the steps, but it feels rehearsed, like you're going through the motions. The Cha-Cha needs personality and energy. It's playful and flirtatious. Let's try a Rumba instead."

Adam's brows furrow slightly, but Kari nods, her confidence unwavering. She adjusts her posture, ready for the shift in tone, while Adam glances at the mirrors, adjusting his frame. Greyson queues the music, and the sultry rhythm of a Rumba begins to play its slow, deliberate beat, filling the room.

They glide into the opening steps, Kari's movements fluid and expressive. Her hips sway naturally with the music, her arms extending in elegant lines. Adam, however, seems more tentative. His steps are careful, almost hesitant, and his frame lacks the presence needed to match Kari's energy. He looks like he's thinking too much, analyzing every step instead of feeling it.

I cross my arms, my critical eyes following every detail. The contrast between Adam and Mateo flashes in my mind unbidden. Mateo's intensity, the way he immerses himself in the music, and the undeniable pull of his movements. Where Mateo commands attention, Adam fades into the background. The comparison makes my cheeks flush, and I quickly refocus on the routine in front of me.

When the music fades, I step forward again. "Your technique is solid," I start, directing my gaze at both of them. "But Adam, you're holding back. The Rumba is a conversation, a dance of tension and release. Right now, it feels one-sided. You need to bring more to the performance."

Adam nods, his expression sheepish. "I'll work on it."

"Good," I reply, glancing briefly at Greyson. He's leaning against the wall, his lips twitching into a smile as he watches me.

"Thank you," Kari says, her voice steady. "We'll keep

refining it."

As they gather their things and leave the floor, Greyson steps forward, his smirk more pronounced. "Not as compelling as Mateo, is he?" he teases, his tone light but pointed.

I roll my eyes, ignoring the heat creeping up my neck. "Kari's technique is better," I counter, though the words feel hollow even as I say them.

Greyson chuckles, clearly not convinced. "Keep telling yourself that, Vae."

The studio is dimly lit as Greyson and I finish cleaning up for the night. The hustle of the day's activities still buzzes faintly in my mind, but the quiet now is a welcome reprieve.

Without having Mateo here in the same room, I can breathe a little easier and see things a little clearer. I wish I could argue with my entire chest about having Adam and Kari representing us in Paris, but I fear Greyson is right. Mateo and Yvonne have that edge, the connection the judges love to see alongside technique.

Now it means endless hours of practice and routines, and endless hours of Mateo. His scent, his presence, his *allure*. All of it will be obstacles I'll have to overcome to ensure we remain professional, in good standing, and come out of this competition in first place.

Gerardo is my rock, the man who picked me back up off my knees when I thought the world was crumbling down around me, and Mateo is like the apple in the Garden of Eden. I must resist.

With Gerardo still in my thoughts, I place the clipboard into my bag and turn to Greyson. "Thanks for staying late. I wanted to talk to you about something."

Greyson raises an eyebrow, intrigued. "What's on your mind?"

"My husband is throwing me a surprise birthday party next weekend," I reveal, my tone dry. "Consider this your official invitation."

Greyson bursts out laughing, his voice echoing in the empty studio. "A surprise party you already know about? Of course. That's so you, Vae. If 'I can do it all by myself' had a picture in the dictionary, it would be yours."

I shrug, a small smile tugging at my lips. "Sir, that's a whole phrase. A dictionary only has words."

"Whatever." He waves me off as he does up his jacket. "The phrase Dictionary then. Did Gerardo spill the beans on the party because he's scared you'll hate it?"

"Gerardo has never been subtle. Besides, when he thinks he's being sneaky, he leaves a trail a mile wide. He told me because he knows I hate surprises, but he wants a party more for himself than anything else. You know how much he loves a good time. It'll be an extravagant event, even though I've asked for something small and intimate."

"Well, I'm honored to be invited." Greyson chuckles, his grin widening. "Should I offer up a naked sushi platter?"

"How about no?" I reply, locking the studio door behind us. "And keep the gifts tasteful please. None of your ridiculous jokes."

"Wouldn't dream of it," he vows, slinging his bag over his shoulder. "Thirty-three, huh? Time truly flies."

"Don't remind me," I mutter, stepping into the cool night air. "Just show up and be on time."

"I'll be there," he promises, his tone softening. "Get some rest, Vae. You deserve it."

As he heads off, I linger by the studio door, the pressure

of the upcoming competition pressing down on me. Despite the exhaustion, there's a small flicker of hope. Everything has been working out, and maybe this year's birthday won't be so bad after all.

MATEO

Roger's car idles at the curb as I jog down the school's steps, pulling my coat tighter against the crisp afternoon air. The vibration of the city energizes me more effectively than coffee, though the sharp wind biting at my cheeks doesn't hurt either. Sliding into the back seat, I offer a small smile as Roger glances at me in the rearview mirror, his familiar hazel eyes warm and kind.

"Good afternoon, Mateo," he greets, his voice carrying the confidence of someone who's prepared for anything. "You're looking more upbeat these days. It's nice to see."

I buckle my seat belt, settling into the plush leather that seems to cradle me like a safety net. "Thanks, Roger. I've been feeling better lately."

"Good to hear," he replies, turning the wheel smoothly as we merge into traffic. "Whatever you're doing, keep it up. It's a big change from a few weeks ago."

His words sit with me, hovering in the air like a small wind funnel, threatening to coax the tornado out of me. It's true though. Dancing again has brought back a piece of myself I thought I'd lost, but even as I let that hope bloom, it's tethered to the mistakes of my past, a shadow that follows me no matter how fast I move.

The city is alive at this time, bustling with purpose. Steam rises from grates in the sidewalks, curling into the chilly air like ghosts escaping the underground. The low rumble of traffic and the occasional wail of a distant siren are the soundtrack to this place, and a reminder that life goes on, indifferent to the battles we individually fight within ourselves.

Roger weaves through the streets, and soon, we pull up to the modest brick building that houses my Narcotics Anonymous meetings. The building looms ahead, its worn facade standing firm against the tide of the city. It's unassuming, the kind of place you wouldn't glance at twice unless you knew what it offered. For me, it's a sanctuary and a battleground all at once.

"I'll be back to pick you up in an hour," Roger says, his voice breaking through my thoughts.

"Thanks," I mutter, pulling the door handle and stepping out into the cold.

The room is already half-full when I walk in, the circle of chairs arranged neatly in the center, the scene set to look like an invitation to your vulnerability. The smell of coffee lingers, mingling with the slight tang of cleaning supplies. A handful of familiar faces nod in greeting as I take a seat, their silent acknowledgment a small comfort.

Marissa begins the meeting as she usually does: introductions, updates, the steady rhythm of people sharing pieces of themselves they'd rather forget but know they can't. When my turn comes, I feel all of their gazes, each one carrying a mixture of understanding and hope.

"Hi, I'm Mateo, and I'm an addict," I begin, my voice steady but low. "I'm… doing okay. Better, actually." A few murmurs of support ripple through the circle, and I take a deep breath, letting it infuse me with courage. "I've started dancing again," I admit, the words feeling both liberating and terrifying as they leave my mouth. "Just classes, nothing serious, but it helps. It's giving me something to focus on, a goal to work toward."

Jack, an older man with a weathered face and kind eyes, leans forward. He's been coming to these meetings as often as I have, and he's become an acquaintance. His presence always carries a certain dignity, the kind born from decades of mistakes and hard-earned wisdom. "Dancing was a part of your life before, right?" he asks, his voice tinged with curiosity and concern. "When you were heavily using?"

I nod, my throat tightening. "Yeah. Dancing was my whole life. Until it wasn't."

Jack's brow furrows, and he pauses as if choosing his words carefully. "Mateo, we're all rooting for you, but going back to something tied so closely to your addiction is risky. You know that."

"I do," I reply quickly, my voice firmer than I expected. "And I'm being careful. I'm not letting it consume me the way it did before."

Lisa, a petite woman with a no-nonsense demeanor, chimes in from across the circle. "What's different this time?" she presses, her gaze searching but not unkind. "What's keeping you from using?"

Her question hangs in the air, and I hesitate, forming an answer that feels true. "Perspective," I say finally. "Before, I danced because I had to. It was about winning, about being the best. Now, it's more about finding myself again. Reclaiming something that was taken from me."

Lisa nods, her expression softening. "That's a good start. Just remember to keep your recovery first. Dancing is great, but it's not worth your sobriety."

The circle hums with agreement, their collective concern both comforting me and giving me anxiety. I nod, forcing a small smile. They mean well, and I appreciate it, but the doubts they've voiced are ones I've already been wrestling with.

The conversation moves on, each person taking their turn to share. Some stories are hard to listen to, filled with regret and struggle; others are easier, small victories celebrated in the face of their dark demons. By the end of the hour, the room feels both lighter and heavier, our shared burdens hanging over our heads.

There was one thing I failed to confess, and it's settling

inside my chest like a weight. I am forming an altogether different addiction, and she has hair that shines like fire in the light.

An hour later, I step outside, the crisp air hitting me like a reset button. Roger's car is parked next to the building, his silhouette visible through the windshield.

Sliding into the back seat, I let out a heavy sigh. Roger glances at me in the rearview mirror, his eyes filled with empathy.

"How'd it go?" he asks, his eyes searching my face for answers.

"Good," I reply, leaning back against the seat. "Tough, but good."

He nods, merging into traffic with practiced ease. "That's what matters. One day at a time, right?"

"Yeah," I murmur, my gaze drifting to the window. The city blurs past, a kaleidoscope of lights and motion. One day at a time. It was a mantra I clung to in the early days of my recovery, even when the days felt endless and the nights lonelier than I could bear.

As we drive, my thoughts return to the studio, to the feel of the music and the rhythm of the steps. It's not just dancing. It's reclaiming a piece of my soul, and this time, I have the chance to experience it in its purest form. Nothing to enhance or blur it. Each step will be made with my mind and body grounded.

Her face morphs into my mind as my eyes slowly shut, and I imagine I'm reaching out to run my finger over the freckles dusting her nose. I've let the drugs and alcohol go, but I've found a new high, and it may prove to be just as dangerous.

CHAPTER NINE

The studio hums with anticipation, the energy crackling as the four dancers warm up. It's one of those Saturday mornings where everything feels amplified. The light spilling through the windows is almost too bright, the polished floor reflects too much, and the music, though soft, feels intrusive. My clipboard rests on the small desk by the mirror, but my focus isn't on the notes. It's on Mateo and Yvonne.

They stand close together, their heads bent as they speak in hushed tones. Yvonne laughs at something he says, her hand lightly brushing his arm. Mateo smiles in return, his usually serious face softening in a way that makes my chest tighten. They start stretching, their movements fluid and synchronized, their camaraderie easy and obvious.

I glance at Greyson, who's adjusting the playlist on his phone, oblivious to my growing irritation. *This isn't about jealousy,* I tell myself. It's about professionalism. About focus. Yet when Yvonne playfully nudges Mateo, and he responds with a low chuckle, I feel a sharp pang of envy.

"Alright," I call out, my voice cutting through the room like a whip. "Let's get started. Show us your routines. Yvonne and Mateo, you're up first."

Adam and Kari sit against the wall, their casual demeanors replaced with honed concentration. Yvonne and Mateo get into position, their Rumba starting with a smooth opening. Yvonne's movements are captivating, every step sensual, and Mateo matches her pace, his form strong and deliberate. But my eyes are drawn to the way his hand rests on her back, the subtle way her fingers linger on the space between his shoulder and neck.

As the music swells, their connection intensifies, their bodies moving as one. The rhythm is hypnotic, the tension between them palpable. By the time they reach the final pose with Yvonne arching gracefully as Mateo supports her, I'm gripping my clipboard so tightly my knuckles ache.

Greyson claps, his enthusiasm genuine. "Excellent work. You've made a lot of progress."

I force myself to nod. "Good control but, Mateo, you're still holding back. Your movements need to come from a deeper place."

He meets my gaze, his brows furrowing slightly. "What do you mean?"

"It's not just about the steps," I say, walking toward him. "It's about the feeling, the emotion behind them. Let me show you."

Yvonne steps back, her features masked as I take her place. I stand close to Mateo, his presence magnetic in a way that unsettles me.

"Hand on my back," I instruct, my voice steady despite the flutter inside my chest. He complies, his touch firm but careful. I place my hand on his shoulder, my fingers brushing the nape of his neck. "Now, follow my lead."

The music begins, a slow and sultry melody that seems to echo in the charged silence of the room. I guide him through the opening steps, our bodies moving in sync.

"Relax," I murmur, my eyes locked on his. "Feel the music."

He nods slightly, his grip adjusting as we glide across the floor. The magnetism between us builds with every step, every turn. When I spin away and back into his hold, his hand catches me effortlessly, his firm hold making my breath hitch.

"Better," I whisper softly, though my voice is barely audible over the music.

We move through the sequence, the rhythm dictating our every motion. He becomes more fluid, his body reading mine like an open book. I move, he moves. I breathe, he inhales. When we reach the dip, his arm supports me with a confidence that sends a shiver down my spine. Our faces are inches apart, his breath warm against my skin, our eyes locked in a moment that feels endless.

The music fades, leaving only the sound of our labored breathing. For a heartbeat, neither of us moves, the charged silence wrapping around us like a cocoon.

"Vaeda," Greyson's voice breaks the spell, accompanied by a sharp clap.

I step back quickly, my cheeks flushing as reality crashes in. Mateo straightens, his expression unreadable, but his eyes linger on mine for a moment longer than necessary. I turn away, desperate to regain my composure.

"You're still a bit too stiff for the Rumba," I say, my words brisk as I address him. "You need to loosen up, to become one with the rhythm. I suggest taking another class. Something outside your comfort zone. Hip-hop, maybe."

Mateo raises an eyebrow, clearly skeptical. "Hip-hop?"

"It'll help you find a connection from your heart to the music," I explain, my tone firm. "You need to feel the rhythm in your body, not just your feet."

He nods slowly, though I can see the doubt in his eyes. Yvonne steps forward, her expression tight as she glances between us.

"Should we do it again, or are we done?" she asks, her voice sharper than usual.

"Yes, you're done." I nod, smoothing my moist palms down the sides of my thighs. "Kari and Adam, you're up next."

As Yvonne and Mateo switch places with Adam and Kari, I catch Yvonne glaring at me, her eyes dark with anger. I ignore it, focusing instead on the notes Greyson is jotting down. The energy in the room is thick, and I can't shake the feeling that I've crossed a line, not just with Yvonne, but with myself.

I lean against the mirrored wall, clipboard back in hand, my pen hovering over a blank line as Greyson begins fiddling with the sound system, his brows furrowed in concentration. Mateo and Yvonne are stretching near the far corner, their quiet chatter punctuated by the occasional laugh. The sound of her voice is grating on my nerves, something akin to nails on a chalkboard.

Kari and Adam stand in the center of the room, their postures straight, their minds focused. They've been refining this Viennese Waltz for days, and today is the moment to see if their work has paid off. Kari's light blonde hair is swept into a tight bun, and her sky-blue practice dress flows gracefully around her ankles. Adam's black shirt is simple, but it emphasizes his clean lines and lean muscles.

"Ready when you are," I say, motioning to Greyson. He nods and presses a button, the lush, sweeping strains of a waltz filling the air.

Kari and Adam take their starting positions, their hands meeting with a practiced elegance. The first few notes act as a cue, and they step into motion, gliding across the floor with a grace that immediately draws the room's attention.

Their movements are mesmerizing. Kari's frame is impeccable, her head tilted just enough to catch the light on her delicate profile. Adam's hold is steady, his steps confident as he leads her through the sweeping rotations and gentle rises and falls of the waltz. Their synchronicity is almost hypnotic, a seamless interplay of strength and softness.

The music crescendos, and Adam guides Kari into a reverse turn, her skirt flaring in a perfect arc. For a brief moment, it's as if they're floating, their feet barely brushing the ground. My breath catches at the sight because this is what dance is supposed to feel like: weightless, timeless, transcendent.

From the corner of my eye, I catch Mateo watching intently. His arms are crossed, but his expression betrays a mixture of admiration and frustration. Yvonne, standing beside him, nudges his arm and whispers something, but his gaze remains fixed on the dancers.

"Beautiful," Greyson murmurs under his breath, his eyes shining with pride as he watches Kari and Adam move through the more intricate steps of the routine. "They've really stepped up."

I nod, scribbling a note on my clipboard. "Kari's technique is flawless. She's carrying the emotion of the dance perfectly." My eyes flick to Adam. "But he's all technique. His moves are perfect, but the passion isn't breaking through."

As if sensing the critique, Adam suddenly takes a risk, adding a subtle flourish to his movement as he leads Kari into a dramatic pivot. It's bold, unexpected, and exactly what was missing. Their connection seems to deepen, their energy crackling as the music swells toward its climax.

By the time they reach the final pose with Kari dipped low, one leg extended gracefully as Adam holds her securely, the room is silent and captivated. The last note fades, and for a moment, no one moves. Then Greyson claps, the sound breaking the spell.

"Well done!" he exclaims, his voice filled with genuine approval. "That was exceptional."

Kari straightens, her cheeks flushed and her breathing quick. Adam releases her with a small smile, his own face damp with exertion. They exchange a glance that speaks of triumph, their hard work finally paying off.

I step forward, my heels clicking softly against the floor. "Much improved," I say, letting my gaze linger on Adam. "That risk you took with the pivot? That's what I've been waiting to see. More of that and you'll take this routine to another level."

Adam nods, his expression serious. "Thank you. We'll keep working on it."

"You should," I stress, my words filled with encouragement. "This is the kind of dancing that gets remembered."

As Kari and Adam move to the side to catch their breath, I glance at Mateo again. He's still watching, his brows furrowed as if dissecting every moment of their performance. I make a mental note to address his focus later, but for now, I let the moment live on, the echoes of the Viennese Waltz still resonating in the studio.

MATEO

The studio falls quiet after Yvonne, Kari, and Adam leave, their chatter fading down the hall. I hover near the mirrors, pretending to fix the laces on my shoes. The truth is, I'm waiting for us to be alone. I watch as Greyson retreats into the office, the door clicking shut behind him. Vaeda remains, her attention fixed on her clipboard as she makes quick notes, her pen moving with purpose.

My heart pounds as I walk toward her. Each step feels like I'm floating, as if the potency of this drug is immediate. She looks up as I approach, her posture stiffening slightly. There's a flicker of unease in her eyes before she schools her expression into nonchalance.

"Vaeda." Just saying her name, having it roll off my tongue, feels seductive. "I wanted to talk to you about what you said earlier."

She arches an eyebrow, her grip tightening on the clipboard. "What about?"

I stop a few feet away, close enough to feel her presence but far enough to keep propriety in check. "You suggested I take another class," I remind her. "Something outside my comfort zone. Hip-hop?"

"Yes," she replies, her tone clipped. "You need to work on your rhythm. It's a good idea."

"I'll do it," I say, stepping closer. Her eyes narrow slightly as she takes a half-step back. "If you come with me."

Her brows knit together in confusion before she lets out a soft, incredulous laugh. "Mateo, I'm not the one who needs the extra practice."

"I'm serious," I insist, my gaze locking onto hers. "This competition in Paris is everything. If I'm going to do this, I want to do it right, and I can't think of anyone better to push me than you."

She hesitates, her lips pressing into a thin line, then her gaze flickers toward the office door as if hoping Greyson will reappear to break the moment, but the room remains silent, just the two of us standing in the charged bubble.

"You're incessant," she mutters, though there's a softness in her voice that wasn't there before.

"I have to be," I reply, taking another step closer. The space between us is nearly nonexistent now, and I feel the air shift, heavy with a pulsing need. My blood begins to sing as the drug of her courses through me. "You said it yourself. I need to loosen up. Who better to teach me than someone who knows exactly what it takes?"

She exhales sharply, the sound almost a sigh of defeat. "I'll think about it," she concedes finally, her voice quieter now, almost unsure. "I'll send you the details of a class I know nearby. No promises though."

I nod, satisfied for the moment. "That's all I ask."

Our eyes lock for a heartbeat longer, the tension simmering just below the surface. There's something magnetic in the way she holds my gaze, something that makes it impossible to look away, but then she shifts slightly, breaking the moment.

"Good night, Mateo," she murmurs, her tone dismissive as she turns back to her clipboard.

"Good night." I grab my bag before heading out of the studio and toward the exit. The electricity between us is only increasing, and even though I tell myself this is wrong, I can't seem to stay away from her. She's made me a junkie all over again.

The thought of doing something together outside of this studio makes my heart race and my hands grow clammy.

She has a husband, a life outside of me and the studio, and she looks at me like I'm a burden, but sometimes her looks flicker with heat.

Vaeda Lewis wants me, even if she doesn't fully accept it yet, and I'm starting to realize I'll do anything to have her.

Tugging my jacket tighter around me, I adjust my bag and head back to my apartment. My mind races, replaying the conversation with Vaeda, dissecting every word, every glance. She's tantalizing in every way, pulling me in until I find myself in her space without realizing it. She's gorgeous, guarded, and yet there are moments when her walls seem to crack, revealing glimpses of vulnerability.

When I reach my building, I head down the side alley and climb the fire escape, the metal clanging under my weight. Thankfully I'm not afraid of heights. The activity of the city fades as I step into the quiet of the building, erasing all thoughts of Vaeda as anxiety about hiding this secret from my family seeps in.

Opening my apartment door, I kick off my shoes and toss my bag onto the kitchen counter. I open the fridge and pull out a bottle of water, drinking the entire thing in one go before throwing the bottle into the recycling under the counter. Then I flick on the light and freeze.

She's sitting there, on the couch, her posture rigid and her expression unreadable, but the flare of her nostrils tells me everything I need to know. My mother is here in New York, and she's pissed.

"Mami," I say, my voice tinged with surprise. "What are you doing here?"

She stands slowly, her movements jerky, her gaze piercing as it locks onto mine. At her full height, my mother stands just a few inches shorter than me at six feet. "Don't play coy with me, Mateo. Where have you been?"

Her words hang in the air, saturated with accusation, and my stomach twists. I force myself to meet her golden gaze, though my mind is already racing, searching for the right answer, the safe answer. My thoughts become scrambled under her scrutiny, the unspoken fears slipping from her light brown eyes.

The apartment feels smaller now, the walls closing in as the silence stretches between us. Whatever I say next will matter, and I'm not sure if I'm ready for this conversation.

"Answer me, Mateo," she demands, her voice steady but laced with the razor edge of a woman who has spent her life commanding attention. My mother doesn't raise her voice often, but when she does, it's like the edge of a blade, dangerous and impossible to ignore.

"I was at a meeting," I hedge carefully, my throat dry. "Then I went for a walk. That's all."

She arches a perfectly sculpted eyebrow, her lips pressing into a thin line. She's wearing a tailored coat, the rich navy fabric perfectly fitted, and her posture is impeccable, as if she's still standing at the barre. "A meeting? And you didn't think to call Roger?"

"Mami, I—"

She cuts me off with a wave of her hand, her gold bracelets jingling softly with the movement. "Do you know how many times I've called you this week? How many messages I've left?" She steps closer, her heels clicking against the floor. "And now I come all the way here, only to find you, what? Wandering the streets?"

"I wasn't wandering," I argue, my voice rising slightly. "I was clearing my head."

"Clearing your head," she repeats, her tone flat, as though the words are foreign to her. "That sounds like an excuse."

My hands clench into fists at my sides, but I force myself to take a deep breath. Losing my temper won't help. "Mami, I'm fine. I'm… I'm clean. I promise."

Her eyes narrow, scanning my face for any hint of deception. After my accident, my mother has gained the uncanny ability to see through me, her intuition as keen as her technique on stage. "Promises mean nothing without proof, Mateo. You know that better than anyone."

"I'm telling you the truth," I vow, my voice softening. "I've been going to my meetings. I've been staying busy."

She folds her arms, her gaze unrelenting. "Staying busy with what? School? Or is it something else?"

My stomach twists, and I hesitate. Telling her about the dance classes feels like stepping onto thin ice. She'll either see it as a positive or as a dangerous slide back into the life I've worked so hard to leave behind.

"I've been trying new things," I say vaguely, avoiding her piercing gaze. "Things to keep me focused."

Her silence stretches as my heart pounds through my chest. Then she sighs, a sound that's equal parts frustration and exhaustion, drawing my attention back to her face. "You think I don't notice the changes in you?" Her eyes soften as she runs a hand through her perfectly straight brown hair, the caramel highlights shimmering. "I'm your mother, Mateo. I see everything."

I look away, the meaning of her words pressing down on me. She steps closer, her hand reaching out to cup my cheek. Her touch is cool, her fingers delicate but firm.

"You look better," she admits, her voice tinged with reluctant pride. "But I can't help worrying. Dancing…" she pauses, the word hanging between us like a ghost. "Dancing brought you so much joy, but it also brought you so much pain. When you admitted to wanting to dance again during our last phone call, I became worried. I needed to see you."

There's no doubt in my mind that she has a sixth sense about my dancing. It's in our blood, the red essence brimming with melody. To deny it now would be a mistake, one she would see as a betrayal of her trust, something I have barely earned back. So I don't admit or deny.

I swallow hard, meeting her gaze again. "It's different this time, Mami. I'm different."

Her lips press together, and for a moment, I think she might argue, but then she nods, her shoulders relaxing slightly. "You have to prove it, Mateo. Not just to me, but to yourself. Every day."

"I know." The apprehension leaves my body with a long exhale. "And I will."

She studies me for a moment longer, then steps back, her poise as perfect as ever. "I'll stay for a little while," she declares as she removes her jacket. "We can have dinner together, and you can tell me more about all these *new things* you're trying."

I chuckle, relief washing over me. "I'd like that."

As she moves to the kitchen, I let out a breath I didn't realize I was holding. The anxiety lingers, but so does the delicate hope that maybe I've taken another step toward earning her trust. She'll be the one to convince my father, and before long, I will be Mateo Sanchez, world champion once again.

Chapter Ten

Mateo

The past few days have been a blur of routine and restraint. My mother hasn't left yet, her presence as steadfast and imposing as a metronome. She rides with me to school, her eyes scanning the world outside the car window as if trying to find the cracks in my story. Roger's usually lighthearted commentary has shifted to an unspoken awkwardness, like he's caught between us and doesn't know which side to take.

She's even started waiting in the car while I attend my meetings, her gaze drilling into me when I climb back in, as if looking for signs of weakness. The city is coming alive with festive decorations, the stores preparing for the holiday season, and I've been taking her shopping, just to keep her busy. Every day, her lingering worry feels like a noose tied around my neck. Tonight is a dance meeting, and I can't afford to miss it. The Paris competition is too important, but how do I leave without her noticing?

I have yet to tell my mother that I've joined a class; we only spoke briefly about me wanting to. I don't know how she would react if she knew I was actually doing it.

Dinner stretches on longer than usual, my mother's conversation warm but laced with subtle probes. She asks about school, about my meetings, about the books stacked neatly on my bedside table. Every answer feels like a carefully balanced step, as if I'm performing a dance with words instead of movement. Finally, after a meal that feels more like an interrogation, she leans back in her chair, a glass of lemonade in hand. Wine is forbidden anywhere in this apartment, as if wine was my problem. Her gaze softens as she lets out a tired sigh.

"It's good to be here with you, Mateo," she hums, her voice losing its usual edge. "I've missed this."

"I've missed you too, Mami," I reply, and I mean it. The guilt gnaws at me, knowing that I'm about to betray her trust.

By the time we clear the table and she settles onto the couch, which she's folded out into a bed, with a book, I'm already formulating my plan. She'll fall asleep soon as she always does after dinner. All I need is patience.

It's an hour later, nearly seven, when I hear her breathing deepen with the telltale rhythm of sleep. I've been sitting on a stool at my kitchen counter, staring at an open textbook but reading none of the words. Quietly, I push my stool back and grab my dance bag from the closet. My heart pounds as I slip on my sneakers and pull on a hoodie, the soft rustle of fabric sounding deafening in the silence.

As I grab my jacket from the hook, I check the living room. She's sprawled on the couch bed, her book resting on her chest, and her expression peaceful. Guilt twists in my gut, but I remind myself of why I'm doing this. The competition. My future. My recovery. It all hinges on my ability to prove I can handle this.

I slip into the hallway, the door clicking softly behind me, and make my way up the stairs to the roof access door. The rooftop is cold, the wind biting against my face as I step outside. I'm careful to close the access door without letting it slam, fear of amplifying every small sound making my movements slower.

The fire escape is sturdy but narrow, the metal groaning faintly under my weight as I descend. My heart races with every slippery step, a mixture of adrenaline and fear. If my mother wakes up and finds me gone, there's no telling what she'll do, but I can't think about that now. My focus needs to be on my routine and the rhythm Vaeda is insisting I find.

The walk to the studio is brisk, the city alive with its festive lights and decorations. I've always loved the way New York feels after dusk, but it's even more electric during the holidays. The energy shifts and the pace slows just enough to notice the details: the way the streetlights create curious shadows, the distant sound of music spilling from open windows, and the occasional laughter of strangers.

When I arrive at Fusion Core, the familiar sight of the building calms me. I open the door and step inside, the polished floors gleaming under the fluorescent lights. The studio is quiet, the air cool and still. I'm early, but I prefer it that way. It gives me time to warm up, to center myself.

As I stretch by the mirrors, I catch my reflection and pause. My face is thinner than it used to be, and my eyes appear older, but there's something else there now, a determination I haven't seen in a long time. I pull my shoulders back, exhaling slowly. All of this is worth it just to see an echo of the man I used to be, the man who found joy on a dance floor and not at the sight of a prescription bottle.

The door opens behind me, and I glance over my shoulder to see Greyson stride in, his ever-present clipboard in hand. He gives me a nod of acknowledgment before heading to the sound system. I know Vaeda will be here soon, and the thought sends a ripple of nerves through me. Not just because of her critiques, but because of the way her presence shifts the air in the room. Intense. Unpredictable. Magnetic. I'm teetering on the edge of my next hit.

I shake off the thought and focus on my routine, the sound of my movements filling the quiet studio. For now, it's just me and the rhythm, the steps etched into my body like muscle memory, and although the weight of my choices hangs over my head precariously, the music offers a fleeting sense of freedom. Each step, each turn, a chance to prove that I'm still standing.

The door opens once again, and I watch as Yvonne, Adam, and Kari walk in together. Their laughter and easy conversation fill the room, and for a moment, I feel a pang of envy. They've become a tight-knit group, their friendship evident in the way they move and talk as though they're a unit.

I keep my distance, focusing on my stretches as they head toward the center of the studio. Yvonne waves at me, her smile bright, but I only nod in return. Sobriety has made me cautious, careful about letting people in. The line between connection and temptation is too thin, too dangerous to tread.

Vaeda arrives shortly after, her presence shifting the energy in the room. Her piercing gaze sweeps over all of us, her clipboard in hand as always. Greyson claps his hands, drawing our attention.

"Alright, everyone, let's sit down for a moment," he says, his tone brisk and punctuating. "We have some news to share."

We gather around, sitting in a loose circle on the polished floor. Vaeda remains standing, her posture as perfect as ever, while Greyson steps forward, his clipboard tucked under his arm.

"As you all know," Greyson begins, "we've been watching your progress closely over the past several weeks. Each of you has shown incredible dedication and growth, and we're proud of what you've accomplished."

Vaeda nods, her expression unreadable. "But as we've

mentioned before, the Paris competition only allows one couple to represent us. We've had to make a difficult decision."

The room feels charged, the air thick with anticipation. My heart pounds as I glance at Yvonne beside me. She's sitting cross-legged, her hands resting lightly on her knees, but there's a stiffness in her shoulders that betrays her nerves.

Greyson takes a deep breath, his gaze sweeping over all of us. "The couple representing Fusion Core in Paris will be Mateo and Yvonne."

The words hit me like a jolt, and for a moment, I can't move. Yvonne gasps softly beside me, her hand flying to her mouth. Adam and Kari exchange a quick glance, their disappointment flashing briefly before they compose themselves.

"Congratulations," Vaeda says, her voice cool and professional. "This is a significant opportunity, and we expect you both to take it seriously. The next few months will be crucial for your preparation."

Yvonne turns to me, her eyes wide with excitement. "We did it," she whispers, her voice barely audible. I manage a small smile, the enormity of the announcement settling over me. Paris. The chance to prove myself again on an international stage. It's everything I've been working toward, but the pressure is already starting to build.

Greyson continues, outlining the next steps and emphasizing the importance of discipline and routine, but my mind is racing, already jumping ahead to the countless hours of practice, the scrutiny, the expectations. When the meeting ends and the others begin to leave, I stay behind, my thoughts spinning like a whirlwind.

VAEDA

The room begins to empty, the echoes of footsteps and laughter fading as Yvonne, Adam, and Kari gather their things and head for the door. I watch from the far end of the studio as Yvonne hesitates, turning back toward Mateo. She shifts her bag on her shoulder, her expression unsure, as though searching for the right words.

"See you later," she says softly, lingering.

Mateo doesn't respond immediately. His eyes are distant, unfocused, as if he's somewhere else entirely. After a beat, he nods, but it's absent and perfunctory. Yvonne's brows knit together, but she doesn't press him. With a small wave, she follows the others out, the studio door closing behind them with a click.

I glance at Greyson, who's finishing notes on his clipboard. He catches my eyes, his lips quirking into a knowing smirk. "Be gentle with him," he mumbles under his breath as he passes me on his way out of the studio.

"Always," I mutter, my tone flat but my heart unexpectedly tight. Greyson's gaze hovers for a moment longer before he disappears through the door, leaving me alone with Mateo.

The silence stretches, filled only by the slight buzz of the fluorescent lights. Mateo stands near the mirror, his hands on his hips, his head tilted downward. His chest rises and falls with steady breaths, but there's something about his stillness that unsettles me.

I take a step forward, my heels clicking softly against the hardwood. "Mateo," I call out, my voice gentler than usual. "Are you okay?"

He looks up, his dark eyes meeting mine. For a moment,

he doesn't answer, his expression guarded. Then he sighs, his shoulders sagging slightly. "Not really."

The honesty in his tone surprises me, and I close the distance between us, stopping a few feet away. "What's going on?"

He hesitates, his gaze flickering to the floor before returning to mine. "I've been coming here in secret," he admits, the words rushing out of him as though he's broken the dam he built to protect himself. "My family doesn't know. They don't trust me, Vaeda. They think if I'm around this world again, I'll fall back into old habits."

My heart tightens at his words. The burden of the secret he carries is evident in the slump of his shoulders, in the anxiety that radiates from him. "But you've stayed clean," I state, keeping my tone steady.

He nods, a small, bitter smile tugging at his lips. "I've worked so hard for it. Every day feels like a battle, and now, with Paris…" he trails off, running a hand through his hair. "What if I let everyone down? What if I can't handle it?"

I step closer, instinct taking over as I reach out and place a hand on his arm. The contact startles him, his eyes snapping to mine. "Listen to me," I demand, my voice stern. "You wouldn't be here if we didn't believe in you. Greyson, the studio, even me. We see what you're capable of."

His gaze softens as he leans in, his eyes searching mine. "And what do you see, Vaeda?"

The question catches me off guard, my breath hitching, and for a moment, I'm not sure how to respond. "I see someone who's stronger than they give themselves credit for," I finally admit, something I wouldn't have said a few months ago. "Someone who's fighting like hell to rewrite their story."

The space between us feels smaller now, charged with electricity. His eyes hold mine, dark and intense, and I'm acutely aware of the warmth of his skin under my hand. The air seems to thicken, the quiet pressing in around us.

"Vaeda," he murmurs, his voice filled with reverence. His hand lifts slowly, as if in slow motion, and his fingers brush against my chin. The touch sends arcs of electricity over my skin as I suck in a breath.

His tongue snakes out along his bottom lip, leaving behind a trail of moisture, the sight nearly making me forget everything I am and all I have. Nearly.

"Mateo," I rasp softly, my hand falling away from his arm. The connection breaks as I draw in a much-needed breath. "We can't do this."

He exhales sharply, nodding once. "I—I'm sorry. I didn't mean to make you uncomfortable."

"You didn't," I assure him, though my voice wavers slightly. "But we both need to stay focused. Paris is what matters right now."

He nods again, his expression unreadable. "You're right."

I take another step back, putting more distance between us. The silence stretches once more, laden with words left unsaid. Then I straighten my shoulders and lift my chin. "Get some rest. We have a lot of work ahead of us."

He offers a small smile, but it doesn't quite reach his eyes. "Good night, Vaeda."

"Good night, Mateo."

I watch as he gathers his bag and heads for the door, his steps soft and uncertain. So unlike the confidence he exudes on the dance floor. When the door closes behind him, I exhale slowly, my hand brushing over my face. Whatever just happened, it's not something I can afford to dwell on. Not now.

The studio is eerily quiet, the thrum of the lights the only sound. I stand there, staring at the door long after Mateo has left. My heart is still racing, my mind replaying the moment he leaned in. I had stepped away, but the intensity lingered, wrapping around me like a ghost.

I'm married. I'm his instructor. I'm ten years older than him. Every reason why this is wrong feels like a boulder on my chest, pressing the air from my lungs, and yet… I can't stop wondering. What if I hadn't stepped back? What if I had let him close the distance? What would his lips feel like against mine? The thought sends a shiver down my spine with equal parts thrill and shame.

I shake my head, forcing the thoughts away. This is dangerous. Reckless. Mateo is vulnerable, trying to piece his life back together. And me? I have a husband waiting for me at home. A man who has stood by me through everything. What kind of person does this make me?

With a sigh, I walk to the mirrored wall and press my palms against the cool surface, letting my forehead rest against the glass. The reflection staring back at me is too raw and exposed. I've always prided myself on my control, my ability to maintain composure no matter the circumstance, but tonight, that composure cracked, and I'm not sure how to piece it back together.

After a long moment, I push away from the mirror and begin locking up the studio. I double-check the doors and turn off the lights, leaving the space shrouded in darkness. When I step outside, the city greets me with a fresh layer of snow. The flakes fall gently, settling on my hair and coat as I stand there, staring up at the sky.

The world feels still, hushed by the snow's quiet insistence. I take a deep breath, the cold air filling my lungs and clearing my mind. Whatever this is, this pull toward Mateo, I have to bury it. For his sake and mine, and for everything I've worked so hard to build.

With that resolve, I pull my coat tighter around me and step onto the sidewalk, the snow crunching softly beneath my boots as I head home.

CHAPTER ELEVEN
Mateo

The apartment is dark when I slip through the door, closing it softly behind me. I'm careful not to make any noise, praying my mother is still asleep, but as I step into the living room, my heart sinks. She's sitting in the armchair by the window, her silhouette illuminated by the glow of the city lights outside.

"Mami," I start, but she cuts me off with a sharp inhale.

"Where have you been?" she demands, her voice low and tight. Her eyes flash in the dim light, and I can feel the weight of her accusations before she even speaks them. "Don't you dare lie to me, Mateo."

"I wasn't doing anything wrong," I quickly defend myself, trying to keep my tone calm. "I promise."

She rises from the chair, her movements graceful but charged with anger. "Do you know how long I've been sitting here? Wondering if you were out there…" she trails off, her voice breaking. "If you were using again?"

"I'm not," I say firmly, stepping closer. "Mami, you have to believe me. I've been clean. I swear."

She shakes her head, her hands trembling as she presses

them to her temples. "How can I believe you when you sneak out like this? When you don't answer my calls or tell me where you're going?"

"Because I've been doing something good," I reveal, my voice rising with desperation. "Something that… that makes me feel like myself again."

Her eyes narrow, suspicion and hurt mingling in her expression. "What are you talking about?"

I take a deep breath, the words catching in my throat. This is the moment. I can't hide it anymore. "I've joined a dance class," I confess, my voice steady despite the storm raging inside me. "And not just any class. It's an advanced class, focusing on competing. Vaeda and Greyson… they've chosen me to compete in Paris."

For a moment, she just stares at me, her face unreadable. Then slowly, she sinks back into the chair, her hand covering her mouth. "Paris?" she whispers. "You… you've been dancing again?"

I nod, stepping closer. "It's different this time, Mami. I'm not doing it to escape. I'm doing it because I love it. It's the one thing that makes me feel alive."

Her hand drops to her lap, and she looks up at me, her eyes shining with unshed tears. "Mateo… why didn't you tell me?"

"I knew you'd worry, and because Dad…" I trail off, shaking my head. "He'd never understand. He'll think I'm making a mistake. That I'm putting myself at risk."

"He's not the only one who worries," she rasps, her voice thick with tears. "Do you know how terrified I've been? Watching you fight so hard to pull yourself back from the edge, only to see you run toward the very thing that almost destroyed you?"

"I know," I admit, my voice cracking. "But I'm not

that person anymore, Mami. Dancing didn't destroy me. My choices did, and I've learned from them. I've changed."

She studies me for a long moment, her gaze searching mine. Then she sighs, leaning back in the chair. "Paris," she murmurs, as if testing the word. "Do you really think you're ready for this?"

"I have to be." I fall onto the couch and run my hand over my eyes. "This is my chance to prove to myself that I can do it. That I'm stronger than my past."

Her lips press into a thin line, but there's a hint of pride in her eyes. "You're going to have to tell your father."

My stomach twists, but I nod. "I know, but I need you to help me. He'll listen to you."

She releases her breath slowly, her fingers brushing through her hair. "I'll talk to him," she relents finally. "But you'll need to show him… show us… that you're serious about this. No more sneaking around. No more secrets."

"I promise," I vow, relief flooding through me. "Thank you, Mami."

She rises from the chair, her movements still graceful despite the burden of our conversation. "Go to bed, Mateo. We'll figure this out tomorrow."

I nod, getting up from the couch to head toward my bedroom. When I get to the top of the stairs, I sink onto the bed, the stress inside my chest finally easing. For the first time in weeks, I feel like I can breathe. It's not over, not by a long shot, because my father won't make this easy, but the secret is out and I can finally be free.

The airport is crowded, the bustle of activity crowding us as travelers rush past with their luggage in tow. My mother stands beside me at the security checkpoint, her arms crossed over her chest, her expression pensive. Roger waits a few feet away, giving us privacy, though I'm certain he's still listening. He always is.

"You'll call me every day?" she asks, her voice softer than usual.

"Every day," I promise, meeting her gaze. "And I'll text you before my meetings and after. You don't have to worry, Mami."

She exhales, her shoulders dropping slightly as she steps forward and pulls me into a tight hug. "I'm your mother. Worrying is what I do. Christmas is coming. Are you sure you do not want to come home with your father and me?"

"No." I shake my head as she pulls back, memories of Christmases flooding my mind. Grace and I would make a mess of gift wrap and toys as we excitedly ran around the room. "I couldn't bear it without Grace and with Dad still mad at me."

"He loves you, Mateo. He just needs time, and so does Grace. Gain their trust like you've started to gain mine." She pulls me back in for another hug, her warmth and scent washing over me.

"I know," I murmur, my voice muffled against her shoulder. "Thank you for trusting me."

When she pulls back, her eyes are glossy but determined. "Don't make me regret it."

"I won't," I assure her.

She gives me one last look before turning toward security, her posture straight and poised, as if she's heading for the stage instead of a plane. I watch her disappear into the crowd, the knot in my stomach easing slightly now that she's gone. Yet the burden of her expectations remains, ramping my anxiety up a notch.

Roger claps a hand on my shoulder as we head back to the car. "She's proud of you, you know," he says, his tone unusually warm. "Even if she doesn't say it outright."

"I hope so," I reply, sliding into the back seat of the SUV. The drive home is quiet, Roger sensing my mood and leaving me to my thoughts. When we pull up to my building, he glances at me in the rearview mirror.

"Need a ride later?" he asks casually. It looks like my mother might have filled Roger in on my dancing. I just don't know how much. It makes me nervous, because what if he feels inclined to tell my father?

"No," I say quickly, too quickly. "I'll just be studying at home today."

His eyebrows lift slightly, but he doesn't push. "Alright. Call me if you need anything."

I nod and step out, my bag slung over my shoulder as I head inside. The doorman greets me with a nod, and I force a smile in return, my mind already racing. I have to be careful now. With my mother gone but still in close contact, and Roger's watchful eyes, every move feels like it's under scrutiny until my father knows everything.

Once inside my apartment, I head straight for my room and change into my dance gear: fitted joggers and a lightweight hoodie. I glance at the clock. It's still early, but I'll need time to make it to the studio. Grabbing my bag and jacket, I take the now-familiar route to the roof, carefully pushing open the access door and stepping onto the fire escape. The cold metal feels shaky under my feet as I descend, my heart pounding with a mixture of anticipation and nerves.

The studio is quiet when I arrive, the Saturday afternoon light streaming through the tall windows and illuminating the polished floor. Greyson is already there, adjusting the sound system, while Yvonne stretches near the mirrors. She glances up when she sees me, flashing a bright smile.

"Hey," she calls out, her tone chipper. "Ready to get your butt kicked?"

"Always," I reply, setting my bag down near the wall.

I try to keep my head down while I hang up my jacket and change into my shoes, but I find myself giving in and looking around the studio for my very own drug. She's nowhere to be seen, and my heart sinks as my stomach rolls. It's been nearly a week since our last interaction, and I can feel myself growing uneasy. I don't know what will come of us, or this attraction that's growing. She's married, happily from what I gather, and I'm a recovering addict who's latched onto a new fixation. None of it is healthy, but just like the first time I succumbed to the magnetism of the forbidden, I find myself doing the same.

Greyson claps his hands to get our attention. "Alright, you two. Let's start with some Jive drills. I want to see hard-hitting footwork and clean lines. Remember, Jive is all about energy and rhythm. If you're not sweating within five minutes, you're doing it wrong."

We line up, and the music starts, its quick tempo setting the pace. Yvonne and I move through the drills, our feet bouncing and our arms snapping into position. The Jive is demanding, both physically and mentally, but it's also exhilarating. The rhythm pulses through me, making my blood rush with excitement.

After a few rounds, Greyson calls us to the center of the floor. "Let's run through the routine again," he says. "From the top."

Yvonne and I take our positions, and the music starts again. The routine is fast and intricate, each movement requiring attention and timing. Yvonne's confidence is palpable, her energy infectious as she grins at me during the turns and spins, but my focus is split. As much as I'm committed to the dance, a part of me can't stop wondering where Vaeda is.

When we finish, Greyson gives us a nod of approval. "Good. That was solid, but there's always room for improvement. With the holidays around the corner, I want you guys to be mindful of the food you eat and the alcohol you consume." His eyes meet mine, but he doesn't point out my sobriety as he continues. "The studio will be open still as Vaeda and I work through the holidays every year. You are still welcome to come and practice. In fact, I insist that you do."

"Thank you, Greyson," Yvonne murmurs before taking a drink of water.

I grab a water bottle from my bag, catching my breath before turning to him. "Where's Vaeda?" I ask, trying to sound casual.

Greyson hesitates, his expression unreadable. "It's her birthday," he reveals finally. "She's taking the day off."

"Her birthday?" Yvonne echoes, her brow lifting. "And she didn't tell us?"

"Vaeda's not exactly the celebratory type," Greyson admits with a grin. "But there's a surprise party for her later. You're both welcome to come."

I glance at Yvonne, who's already nodding enthusiastically. "Of course we'll come," she gushes. "I'll tell Adam and Kari too. Right, Mateo?"

I hesitate, the idea of stepping into Vaeda's personal life feeling strange, but Greyson's expectant gaze and Yvonne's excitement leave little room for refusal.

"Sure," I relent as trepidation trickles down my back. "Why not?"

Greyson claps his hands together. "Perfect. Now, let's get back to work. Paris won't wait for anyone."

As the music starts again, I push thoughts of the party aside, focusing on the here and now. Despite that, the fear of being around alcohol creeps back in. It's been well over a year since I've tempted my weakness, but the idea of seeing Vaeda outside the studio trumps my fears of a relapse, which tells me this is completely reckless.

VAEDA

The penthouse is alive with chatter and the clink of glasses, the warm buzz of conversation mixing with the soft strains of a live jazz trio. Gerardo has outdone himself, as always. The decorations are festive and will remain up as Christmas is just a few days away. The floor-to-ceiling windows showcase the city skyline glittering against the night, and the space is filled with well-dressed guests laughing and toasting in celebration. My birthday. My thirty-third, to be precise.

I've already had three martinis, which is two more than I usually allow myself, and the edges of the evening are starting to blur in a pleasant haze. Gerardo glides effortlessly through the crowd, charming everyone as he goes, his radiant smile making him the perfect host. I should be happy, content even, but there's a knot of guilt inside my chest I can't quite untangle.

I'm standing near the bar when it happens. The shift. It's subtle at first, like the air being sucked out of the room, the kind of change you feel before a thunderstorm. Then I turn, my hand tightening around the stem of my glass, and there they are.

Adam and Kari arrive first, their grins infectious as they gaze around the room. Then I see him. Mateo. And Yvonne. Together.

He's wearing a fitted suit, dark and crisp, his hair styled just enough to look effortless. She's on his arm, radiant in a red cocktail dress that hugs her in all the right places, her smile wide as she says something to him. He nods, his expression polite but distant, his gaze flickering over the room, and I just know he's searching for me.

My stomach twists, the alcohol in my veins amplifying the heat that rises to my cheeks. I force myself to take a slow sip of my drink, but my hand trembles slightly. What the hell is he doing here? My gaze darts to Greyson, who's by the grand piano, chatting with a group of guests. Of course.

I make my way across the room, my heels clicking against the marble floor, each step a strike of frustration. Greyson spots me before I reach him, his expression shifting into something between amusement and trepidation.

"Vae," he says smoothly, lifting his glass in greeting. "Having a good time?"

"Why are they here?" I cut straight to the point, keeping my voice low but laced with irritation.

He takes a measured sip of his champagne, unbothered. "It's your birthday. The more the merrier."

"Don't play coy with me, Grey," I snap, stepping closer. "You know damn well that this isn't about numbers. Why would you invite them?"

His gaze flicks past me, briefly landing on our four students before returning to mine. "They're part of the studio, and it's good for them to see you as more than just their instructor."

"You're unbelievable," I mutter, grabbing his arm and pulling him away from the group he's entertaining. "We need to talk. Now."

I drag him toward my bedroom, ignoring his half-hearted protests. Once inside, I shut the door firmly and turn to face him, my anger bubbling over.

"What were you thinking?" I hiss. "This is my home, Greyson, my personal space, and you invite our students? They're a part of our job, not our personal life."

He leans casually against the doorframe, his expression maddeningly calm. "They're adults, Vae. They can handle a party."

"That's not the point," I say, my voice sharp. "You

know how complicated this is. Mateo is already…" I trail off, shaking my head. "He's vulnerable, and Yvonne…"

"And Yvonne is harmless," he interrupts, his tone firm but not unkind. "You're projecting."

My jaw tightens. "You think this is about me?"

"I think you're overreacting," he replies, crossing his arms. "You've had a few drinks and you're letting your emotions get the better of you. They aren't doing anything wrong. They're just here to celebrate your birthday. That's all."

I glare at him, my frustration spilling over. "You don't understand. This isn't just about tonight. It's about what this could mean for the studio, for them. For *him*."

Greyson's gaze softens slightly, and he steps closer. "Vaeda, I know you care about the studio and about Mateo's sobriety, but you need to trust him. He's stronger than you think."

I look away, my arms wrapping around myself as the weight of his words sinks in. "It's not that simple."

"It never is," he agrees quietly. "But you have to let go a little. Let him make his own choices and let yourself breathe."

The room falls silent, the irritation between us dissipating slightly. I glance at the door, knowing the party is still in full swing on the other side. Somewhere out there, Mateo and Yvonne are mingling, laughing, and living their lives while I'm in here, unraveling.

"Fine," I relent, my voice resigned. "But if this blows up, it's on you."

Greyson smiles faintly, reaching for the door. "It won't. Trust me."

He leaves, the door clicking softly behind him, and I'm left alone in the quiet of my bedroom. I sit down on the edge of the bed, my head in my hands. The martinis swirl in my veins, dulling the edges of my frustration but doing nothing to ease the ache inside my chest.

Forcing myself to stand, I smooth out my dress and straighten my posture. I'm not about to let this ruin my night.

The hallway is quieter than the main room, the sounds of the party sounding farther away as I step out of my bedroom. I'm still reeling from my argument with Greyson, my thoughts tangled and restless, and the alcohol coursing through my veins isn't helping. I run a hand through my hair, exhaling sharply as I turn toward the main room.

And then I collide with him.

Strong hands steady me, gripping my arms gently but firmly. The familiar scent of clean soap and something distinctly Mateo fills my senses before I even look up. When I do, his dark eyes are locked on mine, wide with surprise but lined in appreciation, a lingering look that makes my pulse quicken.

"Vaeda," he says softly, his voice low and filled with gravel. "Are you okay?"

"I..." My words catch in my throat as I nod, his touch alighting my skin with goose bumps I wasn't prepared for. "Yes, I'm fine. Thank you."

We don't move, and his hands remain on my arms, his warmth seeping through the thin fabric of my dress. The hallway seems to shrink around us, the air thickening with an anticipation that makes my skin prickle. He's so close, close enough that I can see the shadow of stubble on his jaw and the way his throat bobs as he swallows.

"Happy birthday," he murmurs after a moment, his lips curving into a small, hesitant smile, then his hands drop away, leaving my skin cold in their absence.

"Thank you," I manage, the words sounding strangled.

He takes a step back, but then he leans in, his movement slow and deliberate. "I hope it's a good one," he rasps, his breath brushing against my cheek and his lips pressing against my skin, soft and warm, just shy of my jawline. I feel the heat of him, the way his presence seems to wrap around me, stealing the air from my lungs.

But then it happens. I shift, barely, instinctively leaning into the moment, and his lips graze the corner of my mouth. It's fleeting, an accidental brush that sends a shockwave through me. My breath catches, and I know he feels it too because he pulls back abruptly, his eyes wide and searching mine.

"I…" he starts, his voice unsteady, but the words don't come. He runs a hand through his hair, his movements tense and unsure. "I should…"

I nod, my heart pounding inside my chest. "Yes, of course."

The sound of footsteps draws my attention, and my stomach twists as I spot Yvonne at the end of the hall. She's standing near the entrance to the main room, her expression frozen somewhere between shock and confusion. Her eyes dart between Mateo and me, her lips parting slightly as if she's about to say something.

Mateo sees her too, his posture stiffening as he takes another step back, putting more distance between us. "I was just coming from the bathroom," he explains quickly, loud enough to be heard by both her and I.

I nod, though the gesture feels hollow, and stand rooted in place, my legs locked. There's no doubt in my mind that she caught the end of our interaction, and now I've put the studio at risk.

He turns and walks toward Yvonne, who doesn't move as he passes her. Her gaze lingers on me, her brows knitting together in a silent question I don't have the answer to. The weight of her stare feels like a judgment, though I'm not sure who she's judging more: him or me.

I stand there, frozen, as the two of them disappear into the party. My hand drifts to my lips, the ghost of his touch still burning against my skin. The knot inside my chest tightens, and for the first time in a long while, I'm not sure what I'm doing anymore.

Chapter Twelve

Varela

The penthouse feels cavernous now that the guests are gone. The jazz trio's instruments have been packed away, the chatter and clinking glasses replaced with silence that settles heavily over the space. I'm alone. Even Gerardo, ever the social butterfly, has gone out dancing with a few friends, his parting kiss on my cheek a reminder that he's always the one to extend the night.

I stayed behind. My excuse had been exhaustion, the weight of hosting a party this grand, but the truth is, I'm not tired. I'm restless, my thoughts tangled and uneasy.

I watched them leave. Mateo and Yvonne. She'd looped her arm through his, her laugh light and carefree as they stepped into the elevator with Adam and Kari, but it was his gaze that lingered, his eyes locking with mine for a moment too long as the doors slid shut. There was something in his expression that sent a shiver down my spine. He let his guard down, just for that moment, and I saw the feral need emanating from his eyes.

I lean against the closed door, the last few stragglers having just left, their laughter echoing faintly in the hallway before fading completely. The lock clicks into place, and I let out a long breath, pressing my forehead against the cool wood.

What am I doing?

The question circles in my mind, a relentless whisper that refuses to be silenced. I'm married. I'm his instructor. I'm supposed to be a professional, someone who holds herself to a standard. Yet every time Mateo looks at me, every time we're in the same room, it's as though the ground shifts beneath my feet.

The memory of his touch, the accidental brush of his lips earlier at the party, is still fresh. My skin tingles where his hands steadied me, and I feel the heat rising to my cheeks even now. How did I let it get this far? How did I let myself...

A loud knock at the door jolts me from my thoughts. My heart jumps, the sound reverberating through the quiet. For a moment, I straighten, staring at the door as if it might open on its own.

Another knock, firmer this time.

I swallow hard, my pulse racing as I push away from the door and reach for the handle. When I pull it open, the breath catches in my throat.

Mateo stands there, his suit jacket gone, the crisp white shirt he'd worn earlier now slightly rumpled. His tie is loosened, and his dark hair is mussed, as though he'd run his hands through it one too many times. His cheeks are red from the cold and his expression is unreadable, his dark eyes shadowed in the dim light of the hallway.

"Mateo," I manage, my voice barely above a whisper. "What are you..."

"I needed to talk to you," he interrupts, his tone quiet but resolute. "And luckily, you don't live too far from me."

I glance down the empty hallway, my mind scrambling for an explanation, an excuse to send him away, but when I look back at him, the intensity of his gaze roots me to the spot.

"It's late," I say, though the words feel hollow even as I speak them.

"Where's your husband?" He's still standing on the threshold, not quite inside but refusing to back away too. I wonder what he would do if Gerardo was home. Would he continue to stand there, invading every one of my senses?

"He went out with a few friends. He's always been a bit of a partyer." The explanation falls from my lips to fill the nervous space between us. "You shouldn't be here."

"I know," he replies, stepping forward just enough to close the distance between us. "But I couldn't sleep without saying this."

"Mateo…" I start, but he shakes his head, cutting me off again.

"Please." His voice softens, the vulnerability in it making my chest tighten. "Just let me say this."

I hesitate, my hand still gripping the edge of the door. Then slowly, I step back, allowing him to enter. He moves past me, his presence filling the room in a way that feels far too significant. I close the door behind him, the click of the latch sounding louder than it should.

He turns to face me, his hands shoved into his pockets, his shoulders stiff. "I don't know what's happening," he admits, his eyes steady on mine. "But I can't stop thinking about you. About us."

My heart pounds inside my chest, the weight of his words settling heavily between us. "Mateo," I groan, forcing my voice to remain calm. "There is no 'us.' This can't… It can't happen."

"Why not?" he asks, his tone tinged with frustration. "Because of Gerardo? Because you're my instructor? If he truly is your person, our feelings wouldn't have happened. You being my instructor was fate."

"Stop," I grind out firmly, crossing my arms over my chest as if to shield myself. "We can't let this go any further. I love Gerardo, and I love teaching you, but whatever is building between us stops tonight because it's wrong."

He takes a step closer, and I feel the pull of him like gravity, impossible to resist. "It doesn't feel wrong to me." His voice drops to a whisper. "It feels real, and I think it feels real to you too."

I'm shaking my head before he even finishes, but the denial feels weak and half-hearted. "You don't understand," I beg, my voice trembling. "This isn't about what feels right or real. It's about what's practical, what's ethical. I can't… I won't cross that line."

His jaw tightens, and for a moment, I think he might argue, but then he takes a step back, his shoulders slumping slightly. "I'm sorry," he breathes out, his features saturated in pain. "I didn't mean to…" he trails off, running a hand through his hair.

"You should go," I press, though the words feel like they're cutting me as I speak them.

He nods, his gaze lingering on mine for a moment longer before he turns and heads for the door. I follow, my steps faltering as he reaches for the handle.

"Happy birthday, Vaeda," he says softly, glancing back at me.

I don't respond, my throat too tight with emotion as I watch him leave. When the door closes behind him, the silence feels deafening. I press my palms to my face, exhaling shakily as I try to steady myself.

Whatever this is, whatever we've become… It's dangerous, and I'm not sure I'm strong enough to continue fighting it.

MATEO

The elevator chimes softly, the glow of the floor numbers flickering as I wait. My hands are shoved deep into my pockets, my heart still hammering from the exchange with Vaeda. The taste of her proximity, the near kiss. All of it is seared into my mind. I glance back at her door, my chest tightening with fear.

It's been my constant companion since the day I woke up in that hospital bed, staring at the ceiling and realizing I'd almost thrown my life away. I've been so damn afraid of making a mistake, of letting people down, of losing control again. Every step since has been cautious, calculated, like I'm walking on a tightrope above a pit I'll never escape if I fall.

But I'm tired of being afraid and fearful that my inhibition is stealing my second chance at life.

The elevator arrives, but I don't get on. I push through the stairwell instead, needing the burn in my legs to distract from the ache twisting inside my chest. By the time I reach the bottom, my legs are trembling and my forehead is lined with sweat.

I push out of the doors, regretting leaving my jacket at home and knowing I risk catching a cold, but I throw the worry away as I curse under my breath. I've been so damn fearful since I woke up in that hospital bed. The city is hushed this late, its sounds muffled by fresh snow and the pounding of my heart in my ears. I walk the few blocks home, every step pressing Vaeda deeper into my thoughts.

She's becoming a problem.

Not because of what she is, my instructor, a married woman, someone entirely off-limits, but because of how she makes me feel. I'm supposed to be clean, clearheaded, in control, but when I'm around her, the urge to spiral is almost too tempting to resist, and I can't tell if that's terrifying or addictive.

I reach my building and climb the ladder to the fire escape, my palms absorbing the sting of the frigid metal. Once inside my apartment, I close the door softly behind me and lean against it, the echo of tonight still ringing in my ears.

I've fought so hard to stay balanced, to be seen as trustworthy again, but the way my heart races when she's near, the way I crave her attention like it's oxygen, feels too close to how I used to crave the numbness of a high. When I would become reckless and dangerous.

Only this time, the high has auburn hair and a voice that unravels me with syllables.

I sink onto the edge of my couch, elbows on my knees, running a hand through my hair. This can't happen, it shouldn't, but the thought of walking away from her… It makes my chest hollow.

There's a fine line between love and addiction. Between beauty and destruction. I've danced along that edge before and almost didn't survive it, and now I'm doing it again, only this time it's Vaeda I can't stop reaching for.

I sink back, staring at the ceiling, forcing my breath to steady. Tomorrow, I'll pretend I can handle this. Tomorrow, I'll go back to being her student, but tonight, I admit the truth to myself: I'm not sure if I want to be saved from her.

The city is hushed beyond the glass, its skyline softened under the shroud of a winter night. I stand in front of the floor-to-ceiling windows of my apartment, barefoot on the warm hardwood, pressing my hand to the pane. The party ended hours ago, but sleep hasn't come. It won't. Everything feels too loud inside my head.

The silence out there, in the city that never sleeps, is deceptive, because inside me, there's noise. Her voice. Her face. The way she looked at me before I left.

I close my eyes and lean my forehead against the glass, letting the cold bleed into my skin. My body still craves her scent, her nearness, the melody between us that keeps getting louder no matter how many times we try to deny it. There's a weight on my chest that won't ease. A need that has nothing to do with pills or powder.

I push off the window and head to the kitchen, needing something to ground me. As I open the fridge, my phone buzzes on the counter, and I glance at the screen.

Voicemail. From my father.

My stomach knots. I don't play it right away. Instead, I open a bottle of water and take a long sip, trying to steady myself. Then I tap the screen and hold the phone to my ear.

His voice is as cold as ever, clipped and direct. "Mateo, your mother says you've been doing well. I hope that's true, but remember why we sent you to New York. Stay focused on the promises you made. Don't get distracted by old habits. Call me."

That's it. No warmth. No questions. Just warnings.

It sounds like he doesn't know I've gone back to dancing yet. My mother must be waiting to break it to him, and that makes me more nervous, but he knows me well enough to suspect, and that suspicion feels like an impending storm, threatening to disrupt everything I've built.

I set the phone down and return to the window, the water still cool in my hand. The city sparkles faintly under the low clouds, and I stare out at it like it might have answers. Like it might tell me who I'm supposed to be.

Should I quit? Should I walk away before I lose everything again? Because I can feel how much she means to me already, and it's too much, too fast, and too dangerous. She could be the reason I spiral, but she's also the reason I feel alive.

Vaeda doesn't offer me anything toxic and doesn't encourage my weaknesses, but the way she sees me, the way she challenges me? It lights something inside me I thought I lost. I press my palm to the window, hoping the chill brings me back to reality, and breathe deeply. My chest hurts. I don't want to let go of this, of her, of the studio, but if I keep holding on, it might break me.

I close my eyes and whisper into the night, "What the hell am I doing?"

The answer doesn't come, and only the ache remains.

CHAPTER THIRTEEN

The morning sun barely filters through the gauzy curtains of our penthouse, but I'm already awake. Gerardo is still asleep, his breathing even beside me, but my body won't rest. My mind won't stop replaying last night. Mateo's eyes. That electricity.

I slip out of bed quietly, not bothering to change out of my leggings and oversized sweatshirt, the crop top underneath bunching under my chest. My ankle still throbs from wearing heels for too long, but I ignore it, grabbing my keys and jacket, then heading out the door before I have time to talk myself down.

Fusion Core is silent when I arrive, a stark contrast to the rushed activity on the streets. This close to Christmas, everyone is scrambling to complete their shopping. The cold fluorescent lights blink on as I walk in, the scent of floor polish lingering in the air. It's my day off, and yet somehow, here I am. There's a comfort in the studio I can't find anywhere else. It's routine and discipline. The one place where my body still listens to me, even if only for a little while.

I settle behind my desk first, sorting through paperwork and registration forms we've neglected since the competition prep began. My ankle pulses, and I curl my toes, trying to stretch it without drawing attention to the pain, though no one is here to see me anyway.

After a while, the stillness becomes too much, so I pull off my sweater and leave the desk to walk onto the floor, the familiar squeak of my sneakers echoing across the space. My hands find the sound system out of habit, fingers scrolling until a piano instrumental sounds through the speakers. I stretch slowly, biting back a wince. Then I start to move.

It's not a routine, nothing polished or planned. Just muscle memory and emotion, pouring out of me one step at a time. My body knows how to speak this language, even when my mind is exhausted. Even when my ankle screams.

I dance through the ache, letting it blend with the frustration, the confusion. Every extension, every turn is sharper than it should be, a reflection of everything I don't say out loud.

I'm breathless and shaking when I finally stop, one hand on the mirror to steady myself. The studio falls quiet again, the music fading to a whisper. That's when I hear the door, and I turn sharply, startled when I see him.

Mateo stands in the doorway, framed by the soft glow of the corridor light behind him. His coat is unzipped, cheeks pink from the cold, and his expression is unreadable.

"I was out walking," he explains, his voice hesitant. "Saw the lights on. Didn't think anyone would be here."

My pulse stutters. "I wasn't expecting company."

He steps slowly inside, like he isn't sure if he should be here. "I can see that." I brush my fingers through my hair and nod, turning slightly so he can't see the way my hand is trembling at my side. "I didn't mean to interrupt."

"You didn't." The lie tastes bitter. "I was just... clearing my head."

He glances at the mirror, our eyes meeting. "I get that."

The silence stretches between us, thick with fear and anticipation. I can't break the contact, and the intensity there knocks the air from my lungs.

"You look like you needed it," he says gently.

"Yeah," I reply, forcing a small smile. "I did." And now, standing in the same room with him again, I'm not sure I can keep pretending that I don't need more than just the dance.

MATEO

Vaeda leans against the barre, her arms crossed, the hint of exertion still glowing in her cheeks. Her hair is pulled back in a loose twist, and a sheen of sweat glistens along her collarbone. My eyes travel downward, over her braless chest and bare midriff, drops of sweat clinging to her porcelain skin. She's toned to perfection, her abs flexing with each labored breath. My eyes glide back up, and I find her watching me like she always does, like she sees more than she should, more than I want her to.

"Did you ever find that Hip-hop class I suggested?" she asks, her voice casual, but her eyes are filled with heat.

I shake my head. "No."

She arches an eyebrow. "No?"

"I was waiting for you." The words hang there, more honest than I meant them to be, but I don't take them back.

Her lips part slightly, and for a second, I think she might ignore it, let it pass unspoken. Instead, she straightens. "There's one happening right now," she reveals. "At a studio just a few blocks up." She glances at the clock on the wall and then back at me. "If we leave now, we can make it before warm-ups are over."

I blink at her, trying to gauge what she's really offering. "Are you coming with me?" I ask, half expecting her to laugh it off, the question asinine.

She gives a small shrug, her breasts moving with the motion as she turns on her heel and heads to her office. "I did say it would help loosen your movement. Might as well see if it works," she calls out as she disappears.

A few moments later, she's hauling a large sweatshirt over her head and grabbing her water bottle, her eyes dancing with excitement. I turn to follow her without another word, heart suddenly racing.

Leaving the studio, I wait patiently as she locks the door, pieces of her hair blowing in the chilly breeze. It feels like a dream, having her alone like this, her scent enveloping me as she steps in closer, her gaze traveling over my face. She nods for me to follow, and then we're off.

We walk side by side through the late morning chill, the sky bruised with the dull light of early winter. She doesn't say much, and neither do I, but the silence between us isn't uncomfortable. It's charged.

We reach the building and climb the stairs, the thump of bass-heavy music seeping through the floor as we approach, rattling something loose inside me. An eagerness.

When Vaeda opens the studio door, the space is full of energy. A group of dancers are already moving through stretches, the instructor calling out from the front with contagious enthusiasm.

Vaeda turns to me, her expression unreadable but open. "You ready?"

I nod, and I mean it. Maybe I don't know what I'm doing, and maybe this is another edge I'm walking, but with her next to me, I'm willing to find out where it leads.

The music pulses rhythmically through the speakers, echoing off mirrored walls and reverberating through the polished hardwood floor. Vaeda stands next to me, discarding her sweater and pulling her hair out of its messy bun and into a high ponytail, exposing the elegant slope of her neck. My pulse quickens as I glance her way, my throat suddenly dry.

The instructor, a dynamic young woman with an infectious energy, steps to the front of the room, clapping her hands sharply to gather our attention. "Alright, everyone! Let's break down today's choreography step-by-step. Watch closely, follow along, and feel the music."

We spread out across the dance floor, giving each other enough space to move freely. I position myself behind Vaeda, acutely aware of her proximity, the warmth of her body emanating like a subtle invitation.

The instructor leads us through the routine slowly at first, demonstrating each fluid movement with precision and grace. I focus intently, mirroring her actions, feeling the rhythm seep into my muscles, coaxing them into motion. In front of me, Vaeda moves effortlessly, her body interpreting the beat with an ease I envy and admire.

"Great, now pick up the pace," the instructor encourages, increasing the tempo slightly. The movements become more pronounced, hips swiveling, arms extending with controlled sensuality. My heart pounds harder, the combination of music and motion making it difficult to concentrate on anything other than the woman in front of me.

"Now," the instructor announces, her voice cutting through the rhythm. "Find a partner. It's time to put what we've learned into practice."

Vaeda turns slowly, eyes locking with mine immediately. There's no hesitation, no questioning glance, just an unspoken understanding pulling us together, closing the short distance between us.

"Ready?" she asks softly, her voice barely registering over the music.

"Always," I respond, my voice carrying more weight than intended.

She takes a small step closer, her eyes flickering with intensity as my hands settle lightly on her waist. The heat of her bare skin sends a jolt of electricity up my spine. Her breath hitches audibly as her fingertips rest on my shoulders, light but unmistakably present.

The instructor restarts the music, louder now, each beat pounding like a heartbeat shared between us. We move as one, bodies instinctively finding a rhythm, hips rolling, limbs weaving together in seamless synchronicity. Every touch is charged, every look smoldering.

The dance demands proximity, encourages intimacy, and I'm all too willing to comply. My fingers grip her hips tighter, pulling her closer until there's barely space left between us. Vaeda doesn't resist; instead, she matches the pressure, leaning into my touch, her body molding to mine.

Our eyes meet, the air heavy with unspoken desire. The room around us fades, the other dancers forgotten. All that remains is the heat of her body pressed against me, the electric sensation of her breath mingling with mine, and the undeniable chemistry that has haunted us from the very start.

As the routine draws us even closer, my fingertips skim the bare skin at her waist, tracing gentle circles that send shivers visibly rippling through her. Her breath fans across my neck, warm and uneven. The temptation to close the final distance, to erase all boundaries between us, nearly overwhelms me.

"Good," the instructor's voice breaks through our trance. "Now slow it down, feel the sensuality in each movement. Let the dance speak for you."

Vaeda's eyes never leave mine as we follow the guidance, each motion deliberate, filled with a restrained intensity that pushes me to the brink of control. Her chest rises and falls rapidly, mirroring my own erratic heartbeat.

My lips brush her ear, my voice barely a whisper, deep and roughened with longing. "Like this?"

She nods subtly, pressing herself even closer, her fingers gripping my shoulders firmly. Our bodies communicate in ways words never could, speaking truths we both fear to admit aloud.

The song eventually fades, leaving only the silence punctuated by our labored breaths. Reluctantly, I loosen my grip, stepping back just enough to let reality seep back in. Vaeda's cheeks are flushed, her eyes glazed with the same overwhelming desire I feel coursing through my veins. We remain in the charged aftermath, neither willing to fully break the connection we've established.

"Mateo," she breathes out, voice unsteady.

I lift my gaze, meeting hers squarely. "I know," I respond quietly, understanding passing silently between us. The consequences are all painfully clear. Yet, I find myself stepping closer once more, drawn inexorably back into her orbit, and she doesn't pull away.

The instructor's voice echoes again, signaling the end of class, breaking our fragile bubble. Vaeda finally steps back fully, inhaling deeply, visibly collecting herself.

"Great job, everyone!" The instructor's cheerful voice feels out of place in our heightened reality. "Keep practicing. Remember, dancing is about feeling. Trust yourselves and trust each other."

Trust.

The word hangs heavily between us as we exit the studio and into the cool afternoon air. Vaeda glances at me from beside me, vulnerability flickering briefly in her eyes before she covers it again with practiced composure.

"That was... intense," she murmurs softly.

I nod, the admission echoing in my mind. "Yes, it was."

We walk in silence for a moment, the sun creating gentle halos around us despite the cold winter day. The intensity of the experience we shared refuses to fade, and it's taking everything in me not to haul her down a darkened alley and do what I've been dreaming of for months.

"Mateo," she says finally, her voice steadying, "this can't—"

"I know," I interrupt gently, even though it pains me. "But right now, let's just… not think about that."

She hesitates, then nods slowly, the smallest smile tugging at her lips. For now, today, we can pretend the rest doesn't exist. Even if we both know it definitely does.

CHAPTER FOURTEEN

Mateo

"Are you hungry?" Vaeda breaks the silence as she points across the street at the diner. It's a popular place for the dancers. Yvonne has praised their sandwiches many times.

"I can eat." I would do just about anything to stay with her a bit longer.

Vaeda walks alongside me, quietly twisting a lock of her hair around a slender finger as we cross the street to the small restaurant. The diner sign flickers above the doorway, emanating an inviting glow.

Inside is quiet, caught in the lull between the lunch and dinner rushes. The waitress greets us warmly, guiding us toward a secluded booth tucked into the back corner. It feels like a private sanctuary, removed from the rest of the world, exactly the kind of intimacy that makes my pulse quicken.

Vaeda slides gracefully onto the vinyl bench across from me, and I settle opposite her, our knees barely brushing beneath the table. A rush of heat floods me at even that minimal contact, but neither of us pulls away. Instead, our eyes meet briefly, a silent acknowledgment of the energy we both feel.

The waitress sets down two menus and a couple of

water glasses, her friendly chatter a gentle backdrop to our charged silence. When she's gone, Vaeda's gaze meets mine again, eyes bright but cautious.

"You danced well," she says softly, interrupting my thoughts.

"I have a good teacher," I respond, smiling slightly.

Her lips curve into a small smile, her eyes softening as she sips from her water glass. "You don't need much teaching. It's natural for you."

"Feels different with you," I confess quietly, holding her gaze. The words slip out before I can stop them, honest and vulnerable.

She hesitates, her eyes flickering with uncertainty before she replies carefully, "Different isn't always good, Mateo."

"It isn't always bad either," I counter gently.

Her cheeks flush faintly, and she glances away, fingers tracing idle patterns on the tabletop. Silence settles between us again, comfortable yet charged, each heartbeat echoing the tension that continues to build relentlessly.

The bell over the diner door jingles softly, interrupting the quiet moment, and my eyes flick instinctively toward the sound. My heart sinks slightly when I see Yvonne stepping inside, her eyes scanning the diner briefly before quickly finding us tucked in our quiet corner.

Her expression shifts immediately, a mixture of surprise and something darker. Jealousy. It hits me abruptly, realization sinking in heavily. I hadn't noticed it before, but the way her eyes linger, narrowing at Vaeda before settling on me, makes her feelings unmistakably clear.

Yvonne strides over, a forced smile on her face. "Hey," she greets, her tone deceptively cheerful. "I wasn't expecting to see you two here."

"We were just grabbing a quick bite," I reply cautiously, glancing at Vaeda, whose expression is now guarded, her body language tense. "I came by the studio today to grab my shoes. I left them there after the last class."

"Mind if I join?" Yvonne asks, not bothering to wait for an answer as she slides into the booth next to Vaeda, her eyes fixed solely on me.

"Actually," Vaeda interjects smoothly, "I was just about to leave. You two go ahead."

My stomach knots as Vaeda crowds into Yvonne, forcing her to get up and let her out of the booth. She stands gracefully, her eyes avoiding mine. "Vaeda—"

"I'll see you both tomorrow," she interrupts gently, her eyes focused ahead as she moves swiftly toward the door before I can respond.

As the bell jingles again, signaling her departure, Yvonne shifts to the spot Vaeda vacated, immediately changing the energy between us.

"Didn't mean to scare her off," Yvonne says, a note of smugness in her voice that irritates me instantly.

"What are you doing here, Yvonne?" I ask, my tone cooler than intended.

She shrugs, feigning innocence as she takes a menu in her hands, eyes not meeting mine. "I come here often, remember? I didn't know you two were that... close."

"We're not," I respond curtly, though it sounds defensive even to my own ears.

Her gaze snaps up sharply, eyes narrowing slightly. "Really? Because that's not how it looked."

"It's not like that," I insist, a lie that tastes bitter on my tongue. The tension in the air thickens, frustration and confusion battling inside me.

"Mateo…" Yvonne sighs, dropping her pretense. "We've been partners for a while now. You must've noticed how well we work together."

"Yeah, we're good partners," I concede warily, sensing where this conversation is heading.

She leans forward slightly, lowering her voice. "It could be more than that. We could be amazing together, both on and off the dance floor."

I sit back, taken aback by her bluntness. "Yvonne, I don't think—"

"Think about it," she presses gently, reaching across the table to rest her fingers lightly over mine. "We have chemistry, Mateo. Real chemistry. Not something forbidden and needing to be hidden away."

Her words sting, a direct jab at my complicated feelings for Vaeda. I withdraw my hand gently but firmly, shaking my head. "I value our partnership, Yvonne, but I don't see us that way," I say quietly, hoping to soften the rejection.

She withdraws her hand slowly, disappointment and hurt flashing briefly across her face before she masks it behind a neutral expression. "Alright," she murmurs, leaning back. "I just thought you should know how I feel."

Silence hangs heavily between us, interrupted only by the quiet clatter of dishes from the kitchen. My appetite gone, I find myself searching for an excuse to leave.

"Look," I finally say, breaking the uncomfortable silence. "I appreciate your honesty, Yvonne, I really do, but I think it's best if we just stay partners, okay?"

She nods as a faint, resigned smile touches her lips. "Understood."

I rise, forcing a smile, unable to shake the lingering discomfort from the conversation. "I'll see you at rehearsal."

"Sure," she mutters softly, watching me carefully as I move toward the exit.

Stepping into the cool afternoon, I exhale heavily, the weight of the situation pressing heavily on my shoulders. My mind races with confusion, guilt, and desire. Yvonne's revelation complicates things even further, yet all I can think about is the pain in Vaeda's eyes as she left.

My feet carry me down the quiet street, but my mind stays tangled in the messy web of emotions. The truth is clear, painful, and unavoidable. My feelings for Vaeda aren't fading; they're deepening with every shared moment, every stolen glance, and every charged touch. And no matter how dangerous or impossible it may be, I'm starting to realize there's no turning back.

VAEDA

The pavement beneath my feet feels unrelenting, harder than usual, as I cross the street back toward Fusion Core. My pulse pounds, frustration simmering beneath my skin. I'm furious, mostly with myself. How could I have been so careless and reckless as to let Mateo draw me in like that? I should have known better, especially with Yvonne's obvious interest in him. The image of her eyes, bright with jealousy and desire, burns vividly in my mind.

The studio door slams shut behind me, echoing harshly in the quiet space. I move quickly, needing privacy and space. Pulling off and dropping my sweater carelessly onto the bench, I head straight to the sound system, my fingers shaking slightly as I flip through songs until I find a driving, relentless Rumba rhythm. The beat immediately fills the room, powerful and consuming.

I step onto the polished floor, the ache in my ankle barely noticeable beneath the fury propelling me forward. My body responds instantly, years of practice guiding my movements as I channel my anger and confusion into every sharp, decisive step. The music builds, wrapping around me like a storm, pulling me deeper into its fierce embrace.

My hips twist sharply, arms sweeping in controlled arcs, each movement punctuated by the rhythmic pulse driving through the speakers. I spin, losing myself completely, the world fading until there's only the dance, only the raw intensity of emotion bleeding from me with every move.

Suddenly, I feel a presence behind me, solid and warm, then Mateo's familiar scent wraps around me as his hands settle confidently on my hips, matching my rhythm effortlessly. My breath catches, heart pounding harder than ever. I tense initially, instinctively preparing to pull away, but his touch and his closeness dissolves my resolve.

He moves with me fluidly, our bodies finding a natural harmony. His chest brushes against my back, his breath hot against the side of my neck, sending goose bumps cascading over my skin. The dance between us shifts from frustration to something deeper, more dangerous, as the lines of professionalism blur into raw, undeniable attraction.

I lean into him slightly, a silent surrender to the inevitable pull between us. Mateo's grip tightens fractionally, possessively, sending an electrifying thrill through my body. His fingers trace along the curve of my waist, teasing at the hem of my crop top, sending fire streaking through every nerve ending. The rhythm guides us, our movements becoming slower, deliberately seductive, each sway and twist filled with unspoken promises.

His lips brush the spot behind my ear, warm breath washing over my skin. I shiver, a soft gasp escaping my lips as he murmurs, "I've wanted to dance with you like this from the first day I saw you."

My head tilts back involuntarily, exposing more of my neck to him. Mateo accepts the silent invitation, pressing gentle, tantalizing kisses along the sensitive skin. The sensation crashes over my senses, leaving me breathless and trembling with need. His hands travel boldly along my sides, pulling me even tighter against him until every inch of our bodies is perfectly aligned.

I reach back, my fingers tangling into his dark hair, urging him closer, deeper into the moment we've both resisted for far too long. The Rumba rhythm intensifies, matching the wild tempo of our heartbeats. We're dangerously lost in each other's embrace, boundaries disappearing beneath the overwhelming force of desire.

Mateo spins me suddenly, bringing me face-to-face with him, his eyes dark and filled with unmistakable hunger, then he presses me against his chest, our bodies still moving sensually in perfect unison. I feel the powerful thrum of his heart through his shirt, mirroring the frantic pace of mine.

His gaze drops to my lips, lingering and filled with intention, and I tilt my head, offering him everything in that single vulnerable gesture. Mateo's eyes meet mine again, searching for permission. My heart pounding wildly, I give the faintest nod before he slowly lowers his mouth toward mine.

Our lips meet in a searing, all-consuming kiss, igniting every inch of my being with raw passion. His tongue sweeps across my lower lip, coaxing my mouth open, and heat floods through me, melting away the last remnants of resistance as our bodies cling desperately together.

Chapter Fifteen

Mateo

The moment Vaeda's lips touch mine, all control I've desperately clung to shatters. A rush of heat ignites between us, searing away every thought and hesitation, every carefully constructed barrier. The taste of her mouth, sweet and utterly intoxicating, draws me in deeper, demanding more.

With a low groan, I tighten my grip around her waist, pulling her flush against me, and her hands slide into my hair, nails lightly scraping against my scalp, sending sparks of pleasure down my spine. Every nerve in my body feels electrified, drawn irresistibly toward her.

My movements become urgent, driven by raw need as I maneuver us backward until Vaeda's back gently hits the mirrored studio wall. A gasp escapes her, swallowed quickly by another fierce kiss. Her lips part willingly, her tongue tangling passionately with mine as our breaths mingle, hot and desperate.

My hands slip beneath the hem of her shirt, fingertips trailing over soft, heated skin. Vaeda arches into my touch, her body trembling slightly under my palms. The sensation fuels my desire further, and with bold determination, I slide my hands higher, fingertips brushing over the bottom swell of her breasts.

"Mateo," she breathes against my lips, voice shaky yet filled with yearning.

"I don't want to stop," I confess, my voice rough and strained, my lips tracing a heated path along her jawline down to her neck.

"Don't," she whispers urgently, her body pressing closer as her hips shift restlessly against mine.

Encouraged, my hands move further, dragging her shirt up and exposing her perfect breasts. My fingertips are tentative against her skin, teasing lightly before finally slipping upward to cup them. Her sharp inhale sends heat pooling deep within me, awakening a primal urgency that drowns out all rational thought.

Her fingers find the edges of my shirt, gripping the fabric desperately as she breaks away from the kiss just long enough to pull it over my head. The cool air against my heated skin barely registers as our bodies collide again, chest to chest, heartbeat to heartbeat. Vaeda's hands explore the expanse of my bare chest, tracing each muscle and dip, igniting flames wherever her fingers touch.

My mouth finds hers again, deepening the kiss with reckless abandon while my thumbs brush against the sensitive peaks of her breasts, eliciting another sharp gasp from Vaeda. Her reaction drives me wild, each soft sound she makes tightening the coil of desire winding tighter within me.

My hips press insistently against hers, letting her feel exactly how much I want and need her. She responds by arching into me further, her body molding perfectly to mine. Every movement, every touch between us, grows more heated and desperate, pushing us closer to the edge of control.

"Vaeda," I murmur huskily, lips brushing against her collarbone, leaving a trail of open-mouthed kisses down to the hollow of her throat. "You have no idea how long I've wanted this."

"Show me," she whispers urgently, her hands tangling roughly in my hair, pulling my mouth back to hers with fierce determination.

Our kiss becomes a tempest, charged with explosive desire. Every boundary and every rule we've set combusts under the force of our need. Our bodies move in sync, pressed against the studio wall, completely lost in each other. There's no turning back, no retreating from this moment, only the potent, overwhelming reality of our undeniable attraction.

In this heated embrace, I know one thing with absolute certainty: I'll risk everything, including myself, just to hold Vaeda this close, even if it's just for this fleeting, dangerous moment.

VAEDA

My breath comes in sharp, uneven gasps, Mateo's taste still lingering on my lips as my hand boldly moves to cup him through his pants. His deep groan vibrates through me, sending shivers along my spine. Desire coils tighter within me, obliterating every rational thought.

Then, abruptly, the subtle but unmistakable sound of the studio's outer door opening splinters our heated moment. The reality crashes back in, sobering and cold. Panic surges through my veins, and I push Mateo away firmly, heart hammering inside my chest.

"Someone's here," I whisper urgently, my voice tight with fear.

Mateo reacts swiftly, grabbing his discarded shirt from the floor and pulling it hastily over his head, his chest still heaving from our passionate embrace. I snatch my sweater from the nearby bench, barely managing to tug it over my head, smoothing my hair down hastily as heavy footsteps echo down the corridor, growing louder with each step.

The studio door swings open just as Mateo steps back from me, putting careful, intentional distance between us. Greyson strides into the room, his face registering surprise as he sees us.

"Vaeda, Mateo," Greyson says loudly over the music still playing, his tone guarded, eyes narrowing slightly as they dart between us. "What are you two doing here this late and on a Sunday?"

My heart races painfully as I move toward the sound system to shut it off. I force my voice into a steady, nonchalant tone as I say, "Just practicing some moves for Paris. Mateo wanted some extra rehearsal time."

Mateo nods quickly, his voice equally composed despite the flush still evident on his cheeks. "Vaeda offered to help refine some steps. We lost track of time."

Greyson eyes us carefully, the silence stretching just long enough to be uncomfortable before he finally nods slowly, accepting our explanation. "Right. Well, don't burn yourselves out. It's late, and we have a full schedule tomorrow."

"Of course," I reply calmly, the forced smile feeling brittle and fake. "We were just finishing up."

Greyson shifts his stance, clearly still unconvinced, his sharp gaze lingering on me longer than necessary. "Actually, I came by to look over this month's expenses. I figured I'd handle them tonight before the rush of Christmas and such."

A surge of fresh anxiety washes over me, realizing Greyson intends to stay. "They're on the desk," I say quickly, motioning vaguely toward our office. "I left everything organized."

"Great," Greyson responds, moving toward the office door, though he pauses briefly, his hand resting on the handle. "I'll be here for a bit. You two should finish up quickly."

He finally disappears into the office, the door clicking softly shut behind him. Mateo and I exchange a tense glance. The charged atmosphere from moments ago has vanished, replaced by overwhelming dread. This close call serves as a sharp reminder of the dangerous path we're walking.

We stand frozen, listening to the rustling sounds from the office, acutely aware of Greyson's proximity. Mateo's eyes meet mine, filled with unspoken questions and residual heat. I shake my head subtly, signaling caution. The risk is too great, the stakes far too high.

Silently, we gather our belongings, each movement almost mechanical. The air between us feels thick, laden with the tension of interrupted passion and the fear of nearly being caught. As we head toward the studio's exit, I cast one final glance toward the office door, my stomach churning with anxiety and unresolved desire.

Stepping into the cool evening, we both inhale deeply, attempting to calm our racing pulses. The city lights blur around us, my mind swirling with uncertainty and longing.

"Vaeda," Mateo begins softly, his voice cautious yet strained.

I stop him, placing a gentle hand on his arm. "Not now," I whisper urgently. "We'll talk later."

He nods reluctantly, his eyes shadowed with understanding and disappointment. We part ways silently, each step pulling me further from Mateo, but not from the turmoil raging within me.

The cold air offers no relief, only amplifying the intensity of emotions I can neither confront nor escape. Today has changed everything, and as I walk alone, I know there will be no turning back from the path we've recklessly started down.

Chapter Sixteen

I open the door to my penthouse, revealing a dimly lit living room. My heart still races from the chaos at the studio, each breath strained by lingering anxiety. I pause in the doorway, willing myself to appear composed, to bury the guilt and turmoil that threaten to surface.

"Gerardo?" I call softly into the quiet space, stepping inside cautiously. He stands by the window, a packed suitcase resting at his feet. The sight stops me abruptly, my stomach tightening painfully. His usually confident posture now slumps with exhaustion and worry, his gaze fixed distantly on the city skyline. "Gerardo?" My voice quivers slightly, betraying my concern. I'm flooded with fear. Does he know what happened? "What's happened?"

He turns slowly, the shadows beneath his eyes deepening in the dim lighting. "It's my mother," he says quietly, his voice strained and thick with suppressed emotion. "She's fallen ill suddenly. My brother just called. I need to fly to Spain tonight. I know it's Christmas, but I cannot wait."

"Oh, Gerardo," I whisper, the genuine ache inside my chest temporarily overpowering my own conflicted emotions.

Swiftly crossing the room, I wrap my arms around him tightly, holding him close. The comfort feels natural but tinged with the shadow of my earlier indiscretion.

He leans into me briefly, then stiffens slightly, pulling back just enough to study my face with confusion etched into his features. "Vaeda, why do you smell like Irish Spring soap?"

Panic jolts through me sharply, my pulse racing again, but I quickly mask my anxiety with a casual smile, offering a plausible explanation, praying it sounds convincing enough. "I was at the studio. Grey and I danced and it got intense, and I guess I must've picked up his scent. You know how passionate he gets during practice."

Gerardo's eyes narrow momentarily, a shadow of doubt lingering in his gaze, but then he exhales slowly, shaking his head. "Of course," he mutters, clearly trying to dismiss his suspicions amid the more pressing concern. "My flight leaves in a few hours. I don't know how long I'll be gone. It could be days, maybe weeks."

I take his hands gently, forcing sincerity and calmness into my tone. "Gerardo, just focus on your mother. I'll be okay here. I'll take care of everything."

He nods slowly, his eyes softening slightly. "I know you will. You've always been strong, Vaeda." He cups my face gently, his thumb brushing tenderly over my cheek. "I promise I'll call as soon as I land."

"Please do," I murmur, pressing my cheek into his palm, guilt tugging painfully at my heart. His gentle touch intensifies the ache, reminding me of the man who has always been there for me, unwaveringly supportive and loyal. How did I let myself stray so far?

We walk quietly to the door, my relief at not being found out only increasing my shame. As he steps out into the corridor, Gerardo turns to me, his eyes reflecting both urgency and sorrow. "Take care of yourself, Vaeda."

"You too," I respond softly, fighting back a swell of unexpected tears.

He heads toward the elevators, leaving me standing alone, enveloped in an unsettling quiet. I press a hand to my chest as I close the door, feeling the rapid thud of my heart beneath my palm. Relief continues to wash over me, mingling painfully with shame and sorrow. I shouldn't be relieved that he's gone, but I am.

My thoughts inevitably drift to Mateo, to the intensity of what transpired at the studio tonight. The memory burns vividly in my mind, the lingering sensations threatening to weaken my resolve. I shake my head firmly, closing my eyes against the wave of longing that surges fiercely.

"This has to stop," I whisper to myself, my voice barely audible in the empty room. "I have to end things with Mateo. I can't keep risking everything like this."

I walk toward the large windows, staring blankly at the twinkling city lights stretching out before me. The beauty of the cityscape does nothing to soothe my restless spirit, my guilt-ridden heart.

A single tear slips down my cheek, a stark reminder of the emotional turmoil I've brought upon myself. My life had been structured, predictable, and secure until Mateo crashed into it, disrupting everything I'd carefully constructed. Despite the chaos, the temptation, and the undeniable attraction, I must remember my obligations, my loyalty to Gerardo, and the integrity I've always valued.

Taking a deep breath, I steel myself against the storm raging within me, determined to reclaim control. This reckless passion with Mateo must end, even if every fiber of my being cries out against it. For Gerardo's sake, and for my own sanity, I must find the strength to walk away.

The following morning arrives too quickly, dawn creeping in with muted shades of winter gray that perfectly match my mood on Christmas Eve. Sleep had been elusive, my night spent staring at the ceiling, haunted by guilt and wavering determination. Gerardo texted me to let me know his plane landed and that he'll call me as soon as he can. There's a disconnect between us, and we've settled into emotionless texts, something we vowed to never let happen.

I dress mechanically, throwing on a black lacy bra, a comfortable cardigan, and a long black skirt, then pull my hair into a loose ponytail before shrugging into my winter jacket and heading to Fusion Core.

When I step into the studio, the warm, inviting aroma of freshly brewed coffee greets me immediately, causing an involuntary groan to escape my lips. I move into our office, finding a familiar Starbucks cup sitting prominently on my desk. The gesture is thoughtful, but under the circumstances, it feels almost mocking.

Greyson sits behind his own desk, head bowed, his expression deep in concentration as he pores over the monthly financial records. I know this look, the rigid set of his shoulders, the slight furrow of his brows. He's been awake for hours, lost in numbers and ledgers, trying to keep us afloat.

We do well in our beginners' classes, but the number of students slowly dwindles over time as the degree of difficulty increases. My wedding Waltz classes do well, but they are only five classes in total. As for our advanced class, Kari, Adam, and Yvonne pay us well, but Greyson made a deal with Mateo. Since we are a secret and he has no other way to pay us, Greyson accepted the deal of taking a portion of any of the winnings he may earn from competitions. Even though he understands the risk of us winning nothing in the end. Greyson truly thinks Mateo's infamy is payment enough, I believe.

"Merry Christmas Eve," I murmur softly, stepping

further into the room and picking up the coffee. I take a tentative sip, the warmth spreading through my chest and offering temporary comfort against the weight of my guilt.

"Vaeda." Greyson's voice is sharp as his gaze lifts slowly from the books to meet mine. His eyes narrow slightly, suspicion evident in his guarded expression. "We need to talk."

My stomach churns uneasily, but I maintain a neutral expression, hoping to deflect whatever he suspects. "About?"

"You know exactly what," he snaps, a harsh edge slipping into his voice. He leans back in his chair, fingers steepled in front of him. "What the hell were you really doing with Mateo last night?"

The blunt question lands between us, loaded with accusation and tension. I pause, taking another slow sip of coffee to gather my thoughts before taking a seat at my desk. "We were rehearsing for Paris like I told you. Mateo wanted extra practice, and I agreed to help him. Nothing more."

Greyson snorts, shaking his head dismissively. "Don't insult my intelligence, Vae. I know you better than that. I've known you for years and I see things others miss. You were acting strangely. Mateo was too."

I press my lips together tightly, refusing to admit the truth, even though my pulse betrays my anxiety. "I told you, Grey. It was just practice."

He watches me carefully, eyes piercing through my defenses, before exhaling deeply and leaning forward. "Look, I didn't show up here last night to work on the ledgers. I received a call from Yvonne, and she told me the lights were on in the studio. She was worried someone broke in."

Anger courses through me as Yvonne's obvious intentions hit me. She saw me and Mateo together at the diner. When he left, she must've watched him come straight here. She knew what she was doing by calling Greyson, and I'll never forgive her for that.

"I'm sorry you were disturbed. She should've called me instead—"

"I won't pretend to understand all your choices, especially your marriage to Gerardo, but he doesn't deserve to be hurt. He's always been good to you," he interrupts me, cutting off any other excuses I might have said.

His words cut deep, stirring up a wave of guilt that nearly overwhelms me. I nod slowly, swallowing hard as I set down my coffee cup. When Gerardo and I decided to get married, Greyson was the only one to advise me not to. He was worried that the love Gerardo and I felt was confusion for the tension that comes with being longtime partners on the floor. Even now, Greyson questions if we are truly meant to be together, and even though I haven't been acting as such, I love Gerardo.

"I know. There was a fleeting moment. The dance, the music, it all became distorted and… I don't intend to let this get out of—"

Greyson interrupts me once more, his voice softer but no less firm. "Intentions don't matter, Vae. Actions do, and right now, your actions are speaking volumes."

I avert my gaze, staring blankly at the polished surface of my desk, unable to meet his disappointed stare. "I understand."

"Do you?" he challenges gently, his tone now heavy with genuine concern. "Because this could ruin everything you've worked for. Not just your marriage, but the studio, your career, and your reputation."

His words ring with undeniable truth, echoing the warnings I've whispered to myself countless times. The stakes are impossibly high, the consequences devastatingly real.

"I'll handle it," I assure him softly, conviction

strengthening my voice. "Nothing more will happen."

Greyson studies me for a long moment, as though measuring the sincerity of my promise. Finally, he nods once, turning back to his books. "Make sure it doesn't."

I rise from my seat, the coffee now cold and forgotten. The weight of his words presses heavily on my chest, reminding me that my actions have repercussions far beyond my own desires. As I step out of the office, a renewed resolve forms within me. For Gerardo, for Greyson, and for myself, I must find the strength to end this reckless attraction to Mateo once and for all, no matter the cost.

MATEO

The hallway echoes with the usual bustling chatter of students between classes, but it barely registers in my mind. Christmas break started yesterday, but today was the last day to grab any final materials before the school closes. My phone vibrates in my pocket, an incessant reminder that life refuses to pause, even when all I crave is stillness. Pulling it out, my stomach drops when I see my father's name flashing brightly on the screen.

"Hello?" My voice wavers slightly, betraying my immediate apprehension.

"Mateo." My father's voice is laced with barely restrained anger, cutting straight to the core of my anxiety. "We need to talk."

I swallow thickly, stepping into the nearest bathroom and locking myself into a stall, seeking privacy from prying ears and curious eyes. "What about?"

"Don't play games with me," he barks harshly. "Your mother finally told me you're dancing again. I warned you about this. I won't allow you to ruin your life again, or ours."

My heart pounds painfully against my ribs, each beat punctuating his anger. "Dad, please, just listen—"

"Listen? Listen to what, Mateo? More promises? More lies? Do you even understand what you've put this family through?"

His words slice through me, forcing memories I've desperately tried to bury to surge to the surface. My vision blurs with hot tears as his anger sharpens. "I remember, Dad. Every single moment. I know what I did."

His voice softens marginally, but the fury remains evident. "Do you, Mateo? Do you remember us finding you barely alive in that hospital bed? Your mother's cries echoing through the halls? Do you remember your sister, Grace, sobbing because she thought she'd lost you forever?"

A painful lump forms in my throat, choking off my breath. The image of Grace's tear-streaked face flashes vividly through my mind, her words still ringing clearly, as if she'd just spoken them: *"I can't do this anymore, Mateo. You almost died. I can't keep watching you destroy yourself."*

I grip the phone tightly, knuckles whitening with the strain as my voice trembles with raw desperation. "Dad, please. I'm begging you. I'm not that person anymore. I'm fighting so hard every day to prove that to you, to Mami, to Grace—"

"Grace won't even say your name," he interrupts bitterly. "You've broken something inside her that's still not healed. Dancing is what helped put you in that hospital bed, Mateo. How can we trust that this won't lead you straight back there?"

A tear slips down my cheek, silently betraying my crumbling resolve, and my voice cracks painfully. "Because I need to prove to myself that I'm stronger than my mistakes. Dancing was never the problem, Dad. It was me. The drugs, the recklessness, the desperation to escape. I need to dance now more than ever because it reminds me of who I am meant to be."

Silence stretches agonizingly on the other end, broken only by his ragged breathing. Finally, his voice returns, low and strained with raw emotion. "If you fall again, Mateo, if you spiral… I'm coming to New York myself and dragging you back home. Do you understand?"

"I understand," I whisper brokenly, the sound of his disbelief ringing in every word he says.

The call ends abruptly, leaving me trembling and leaning against the cold bathroom wall. The tears fall freely now, my heart shattering with everything I've put my family through. The crushing guilt I'd worked so hard to bury returns tenfold, gripping my soul mercilessly.

I slide down the wall, sinking to the cold, tiled floor, burying my face in my shaking hands. I sob quietly, alone in the sterile silence, each tear a silent plea for forgiveness I fear may never come.

Yet even in this moment of deep despair, an undeniable truth whispers softly within me. I can't give up. I won't. Not when I'm finally learning how to breathe again.

"Merry Christmas," I whisper as my heart incinerates to ash.

The world outside feels distant and muffled, as if I'm submerged underwater. Each breath I take is labored and piercing as splintered glass, filled with echoes of my father's harsh words and unrelenting accusations. They replay incessantly, like a needle stuck on a broken record, burrowing deeper with each painful repetition.

Roger's SUV sits idling at the curb, its glossy black surface reflecting distorted images of passing life, entirely disconnected from my reality. I slip into the leather seat, letting the car door shut with a hollow thud. My silence is deafening, speaking volumes to Roger, who studies me briefly through the rearview mirror. His eyes—always kind and patient—hold quiet concern now.

"Everything alright, Mateo?" His voice is gentle, yet hesitant.

Words crowd my throat, bitter and raw, but I choke them back, unwilling to release the flood just yet. The city outside blurs into meaningless streaks of color, vibrant but lacking clarity. My fingers curl into my palms, nails biting into flesh, grounding me briefly. Finally, I manage a response, forced through clenched teeth. "Just take me to Fusion Core."

A pregnant pause hangs between us, heavy with unspoken truths. "Are you sure? It's Christmas Eve, Mateo."

His compassion only fuels my frustration. "I suppose Dad already told you about my dancing," I mutter bitterly.

He doesn't answer immediately, his silence louder than any confession. I stare into his reflected gaze, the muted sympathy confirming my suspicions. Resentment surges inside my chest, hot and merciless, further poisoning my already turbulent emotions.

When we arrive at Fusion Core, I push out of the SUV hastily, leaving Roger's silence behind. The studio's familiarity, its bright mirrors and polished floors, feels stark and invasive today. Instead of offering comfort, it exposes me, mirrors amplifying every painful emotion etched on my face.

Yvonne moves toward me immediately, her eyes wide with concern, her voice soft with cautious inquiry. "Mateo, what's wrong?" Her sweet tone grates against my raw nerves, irritating rather than soothing.

"Nothing," I growl, my voice harsh, hoping she'll leave it at that.

She steps closer, her gaze earnest, trying to read the storm that undoubtedly darkens my features. "Please, Mateo, let me help. Just talk to me—"

"Damn it, Yvonne!" My voice erupts, loud and jagged, slicing through the air. Her face pales, the hurt blossoming instantly in her eyes. "Not everything is your business! Just back off!"

Silence descends upon the studio like a blanket, thick and suffocating, and I sense the shock reverberating through the others, the weight of their judgment pressing in from all sides.

Acidic shame trickles through the cracks of my bitter anger as I spin on my heel, pushing through the heavy doors into the twilight, the cool evening air biting at my flushed skin. Each step away from the studio is an attempt to outrun the chaos inside me, a futile escape from a relentless internal tempest.

"Mateo!"

Vaeda's voice reaches me, pulling me to a halt. My body tenses, poised between flight and longing, torn between isolation and the ache for her comforting presence. She approaches cautiously, like one might approach a frightened, wounded animal.

"Wait," she whispers, her voice a soothing balm over the ripped edges of my soul. "Please talk to me."

My throat tightens painfully, emotion swelling behind my ribs until breathing becomes nearly impossible. I turn slowly, facing her, my defenses crumbling under the weight of her gaze. The streetlights halo her figure, enveloping her in a soft glow, making her appear ethereal and untouchable. A vision just beyond my grasp. She's wearing a soft-looking cardigan, the top buttons undone to show just enough cleavage to be tantalizing, and her legs are covered by a long flowing skirt.

"Vaeda," I manage hoarsely, my voice fractured by vulnerability. "My father found out about this, about Fusion Core. I ruined our family once, and he refuses to let me do it again. I could be dragged back to California."

"You're attending your meetings and going to school though, right? You haven't slipped, have you?" Her voice trembles as I let out a harsh laugh. It's hard to remember that Vaeda doesn't really know me, not the true me.

She sees my technique inside her studio walls, the way my feet kiss the hardwood floors with precision and passion, but beyond that, Vaeda doesn't know anything about me except for rumors.

"Have I slipped?" I repeat as my eyes crash with hers, fear dancing along her irises. "For drugs? No. For alcohol? Not even tempted." I step closer to her, her chest rising and falling rapidly as she struggles with my proximity. "But... for you? I'm fucking drowning."

She sucks in a breath and steps back, shaking her head as she lets loose a loud scoff. "Greyson knows." Her words make the breath inside my chest stutter as I let them absorb. "At least he has his suspicions... because of last night."

"Who cares?" As soon as I say the words, I realize I mean them. "Who cares if people know we're together?"

"My husband might?" she fires back as she throws up her hands. "Not to mention, I am way too old for you." She's dismissing our feelings because of the years separating us?

"That's absurd," I retort, making her drop her arms and deflate. "Ten years is nothing."

"Ten years is the difference between a college student and a woman with a renowned career. Ten years is the difference between living off your parents and being married and paying your own bills." Her eyes harden as my jaw tightens, forcing me not to explode with anger. "Ten years is the reason I'm saying this is over, but I'm still your friend if you need me."

"Still my friend?" I ground out, my words sounding harsh. I step closer to her and huff through a sarcastic laugh. "You don't even know me." Then I turn on my heel and walk away, leaving behind the woman with a husband and bills of her own while I decide to become the *student* she sees me as.

Chapter Seventeen

Mateo

The pounding bass reverberates through my chest as I step onto the sidewalk outside the club, neon lights illuminating the night in brilliant flashes of color. The line wraps around the building despite it being Christmas Eve, bodies shivering against the chill, but I'm too wired and lost in my own turmoil to feel the cold. Without hesitation, I slip the bouncer a crisp hundred-dollar bill, earning myself a nod of acknowledgement as he unhooks the velvet rope and gestures me inside.

The dim lighting engulfs me as I step into the club, the pulse of music vibrating through every cell in my body. The atmosphere is intoxicatingly seductive. Every corner is an invitation to lose myself, to forget the harshness of reality. Drinks flow freely, glistening in glasses under the sporadic beams of colored light. Beautiful faces laugh, flirt, and lose themselves to the hypnotic rhythm. The air is thick with temptation, a heady mixture of perfume, alcohol, and glistening skin on display.

I navigate through the crowded dance floor, bodies brushing against me, every touch an electric jolt, reminding me of everything I came here to forget. My father's harsh disappointment, Grace's silence, and most of all, Vaeda. Her words echo in my mind, taunting me with a truth that cuts deeper each time it replays: her marriage and the ten years between us.

Reaching the bar, I lean heavily against the polished surface, catching my reflection in the mirrored backdrop. My eyes look dark and troubled, searching for answers at the bottom of a glass. *Just one drink,* I reason silently, fingers tapping anxiously against the bar. It won't hurt. Alcohol was never the vice that nearly killed me. It was the pills, the powder, and the desperation for escape.

The bartender approaches, an eyebrow raised in silent inquiry. My throat feels tight, but I push through the hesitation, my voice sounding foreign to my ears. "Whiskey sour," I manage, my voice raspy, barely audible above the music.

The bartender nods, moving away swiftly, leaving me alone once again with my spiraling thoughts. I grip the cool edge of the bar, my knuckles whitening as I battle with myself. One drink won't hurt, but deep down, I know the truth. It's not about the drink. It's about surrendering control, slipping back into the oblivion where nothing matters and the pain finally numbs.

As the bartender returns, sliding the amber liquid toward me, my phone buzzes insistently in my pocket. I fumble for it, irritation sparking momentarily until I see Yvonne's name flashing across the screen. A slow smile spreads across my lips, dangerous yet enticing.

Yvonne likes me, parties without apologies, and she isn't complicated by marriage vows or professional boundaries. She's safe in her simplicity, the opposite of Vaeda's complex allure. Maybe she's exactly what I need tonight.

I answer, raising the phone to my ear as I stare at the untouched drink, fingers wrapped tightly around the cool glass.

"Hey."

"Mateo!" Her voice is bright, yet tinged with worry. "I wanted to check on you. You seemed really upset earlier. Where are you?"

I pause, the thrum of the music beating through my silence. "I know it's Christmas Eve, but I'm at Pulse. Come join me?"

She laughs lightly, clearly surprised and delighted by my invitation. "Absolutely. I'll be there in ten."

Ending the call, I finally lift the glass, studying the swirling liquid. This is reckless, but tonight I crave recklessness. My gaze drifts to the crowded dance floor, the rhythm calling to me, promising distraction and release.

Yet as I stand poised at this edge, drink in hand, waiting for Yvonne's arrival, a nagging thought gnaws at the back of my mind, whispering dangerously, *Once you cross this line, can you ever really turn back?*

VAEDA

I stand frozen just inside Fusion Core's studio doors, watching as Yvonne paces restlessly across the polished hardwood floors. Her cell phone is pressed urgently against her ear, her face alight with anticipation and excitement. My stomach twists uncomfortably, a growing knot of suspicion and jealousy tightening inside my chest.

She laughs, a bright, carefree sound that sends a pang of irritation straight through me. My jaw clenches as the unsettling thought takes root. *She's talking to Mateo.* I'd meant every word about our age difference, the gap that seemed insurmountable, but the idea of Mateo turning his affections toward Yvonne fills me with irrational jealousy. A jealousy I don't want to acknowledge, let alone feel.

Suddenly, Yvonne grabs her coat from the rack by the door, her movements hurried and eager. She hangs up quickly, a smile still curving her lips, oblivious to my watchful gaze.

"Everything alright, Yvonne?" I call out, forcing my voice into neutrality even as my pulse races in my veins.

Yvonne glances up, startled, her eyes briefly flickering with surprise and irritation before quickly masking it with a casual shrug. "Yeah, everything's great. Just going to meet a friend."

The vague response only sharpens the sting of jealousy, the sensation burning through my chest like wildfire. I try to maintain composure, offering a faint, polite nod. "Be careful out there. It's getting late, and Merry Christmas."

"I will," she promises quickly, clearly distracted. "Merry Christmas!" Then she rushes out of the studio, taking my patience and propriety with her.

An uneasy feeling settles over me, gnawing at the edges

of my awareness. Something about her hurried departure and barely concealed excitement sends a chill down my spine. Before rational thought can intervene, I'm grabbing my jacket, pulling it tightly around myself as I follow swiftly behind her.

Outside, the city streets glisten beneath fresh snow flurries, streetlights radiating a hazy, golden glow across the wet pavement. Yvonne strides confidently ahead, unaware of my presence, her steps hurried. My heart pounds heavily, anxiety and uncertainty warring within me as I keep pace at a careful distance.

Every step that takes me closer to uncovering her destination brings a fresh surge of dread. Yet beneath the apprehension lies a darker truth. I'm driven by jealousy, by a possessiveness I have no right to feel. Mateo's face flashes vividly through my mind, his intense eyes, then the passionate edge of his voice when he spoke of his feelings for me. I've pushed him away, yet I can't bear the thought of someone else holding him close.

The thought sends an agonizing ache through my heart, clawing painfully at my insides, but beneath this jealousy, another emotion surfaces, powerful and insistent. Worry. Mateo is vulnerable, standing at the precipice of temptation, and I know all too well how quickly a single misstep can unravel everything.

My footsteps quicken as Yvonne turns a corner, a sinking feeling pulling me deeper into this reckless chase. I know this is dangerous, risky, and possibly foolish, but my heart overrides every rational argument.

Fear tightens its grip around my chest, suffocating in its intensity. If Mateo spirals, it could cost him everything he's fought so hard to rebuild, and suddenly, the jealousy fades to the background, replaced by a profound sense of urgency and dread. Tonight, boundaries blur, and I can't help but follow the trail, even if it leads me into the very chaos I've desperately sought to avoid. Because beneath everything, the one undeniable truth remains: I've finally realized that I'm terrified of losing him.

I continue to follow Yvonne from a safe distance, ducking beneath the streetlights and pressing into the shadows. The streets are slick, reflecting the neon buzz of storefronts and car headlights in a distorted mirror. Every time Yvonne glances over her shoulder, I duck behind parked cars and awnings, heart hammering. I should feel ridiculous, but I don't. I feel sick, because I have a feeling I know where she's going.

The moment I see the glowing red letters of Pulse Nightclub come into view, another wave of dread washes over me. I stop in the middle of the sidewalk, staring at the line of well-dressed men and women, the thrumming beat of bass vibrating in my chest like a second heartbeat.

He's here, and she's going to him.

I pick up my pace, eyes locked on her light brown hair bobbing through the crowd until she stops at the end of the line. She's checking her reflection in the darkened glass, applying a fresh coat of lipstick, smiling like she's ready to party. Like this is a date.

No. Fucking. Way.

I push through the crowd, ignoring the annoyed murmurs, and march straight up to the bouncer at the door. He eyes me with a mixture of boredom and irritation, arms folded across his chest.

"Please," I gasp. "I need to get inside. My boyfriend's in there. He's an addict, and he's... he's not okay."

The bouncer raises an eyebrow. "Because that isn't a line I've heard before."

"I don't have time for this." My voice cracks, more raw and real than I intended. "If he drinks tonight, he'll relapse, and if he relapses, he could die. Please."

He stares at me for a long moment, as if weighing my sincerity in his hands. Then he jerks his chin toward the door. "Go."

I push past him and into the club.

The bass hits me like a wall, vibrating through my ribs. The air is thick with sweat, smoke, and desperation. Lights strobe over a sea of dancing bodies, arms raised, mouths open in joy or lust or oblivion. My eyes sweep the chaos, searching and hoping I'm not too late.

I weave through the crowd, breath shallow and chest tight. I move past couples grinding against each other, past the press of bodies too lost in their own worlds to notice the storm inside me, and then I see him.

Mateo is standing at the bar, shoulders tense, and eyes glassy. A glass glistens in his hand, the amber liquid trembling as his fingers twitch around it. He's not drunk. Not yet, but he's right there and he looks on the edge.

Glancing back toward the entrance, I watch as the bouncer lets in a few more girls and still no Yvonne. I move to him without thinking, and once I'm within touching distance, I reach out, rip the glass from his hand, and hurl it over the bar. It shatters against the wall, shards flying like crystal confetti. The bartender curses as people turn.

Mateo stares at me, stunned, his lips parted in disbelief. "Vaeda?"

"You can't do this," I snarl, stepping into his space, trembling with adrenaline. "Not like this. Not now when you have so much to lose."

His expression crumples, and something inside me breaks with it. "I wasn't going to drink it," he says, voice hoarse.

"You ordered it."

"I know."

I reach for his chest, splaying my hand over his heart and feeling the rapid thud beneath my palm. "What are you doing here, Mateo?"

He laughs bitterly. "Trying to forget. Trying to feel normal. Trying not to think about you and how badly I want something I can't have."

I close my eyes. "And you called Yvonne?"

"She called me." He exhales, long and broken. "And I answered because... I thought maybe if I wanted someone else, this wouldn't hurt so much." The words slice through me, equal parts painful and true. "I'm fucked-up over you," he confesses, his eyes glassy with emotion. "And I hate that. I hate how much power you have over me."

My hand trembles against his chest. "Then why didn't you drink it?"

His eyes flick to mine, stormy and desperate. "Because I still want to be the kind of man who deserves to stand next to you."

My tears come fast, hot and helpless. In the chaos of this place, in the glow of temptation and noise, he's holding on by the thinnest thread, and somehow, miraculously, he chose to keep fighting.

"Let's get out of here," I suggest as the music attacks my eardrums. I want to talk to him, let him know just how special he is.

The beat of the music pulses behind us as we reach the edge of the dance floor. I'm ready to drag him straight out of this place, but then a familiar rhythm rolls through the speakers, a beat we know intimately. My breath catches.

It's the same track we danced to in that hip-hop class, the one where his hands held my hips like they belonged there, the one where our bodies aligned too perfectly to be innocent.

He recognizes it too. I feel it in the way his hand tightens around mine, the shift in his posture, the pull of something we both try so hard to resist. Mateo turns toward me slowly, his expression unreadable, but I see the flicker of memory in his eyes.

The song commands us and we answer.

I don't think as I let him draw me back into the crowd until we find a pocket of space near the center. Bodies sway all around us, but I feel only him. The first step is natural, the second is instinctual, and then we move together effortlessly.

His hands find my hips again, not tentative this time. His touch is firm, knowing. My back arches into him, and I feel the press of his chest against mine, the heat of him a live wire along every nerve. I raise my arms around his neck, fingers sliding into his hair, tugging lightly, and his breath hitches against the shell of my ear.

We move like a current, lost in the beat. The music fades to background noise and the lights become a blur, and there's only the tension between us, electric and reckless and real.

Mateo's forehead brushes mine, his breath warm against my lips. We don't speak. We don't need to. My eyes close, and then he kisses me.

Hard.

Hungry.

His mouth claims mine in a way that steals all logic, all fear and restraint, while his hands slide up my back, pulling me closer, and I let him. I fall into the kiss like it's the only place I've ever wanted to be. Our bodies move in sync, the dance forgotten, replaced by something deeper.

My hands slip beneath the collar of his shirt, fingers spreading across his skin. His hands roam my sides beneath my jacket, fingertips tracing reverently, as if committing me to memory. He kisses me like he's trying to forget everything but this moment.

When we finally break apart, breathless and shaken, I look up at him, heart pounding. "You can't be alone tonight," I tell him. "It's Christmas."

He searches my face, eyes wide with disbelief. "Are you sure?"

"I don't know what I'm doing," I admit, brushing my fingers along his jaw. "But I know I'll never forgive myself if I let you leave here alone."

He nods, the stiffness in his shoulders easing ever so slightly, then reaches for my hand again, threading our fingers together before we push through the crowd once more. This time, toward the door.

CHAPTER EIGHTEEN

The city rushes past in smears of festive gold and drab gray, streetlights blurring through the cab window as if the world itself can't decide what it wants to be, bright or dark. The warmth of Vaeda's hand in mine anchors me to the seat, her touch steady and real against the tide of chaos still churning inside my chest. She hasn't let go. Even after everything tonight, she's still here. Still beside me.

The high from being near her still vibrates through my veins, her scent clinging to my skin. My lips are tinged with the memory of hers, and yet beneath it all, something sinister pulses. Guilt. Fear. The aftershock of how close I came to falling.

I almost drank.

The words are quiet in my mind, but their echo is deafening. I almost let it all go, almost let one moment of weakness unravel the fragile thread I've been walking since the day I opened my eyes in that hospital bed. For a heartbeat tonight, I thought maybe giving up would feel like freedom. Then she appeared, shattered the glass in my hand, and chased away the fog in my mind. Now she sits next to me, silent and unreadable. Her jaw is tense, lips set, her eyes fixed out the window, reflecting the city's glow without revealing anything inside.

My phone buzzes against my leg and I pull it out of my pocket. Yvonne's name blinks on the screen like a warning. I hit the side button and silence it, but not fast enough because Vaeda sees it. She doesn't say anything at first, but her lips press together more tightly. Then I feel the crack in the moment. The shift.

"There's nothing there," I say quietly, but the words taste thin.

She turns slowly, her eyes guarded and knowing. "Except she's the one you answered. When everything was falling apart, she's the one you chose to let in when you were so close to tipping over that edge." Her voice isn't cruel. It's worse, filled with disappointment and sounding wounded.

"I didn't drink," I offer, my voice tighter than I want it to be. "I didn't even touch it."

"But you almost did," she replies, eyes narrowing just slightly. "And you almost let her be the one to catch you."

"I didn't think you'd care." My hand tightens around hers when she tries to release mine. "Don't you remember your marriage and the ten years between us?"

She blinks, her mouth parting just slightly. "Why would you think that I wouldn't care?" She ignores everything else, choosing to focus on the first part instead.

My throat feels like sand and I swallow hard. "Because you keep pushing me away."

Her gaze drops, shame flickering briefly across her features. "I push because I'm scared. Because I don't trust myself. Because I'm married, Mateo."

"I know," I whisper. "But I never stopped hoping you'd show up anyway." A beat of silence stretches between us, laden with everything we've said and haven't said. "I'm not a saint," I admit, my voice trembling now. "But you... You're the only thing that makes me want to be better. Not for the program. Not for my family. For me. For you. For us. If we ever get to have that."

Her hand tightens in mine, just barely, and I look down at the way our fingers fit, like they were made to. "I'm not your redemption," she counters, but there's no bite behind it.

"I'm not asking you to be," I say. "But you make me want to stay clean. You make me want to fight harder." The cab rolls to a stop outside her building, but neither of us moves. "I wanted to forget you tonight," I confess. "That's why I picked up when Yvonne called. That's why I went to that bar. I wanted to lose you in the noise." Her breath catches. "But even in that place, with temptation all around me, you were the only thing I could feel."

She turns to me then, her expression cracked wide open, flooded with potent fear. "You scare the hell out of me," she whispers.

I nod slowly. "You do the same to me."

We ride the elevator in silence. Vaeda leans against the back wall, arms crossed, the soft glow from the overhead light illuminating the muscle in her jaw. I can feel her retreating already, slipping into that unreachable place she disappears to when the world edges too close.

When the doors open, I follow her down the hallway to her penthouse. She unlocks the door and pushes it open with a quiet sigh, stepping inside and toeing off her shoes before hanging up her jacket.

"Where's your husband?" I ask, my voice low.

Her back stiffens before she answers. "He had to fly to Spain. His mother isn't well."

"Oh," I murmur, stepping in behind her. The door closes with a soft click that somehow feels too loud in the stillness. Now it makes sense why she even invited me over here. I should've realized that the moment she offered at the club.

The space is familiar and still adorned with the holiday decorations. The last time I stood here was the night of her birthday party, when the air was electric with possibilities. When I almost kissed her. When we stood so close, I could feel her breath on my cheek.

She heads to the kitchen, not bothering to turn on any lights. Only the under-cabinet glow spills across the marble countertops. I follow slowly, memories pressing at my ribs. The laughter of her guests, the sound of expensive wine being poured, and the desire of wanting her and knowing I shouldn't.

She pulls two glasses down, fills one with water and hands it to me. Her fingers brush mine as I take it. Cold glass. Warm skin. A pulse of anticipation. The silence is heavy now. I open my mouth to say something, anything, then my phone buzzes. I glance down and see my mother's name flash on the screen.

I hold it up, muttering, "It's my mom. I need to take this." Vaeda nods silently and turns her back, busying herself at the sink. I set the glass of water down and step into the adjacent room, lifting the phone to my ear. "Hi, Mami."

"Where are you?" Her voice is tight, frayed with panic. "I called the doorman. He said you didn't come home."

"I'm okay," I say quickly. "I'm just... I'm at my instructor's place with a few people. We were practicing late."

There's a beat of silence. Then, quieter, "On Christmas Eve? You're not lying to me, Mateo?"

"No, I swear. I'm okay."

She exhales, and I can picture her pacing the kitchen at home, one hand pressed to her chest. "Your father will come around. He always does. You just need to stay focused. Don't give him a reason to drag you back."

"I won't."

"Merry Christmas. I will speak to you tomorrow. I love you, mi cielo."

"Merry Christmas. Love you too."

I hang up and turn to find Vaeda standing in the doorway, her figure a shadow haloed by soft light from the kitchen behind her.

VAEDA

I heard every word.

From the moment his voice dropped to that aching hush, to the soft, worried cadence of his mother's plea. I heard it all, and now I stand frozen in the doorway to my living room, having gravitated here as soon as he picked up the call, staring at him and hoping for answers I've been too afraid to ask. His sobriety is fragile and I'm not helping.

I'm the tremor beneath his feet, the pothole on a road that should be smooth. I see it now, more clearly than ever. The way his voice cracked when he reassured her, the subtle tremble in his breath when he swore he was okay. He's not. Not really. He's just clinging to something that feels steady, and that something—God help us both—is me.

The guilt comes swiftly and strongly. My stomach clenches, a wave of nausea curling under my ribs. I've never made anyone feel like that before, as though I'm their lifeline. Gerardo never looked at me that way. Never needed me with that kind of desperate hope. And the worst part? I wouldn't have noticed, because I've never wanted anyone the way I want Mateo.

I don't move when he makes his way over to me, don't lift my head, but I feel him come closer. The air shifts with him, his presence coiling around my spine like a cord being drawn tight.

"Vaeda," he says, his voice low and tentative.

I look up, and he's already there. Close. So very close. His brows are pinched, his eyes wide and brimming with raw and tender emotion. He looks at me like I'm gravity, and then he touches me.

His hands lift slowly, fingers brushing the line of my

jaw. He holds my face so gently, as if I'm sacred. As if I'm not the one who might ruin him. His touch is hesitant at first, but I can feel the restraint in him, the effort it takes to move slowly when his entire body pulses with urgency.

"I shouldn't want this," I whisper, but the moment the words leave my lips, I know they're a lie. I've never wanted anything more.

His thumb brushes across my cheek, and the warmth of his breath dances across my mouth. He leans in and kisses me. It isn't rushed, or messy, or desperate. It's reverent. Devotional. A prayer disguised as a touch. My knees go weak, my heart stuttering against my ribs. I tremble as his lips linger on mine, and when he pulls back, I see the reflection of my own longing mirrored in his eyes.

He looks at me like I'm his salvation, and I can't stand it.

Mateo guides me gently, leading me farther into the room. The apartment feels too quiet, too intimate, like it's holding its breath right along with me. He sinks onto the couch, his hand still clasping mine, and with the softest tug, he draws me down onto his lap.

I hesitate for a split second. Not out of doubt, but out of fear. Fear that I won't be able to stop. That this will become a wildfire I can't control, but I follow the pull anyway, letting him guide me down, my thighs sliding along either side of his. His hands immediately come to my hips, firm and possessive.

My breath catches as I straddle him, the feel of him pulsing between my legs making it hard to breathe. I brace my hands on his shoulders, but it's not to steady myself. It's to stop myself from falling too far because I already know I won't come back from this.

His fingers move along my sides, slow but deliberate, as he makes his way up toward my chest. His touch is soft, but it simmers just beneath the surface, brimming with a barely restrained hunger.

He presses his forehead to mine, his lashes brushing my skin as his hands curl into the fabric of my cardigan. "You feel like a dream," he whispers.

I close my eyes, because if I keep them open, I'll see everything I stand to lose. Gerardo. Greyson. The studio. All of it.

Instead, I let myself just feel him. God help me, I let myself *have* him.

His hands are on my waist, warm and certain as his mouth moves hungrily against mine. The kisses grow deeper, urgent and full of need, and I can't stop myself from responding.

Mateo pulls my cardigan up and over my head, casting it aside without a glance, then his lips return to mine instantly, as if the separation had been agony. I can feel the tremble in his fingers, the eagerness in his grip, but there's still tenderness in every motion, like he's painting each inch of my skin to memory. My bra is next, the black lace joining my cardigan on the floor at his feet.

He pulls off his own sweater, then we press together, skin to skin, bare and burning. I rake my fingers along his back, relishing the strength there, the way his muscles flex beneath my hands. My skirt pools higher on my thighs as I shift my weight and roll my hips instinctively against him.

We fall deeper into this forbidden space, this heady blend of lust and longing. His mouth finds my neck, my collarbone, and I gasp when his hands slide up my sides. I can't think. I can't breathe. All I know is him.

My fingers move to the waistband of his jeans, unfastening the button, slowly tugging at the zipper. My breath hitches as I lean in to kiss his jaw, ready to give in completely.

"When will you leave him?" The words are soft, but earnest, and they rupture the bubble of rapture.

I still as his question slices through the haze of lust. My hands stop moving. My lips freeze against his skin. I feel his heart racing beneath my palm, and for a moment, I swear the whole world holds its breath. I sit back slightly, straddling him still, but all the fire inside my chest has turned to ash.

Mateo looks up at me, his eyes open, vulnerable. He's not pressuring. Not demanding. Just... hoping. And I can't answer. My mouth parts, but nothing comes.

His hands, once tight on my hips, loosen their grip. "You won't," he says, voice quiet but laced with agony. He nods to himself, almost as if he'd known. As if he'd been bracing for it.

I shift off his lap, hugging my arms around myself as shame curls like smoke in my lungs. "I'm sorry," I whisper, unable to meet his gaze, though the words feel pathetic. Useless.

Mateo exhales, long and slow. "I don't want to be someone you come to in the dark and hide from in the light."

"You're not," I protest too quickly, but even I don't believe it.

He stands, moving around the coffee table to gather his clothing from the floor. "I should go."

"Please don't—"

He pulls the sweater over his head and turns to face me. "I would've given you anything," he states. "But not as an illicit secret."

I nod, swallowing the tears that threaten to spill. "And it would've wrecked us both."

He watches me for a moment longer, then heads for the door. He doesn't slam it, doesn't curse. Just quietly walks out, and I'm left in the silence, with the heat of his touch still on my skin, and the ghost of his question echoing in my chest.

CHAPTER NINETEEN
Mateo

The cab's interior is filled with silence, broken only by the occasional rattle of loose change in the driver's console. The city blurs past the window, streetlights flickering like dying stars in the heavily falling snow. I lean my head against the glass, still tasting Vaeda on my lips, still feeling the sting of her silence.

She didn't say it out loud, but she didn't have to. I already know. She's never going to leave him.

My chest feels hollow as the weight of that truth settles deep inside me. For a moment, I think about asking the driver to keep going, to take me somewhere away from this part of the city, but I don't. I'm too tired to run.

The vibration of my phone startles me, and I pull it from my pocket, glancing down and seeing Yvonne's name. I hesitate, thumb hovering over the answer button, but then I think about her waiting at the club, about the phone call I never returned. She didn't deserve to be left in the dark like that.

So I answer. "Hey," I say, my voice flat, empty.

"Mateo? What happened?" Her voice is high-pitched with concern. "You weren't at Pulse when I got there. I waited for like an hour. Are you okay?"

I close my eyes, exhaustion rolling through me like a tide. "Not really."

There's a pause. Then softer, "Where are you now?"

"Heading home." I swallow. "I know it's Christmas Eve and you should be with your family, but can you come over for a little bit? I... I need to talk."

Another pause, then, "Yeah. Yeah, of course. I'll grab a cab."

I give her my building and apartment number, then hang up. I don't know why I'm doing this. Maybe it's guilt. Maybe it's desperation. Or maybe I'm just tired of carrying it all alone.

When I get home, the apartment feels too quiet, too clean, like nothing here knows how messy I am inside. I flick on a lamp and sit down on the edge of the couch, hands pressed together, elbows on my knees. It doesn't take long before there's a knock at the door.

"Come in!" I call out.

Yvonne steps inside, cheeks pink from the cold, a curious look on her face as she shrugs off her coat. "Your place is nice! Why didn't you decorate?" She finally gets a good look at me and the smile falls from her face. "You look like hell."

"I feel worse." She joins me on the couch, turning slightly to face me. Her eyes roam my face, searching for clues. I stare down at my hands before looking at her once more. "I've never told anyone this before, not outside of meetings. Not anyone who wasn't... obligated to care."

She blinks. "Okay."

"I'm a recovering addict," I say simply. "Oxy and coke. It almost killed me. I overdosed. I flatlined."

Her face pales, lips parting with a soft gasp. "Jesus."

"I've been clean for over a year now, I don't even drink, but tonight... Tonight I almost lost it. I ordered a drink. A whiskey sour. I didn't take a sip, but it was in my hand."

Yvonne doesn't speak right away, and her expression is unreadable. "Why are you telling me this?"

"Because I need someone to know," I murmur, my voice shaking. "Someone who isn't a part of my meetings or my family. Someone who might still look at me like I'm not broken."

She places a hand gently on my knee. "Mateo, you're not broken. You're human."

Yvonne curls slightly toward me, her eyes soft and patient. I stare down at my hands, which are trembling again, but not from withdrawal. From memory.

"This is why I need a friend more than a girlfriend," I explain quietly. "I lost all of mine the night I overdosed." Yvonne doesn't interrupt. She just nods, giving me space to unravel. "One minute, I was the guy everyone wanted to train with. Next, I was the guy they warned others about. People in the circuit stopped returning my calls. Some made jokes about it. Others just disappeared. Like I was contagious." I press my thumb against the center of my palm, grounding myself. "But worse than all of that was losing my sister, Grace."

Her name cracks something open inside my chest.

"She was my best friend. We grew up in each other's shadows. We used to choreograph dances together in the living room, take turns sneaking each other out of the house. She was always the one person who saw me completely."

Yvonne shifts a little closer, her hand finding mine. Her warmth anchors me, helps me keep going.

"When I woke up in the hospital... she wasn't the same sister I once knew. She was devastated. I broke her." The silence between us stretches, and I force myself to speak through it. "She stopped answering my texts. Didn't visit, didn't call. I think she couldn't look at me without seeing all the pain I caused our parents. She left for Paris before I was even released from the hospital. She wanted to be as far from me as she could get. Grace doesn't say it, but she's grieving me as if I truly died that night." My voice breaks on the last word, the ache behind it too large to contain, pouring out in a shuddering breath.

Yvonne leans in, wrapping her arms around me in a slow, protective hug. Her embrace is quiet and strong, like she knows there's nothing to say that will fix it, but that being here is enough.

"You didn't die," she whispers. "You fought your way back. That counts for something."

I bury my face into her shoulder, breathing in the laundry detergent scent clinging to her sweater. I stay like that for a while, letting her presence fill the gaps where my courage frayed.

"I just want one person to still believe in me," I murmur. "To see more than the mistake."

Yvonne pulls back just enough to look at me, her eyes shimmering. "I do. I see you. The real you, Mateo. You're still here. Still trying. That's not a weakness. That's strength."

Something inside me cracks open at her words, and the breath that was trapped in my chest slips free. I don't say anything, just lean back against the couch, the exhaustion of my confession washing over me. She stays beside me, her fingers gently threading through mine.

Yvonne's steady, whereas Vaeda feels like the edge of a cliff during a thunderstorm. One is comforting and dependable, while the other is exciting and overwhelming. For me, for the part of me that craves the rush, I'll always want Vaeda, but the rest of me knows I need the strength and comfort of a true friend more.

VAEDA

The metronome clicks steadily, echoing off the mirrored walls of Fusion Core, but I can't focus on the rhythm. My body goes through the motions, arms slicing through the air, hips twisting in a sharp rumba accent, but my mind is a thousand miles away, or maybe just a few blocks. Wherever Mateo is.

It's been a week. Seven entire days without him showing up for class. No texts, no updates, no excuses, and it's killing me more than it should. I've given him space, hoping he has been absent because of the holidays and the New Year, but I can't deny how concerned I am. As much as I worry about his sobriety and fragility, I can't be his salvation. Only he can save himself. The thought of losing everything I've worked for just to have a fleeting moment in time with him is stupid.

We're three weeks out from Paris now, and it's been grueling days of routines and exhaustion, then lonely nights at home while Gerardo remains in Spain. The pressure to deliver something bold and unforgettable pulses under my skin, but even Greyson's perfectionism hasn't managed to break me out of this haze.

"Again," I demand, trying to mask the weariness in my voice as I cue the music for the next dance. Greyson starts the Paso Doble section, stomping into the opening pose with the kind of flare that would've thrilled judges back in our prime.

I mimic the steps beside him, pushing through the aching stiffness in my ankle. The music blares, and I manage to let it swallow me whole for just a moment. Until Greyson kills the music with a single flick of his wrist.

"Alright, what gives?" I blink, breathless, and glance over. Greyson stands beside the soundboard, towel slung over his shoulder, eyes narrowed with quiet suspicion. "You've been off all morning."

"I'm fine." I swipe sweat from my brows and lean on the barre, stretching one leg out behind me.

He scoffs. "Don't lie to me, Vae. I can smell it when something's festering. Is everything okay between you and Mateo?"

I freeze. My knee tenses in the stretch, heart skipping a beat as I slowly lower my leg. I don't answer right away, which only makes the silence heavier.

"I haven't seen him," I finally admit. "He hasn't come to class. No explanation. No word."

Greyson studies me, maddeningly quiet for a moment. "It's the holidays, Vae. Some people have lives, unlike us. Did something happen?"

Yes.

But I don't answer. I don't even nod. Instead, I turn my back and grab the choreography sheet, pretending to reread the notes I've already memorized.

He sighs. "You know, it's not just about getting to Paris. That boy's trying to move on. I don't think he can afford to get burned again."

My spine stiffens. "You think I don't know that?" I whisper.

"I think you forget," Greyson says gently, stepping closer, "that there's a difference between being careful and being cold."

"I'm not cold," I snap, whirling to face him. "I'm—" I falter. "I'm trying to protect both of us… from a disaster we can't afford."

Greyson's face softens. "Then make sure he knows that, because right now, it feels like he's been left to figure that out on his own."

My throat tightens as I nod. He turns back to the speaker, giving me a moment to gather myself, but my hands shake as I retie the knot on my hip scarf. Greyson's right. Mateo didn't just disappear, he shut down, and I know what that means for someone like him. For someone clawing their way back from addiction and loss.

I tell myself I've done the right thing by stepping back, but deep down, the guilt twists inside my gut like a knife. I haven't just stayed away from him. I've abandoned him, and the worst part? I miss him so badly, I can't even breathe.

The air is thick with sweat and music. Greyson and I have been at it for hours, fine-tuning the tempo on the Jive until my joints ache and my patience wears thin, but I need the pain, because it gives my guilt something to anchor itself to.

"Let's try the breakaway again," I murmur, repositioning Adam and Kari. My voice is tight. Clipped. Anything to keep myself from drifting back into thoughts of Mateo and where the hell he's been. Greyson gives me a look, one that says he knows I'm pushing myself harder than usual, but he doesn't stop me. He just queues the music and we count it in.

Eight… seven… six…

Laughter breaks across the studio, and I stiffen. Not just any laughter. *His.*

My head snaps toward the entrance, heart jerking inside my chest like it's been plucked by a string. Mateo's walking through the front doors, sunlight chasing his heels, arm slung casually around Yvonne's shoulders. They're both smiling and laughing. His head dips close to hers as she says something that makes him grin wider.

The sound is warm, effortless and free, and it cleaves me clean open.

I can't move. I just stand there, frozen, the music still blaring behind me, watching him like a ghost haunting a place he no longer belongs in. He looks so alive. The bruised shadows that clung beneath his eyes for weeks are gone, and in their place is something brighter.

Relief surges through me first. He's here, he's smiling, and he's okay. Then jealousy slides in behind it, unwelcome but impossible to ignore, because it's not me who's making him laugh. It's her.

Yvonne catches my eye across the room, her expression unreadable for half a second, until it isn't. Her smile widens, lips curling as she leans just a little closer into Mateo's side. It's a subtle dig, but she might as well have screamed it. *I know you want him, and now he's all mine.*

My throat tightens, but I refuse to show it. I turn away, spine stiff and chin high, and clap my hands sharply to get the group's attention. "Alright, everyone. That's enough warm-up. Let's run through the full routine."

My voice rings out, professional and steady, and the dancers fall into place around me. I see Greyson shoot a quick glance in Mateo's direction, but he doesn't say anything. He doesn't need to. The unspoken tension is its own presence in the room.

Mateo finally pulls away from Yvonne and starts stretching near the mirrors. Our eyes don't meet. Good, that's how it should be.

I turn toward the stereo and cue the track, letting the pulse of the Jive beat drown out the thoughts clawing at the inside of my skull. It's better this way.

Isn't it?

CHAPTER TWENTY
Mateo

It's been two days since I saw Vaeda at Fusion Core and two days of ignoring her texts.

Two days since I walked in with Yvonne, feeling lighter than I had in weeks, until my eyes found hers. Until that sharp ache pierced the air between us like static before a storm. I didn't think I'd make it through the session. My whole body felt like it was vibrating with the pull to speak to her, to touch her, to beg, but I didn't. I danced. I laughed with Yvonne. I kept myself moving because stillness, for me, always invites the darkness.

And thank God for Yvonne.

She's been my anchor and shield. Not in the same way Vaeda was. No, not that raw, electric tether, but steady in her own right. She shows up. She makes me laugh. She doesn't ask for more than I can give, and after everything that happened at the club, and then what almost happened after... It's nice to have a connection that feels safe.

Tonight, we're all meeting up: me, Yvonne, Adam, and Kari. It's been weeks since the four of us had a moment outside of class. After Greyson split us into two different pairs to prepare for Paris, our rehearsals became staggered and far between. That closeness and camaraderie slipped through the cracks, but tonight, we're taking it back. Just a lounge. Good music. Maybe some fries to split. Nothing crazy.

Nothing I can't handle.

I finish buttoning the collar of my black shirt and check the clock. I'm supposed to meet Yvonne downstairs in five minutes. I run my fingers through my hair and grab my coat, sliding my phone into my back pocket as I step into the hallway.

By the time I get to the lobby, she's already waiting. Yvonne looks effortlessly cool in a cropped leather jacket, her eyes lighting up when she spots me.

"There he is," she says, looping her arm through mine. "I was starting to think you'd stood me up."

"Never." I flash her a small smile. "I need your presence to keep me from brooding into a drink menu."

She laughs as we walk out toward the cab, the city wind brushing between us like a memory I can't quite shake.

"You doing okay?" she asks as we settle into the back seat. "You've been quiet since Tuesday."

I glance out the window, watching the lights smear across the glass like streaks of gold and red. "I'm trying. That counts for something, right?"

"Yeah." She leans her head back. "It does."

The lounge is buzzing when we arrive. Dim lighting, amber-toned booths, and the low thrum of a live band playing something jazzy in the corner adds ambiance to the place. It's not packed, but it's full enough to make it feel alive.

Adam and Kari are already at a table near the back. They wave us over, Kari lifting a half-empty mojito in greeting. Her cheeks are already flushed with laughter. Adam claps me on the back as I slide into the booth beside him.

"It's about time," he exclaims. "We were starting to think you two were off rehearsing some secret Rumba."

Yvonne grins, nudging me. "Please. Mateo's been rehearsing how to survive another stare-down from Vaeda."

My stomach twists, but I manage to laugh. "I think I've mastered the technique: avoid eye contact, count backward from ten, and pretend I'm not dying inside."

They all laugh, and for a moment, it feels good. Easy. Like I haven't been unraveling piece by piece since the night I asked Vaeda when she was leaving her husband and she revealed the truth.

As we fall into conversation, reminiscing about our first awkward group rehearsal, trading horror stories from past competitions, and making fun of Greyson's obsession with the Paso Doble flair, I realize something. This is what I needed. Not a distraction. Not an escape. I needed connection and belonging. People who see me for who I am now, not just who I used to be.

The rim of my water glass sweats between my fingers as I twirl it in slow, anxious circles. The chatter at our booth has grown louder, looser, and funnier, like the kind of night that could easily slip into something messier if we aren't careful.

"I think it's time," Adam announces as he waves over a server, a crooked grin stretching across his face. "We've earned it. A round of tequila shots for the table."

My stomach drops as I try to keep the reaction off my face, but the moment the words leave his mouth, my body stiffens. Yvonne must feel it, because she shifts beside me, brushing her leg gently against mine under the table.

The server nods and disappears into the crowd, leaving me sitting in silence, heart pounding against my ribs like it's trapped. Adam's laughing with Kari, tossing an arm around her shoulder as they argue over who can handle tequila better. It's a perfectly normal night for them. This is what twenty-somethings do. Celebrate, drink, and let go, but for me, it's a cliff's edge.

I press my palms flat to my thighs, suddenly aware of how cold the room feels despite the crowd and the low warmth of the candles flickering between us.

Yvonne leans toward me, her voice low enough that only I can hear it. "Don't worry, I got this. I'm not drinking," she breathes into my ear. Then she straightens and says, "Training's been hell, and I can't risk the dehydration." She groans loud enough for the table to hear. I turn to her sharply, my breath catching, and she meets my eyes before shrugging lightly.

Relief crashes over me so fast and hard that I nearly sag in my seat. "Yeah," I agree, my voice steadier than I feel. "Same here. I've been cramping like crazy during rehearsals. No way I'm making it worse."

Adam's mouth splits into a wide grin when the tray of shots arrives, and Yvonne casually waves her hand, refusing one. "C'mon," he teases. "What happened to the fearless Yvonne who drank whiskey straight after nationals?"

"She got tired of puking in rental car parking lots," she fires back coolly, making Kari laugh.

I follow her lead, nodding as I decline mine. "Same. I'd like to keep what's left of my dignity intact."

"Lame." Adam grins, then promptly downs his shot. Kari joins him with an overzealous cheer, the two of them giggling like it's their first time tasting tequila.

I can't even look at the glasses. My pulse is still erratic, but the danger has passed, for now.

Yvonne pushes back from the booth a moment later, stretching her arms. "I think I'm going to call it a night," she announces. "It's been a long week."

"Already?" Kari pouts.

"Early class tomorrow," Yvonne states simply, and then glances toward me. "Mateo?"

I don't hesitate. "Yeah. I should head out too."

No one protests. The night has mellowed into background music and inside jokes. I slip into my coat as Yvonne does the same. I'm so damn grateful she didn't make a big deal about the lifeline she tossed me.

Once we step outside, the biting chill hits my face, leaving me feeling refreshed. I take a deep breath, letting the cool air soak through me. My body is still humming from the anxiety, but I can already feel it starting to ease.

"You okay?" she asks quietly as we walk toward the curb.

"Yeah," I say, and I mean it, but only because of her.

VAEDA

It's been two days since our last studio session. I've sent three simple texts. Neutral. Just checking in. A quiet "Hope your classes are going well," or "Let me know if you need anything." I told myself I was doing the right thing by backing off. That the distance was healthy. Necessary. That his silence is proof that he's doing better without me, but my chest feels like it's caving in.

Fusion Core was where I was supposed to be this morning. Greyson and I had plans to finish the dance sequences for Paris, finalize the costume notes, and review music cues, but somehow, my feet carried me here instead.

I'm standing outside the hip-hop studio Mateo and I visited together, the one with the graffiti-painted door and the faded gold lettering. I haven't been back since that day. Since his fingers gripped my hips and the music made my skin feel too tight for my body. Since he pressed his mouth to my ear and asked if he was doing it right.

I told myself it was a mistake, a line crossed in a moment of heat and confusion. I told myself the kisses we shared were reckless, born of too much chemistry and not enough clarity, and yet... here I am.

The sun is still low in the sky, spilling amber light across the cracked sidewalk as I step toward the building. I'm not even sure what I'm doing or why I came. There's no class right now. No reason for me to be here.

Except him.

I press my hand to the cold metal of the studio's doorframe and inhale deeply. The scent of the city, of asphalt and coffee, and something slightly burnt floods my lungs.

I miss him. It's that simple. That stupid. That

devastating.

I miss the way his gaze cuts through a room and lands on me like it's the only place he wants to look. I miss the honesty in his voice, even when it rattles me. I miss the way his dancing holds a kind of pain no choreography could tame. I miss the boy who looked at me like I was his beginning.

And now? Now he's with Yvonne. Young, bright-eyed, uncomplicated Yvonne.

I watched them again two days ago, walking into rehearsal five minutes late, laughing about something private. She touched his arm. He didn't flinch. I should be relieved. He's healing. That's what I wanted, isn't it? For him to be okay. For him to have a future, but I didn't expect it to feel like grief.

The studio door doesn't open when I press the handle—it's locked, of course—but I stand there anyway, forehead resting against the glass. Maybe this was a mistake, maybe I'm chasing ghosts, or maybe I just needed to come here and remember that once, for a moment, he danced with me like I was more than an instructor. More than a married woman. More than a mistake waiting to happen.

He danced with me like I was his, and I don't know if I'll ever forgive myself for not completely giving in.

The glass is cold against my forehead, my breath fogging the lower corner of the door as I try to convince myself to leave. This was foolish and sentimental. I should go.

"Hey," a voice says behind me, soft but full of life. I turn quickly to find a woman in joggers and a cropped hoodie, earbuds dangling from around her neck. "You here for the free intro class?"

I blink. "What?"

"The hip-hop class. It starts in ten." She grins, thumb hooked toward the door as she pulls out a key and unlocks it. "Come on in."

For a second, I hesitate, but then I hear myself say, "Yeah, I am." And I follow her inside.

The studio smells like hardwood polish and traces of vanilla from someone's perfume. The mirrored wall reflects my hesitation as I find a spot near the back corner, rolling out my shoulders and slowly easing into a stretch. My ankle gives a slight protest, but I push through it. The music playing overhead is just a warm-up beat, but already it makes something loosen inside my chest.

People trickle in. Men and women in sweats, sneakers, cropped shirts, and beat-up dance shoes. Most of them are young. A few smile at me. I give a tight nod, keeping my head down as I fall into a deeper lunge.

Then I feel it. A prickle of energy in the air. A current I recognize without needing to see it. I look up with instinct more than thought, and there he is.

Mateo steps into the studio casually, eyes half-lidded, headphones slung around his neck, dressed in black joggers and a fitted tee that clings to the ridges of his chest and shoulders. He doesn't see me at first, focused on tying the laces of his sneakers, but I see him and I can't breathe.

The noise of the studio fades until all I hear is my pulse pounding in my ears. My fingertips tremble where they rest on the floor. Then he straightens, his gaze sweeping the room, distracted, until it lands on me like a lightning strike. His whole body goes still as shock washes across his face, raw, exposed, and real. His lips part like he might say something, but then someone walks in front of him and the moment breaks.

The instructor's voice booms, calling us to the center. I force myself to stand, joints stiff from more than just stretching. Mateo doesn't move right away, then he drifts into the line beside another dancer, keeping a distance from me, but not so far that I can't feel him there.

The music starts, hard beats, pulsing rhythm, and the instructor throws us into movement. It takes everything I have to follow along. My body is capable, trained, but my head? My heart? They're in pieces. The bass drives through the floor and into my ribs, demanding I keep up.

Halfway through the final routine, I feel a presence behind me, then I feel his hands. Light, hesitant, and familiar.

Mateo slides in behind me with a confidence that belies the aching look he gave me earlier. His palms graze my hips, his chest brushing my back as we mirror the movement together, caught in a moment no one else sees.

His breath ghosts over my neck as we fall into step, synchronized and seamless. The rhythm grows more sensual, and his grip firms slightly, guiding the arc of my hips into his. My hands find his at my waist without thinking, grinding myself into him as my body forgets to care about everything else. There's no instruction here. No choreography. Just memory, desire, and regret.

I tilt my head back slightly, just enough to feel his exhale on my skin as his fingertips tighten, then drop away. By the time I turn to face him, the song is over and he's walking away. No words. Not even a glance. Just the hollow echo of the door closing behind him.

And I let him go.

Even though my legs threaten to collapse beneath me.

CHAPTER TWENTY-ONE

Mateo

I shouldn't have touched her.

The door of the studio clicks shut behind me as I step into the piercing light of late morning, the sun sitting low but still fierce above the skyline, fighting the chilly January day. It feels as though the sun can't fully reach me here at ground level as the buildings block it from view most of the time, but in those breaks, when the sun kisses my cheeks, it feels a lot like hope.

I shouldn't have danced with her, but the second I saw Vaeda in that studio, her silhouette lit in the mirror, eyes locking with mine like a fuse, I forgot every rule I've been clinging to. I'd been building distance. I told myself I was done letting her pull me back under, but then she showed up.

She's never come back to that studio since our first time there. I've been going for weeks. It became my sanctuary. It was uncomplicated and all mine, but the second she stepped into the room, that illusion fractured.

I move fast down the street, my sneakers hitting pavement harder than necessary, trying to outrun the heat still buzzing in my veins. I can still feel the brush of her back against my chest, the way her breath hitched when I touched her hips. Every step of that dance felt like falling again, and I'm not sure I have anything left to catch myself with. I don't want to want her. Not like this. Not in this endless agony of almost being mine and then never going to happen.

My building comes into view, the sun reflecting off the large glass panes like a beacon directing me home, but it no longer feels like home. I don't know if it ever did. I've been here since late August, in preparation for the new school year, which puts me at six months. I've been in New York for six months and it still hasn't really sunk in that this is home.

The doorman straightens as I approach. "Afternoon, Mr. Sanchez."

I nod silently, pulse still racing. He'll call my father, like always. Maybe he'll say nothing, or maybe he'll tell him I looked distracted, tight-jawed, like I was about to spin out. Or maybe he'll say I was quiet. Controlled. Back home before lunch on a Saturday. Either way, it's a report I didn't ask for.

I head to the elevator and press the button, and the glow of the floor numbers blinking back at me feels hollow. By the time the doors open and I step inside, I already know the afternoon is shot. There will be no studying. No rest. Just the echo of her.

When I get to my apartment, I drop my keys and bag, then freeze in the center of the room. Light pours through the floor-to-ceiling windows, draping gold over everything. It should feel warm and safe, but it doesn't. All I feel is the emptiness where she should be, and if Vaeda's the only thing making me feel whole, then I've already relapsed in the worst way.

The textbook is open in my lap, pages lined with

notes, highlighter strokes, and scribbled margin questions, but I haven't absorbed a single word in the past hour. My mind keeps drifting to the studio, to the heat of Vaeda's body when we moved together and the way she didn't stop me.

I shift on the couch, trying to force focus, but I'm fooling myself. Closing my eyes, I try to breathe through it, grounding myself with the familiar texture of the throw blanket under my palm and the low buzz of traffic outside.

My phone rings and I look down at the screen, my father's name stabbing through me. I hesitate, my hand hovering over the phone. It's always like this, me wondering which version of him I'm going to get.

I swipe to answer. "Hey."

"Mateo." His voice is brisk, deep, and all business. "We need to talk."

I sit up straighter. "Is everything okay?"

"I got your mother's message," he states perfunctorily. "About Paris."

My stomach knots instantly. "Okay…"

"She said you're competing again. At an international level."

"I am." Silence stretches across the line. I don't fill it. I know better.

"I've booked a flight," he informs me. "I'll be there tomorrow."

The textbook slides off my lap and onto the floor. "You—you're flying in?"

"I want to see all of it for myself. The studio, the instructors, and the environment."

I run a hand down my face. "Dad, I'm fine. You don't need—"

"I do need to." His voice sharpens. "You know why."

I swallow hard, throat tightening. "It's not like before. I'm not the same—"

"Don't lie to yourself," he snaps, then catches himself. A pause. "I'm not saying you've done anything wrong, but I have to make sure. Your mother says you're stable and you're happy, but happiness doesn't protect you from temptation."

I press my fingertips to my temples. "So what, you're coming to the studio to interrogate everyone?"

"I'm coming to speak with your instructors. I want them to know what they're dealing with. You may not like it, but if they're responsible for you, then they should understand what relapse looks like. What stress does to you."

My heart drops into my stomach. "They already know about what happened, and I'm not a kid anymore."

"You're not invincible either," he says, quieter now. "You're my son, and I almost lost you once." That makes something fracture inside me.

He doesn't say it often, about what my overdose did to him, how close he came to losing me. Usually he buries it in anger or silence, but I hear it now—the fear buried beneath the control.

"There's something else," he continues. "Roger may be going to Paris with you, depending on how I feel about these instructors."

"What?"

"You'll need someone there. You'll be too far from your family. You'll be under pressure, in a foreign country, surrounded by God knows what. Roger can keep an eye on you."

I want to argue. I want to tell him he's overreacting, but deep down, a part of me is grateful. The part that's still scared of who I was. The part that knows how easy it would be to fall again.

"Alright," I agree quietly. "Okay."

"I'll see you tomorrow. Be ready to take me to the studio." He hangs up before I can say anything else.

I stare at the phone in my hand, the silence in my apartment pressing in like a vise. Tomorrow, my father will walk into the only part of my life that's felt like just mine in a long time, and I don't know if that will burst the comfortable bubble I've built around it.

VAEDA

The Paso Doble rhythm pounds through the studio, each beat snapping like a whip across the floor. My footwork is exact and confident, every sweep of my arm calculated. My back is arched, chin high, chest forward, exactly as it should be, but nothing about this feels right.

Yvonne mirrors my every movement, her eyes locked on mine through the mirror's reflection. There's tension in her posture, not just the usual sharp, deliberate style of the Paso, but something more venomous beneath it. Her jaw clenches as she steps into me with the next pass, our shoulders nearly brushing, her arm cutting a fraction closer than necessary. She's trying to dominate the space.

I match her intensity, refusing to be overshadowed in my own studio. Sweat slides along my spine, heat licking down my neck, and my ankle—God, my ankle—is screaming. Every pivot feels like it might snap something, but I press forward because I refuse to stop. Not with her watching me like that. Not with whatever unspoken battle she's waging.

Did Mateo tell her about what happened between us?

That's the question burning in my mind. Did he confess? Did he explain what we were, or what we became in between the moments and the lies we never meant to tell?

Her movements are like weapons, filled with a feral energy. She's not dancing beside me, she's honing her blade and planning the next strike. Only she doesn't realize I won't lose the damn war. Her hair clings to her temple, breath ragged as she lunges into the final paso line, our bodies angling toward the mirror in dramatic stillness.

We hold it. One breath. Two.

I try to soften my stance without letting the pain show,

and that's when I notice Mateo standing in the doorway, frozen. His gaze is locked not on Yvonne, but on me, and beside him, stiff-backed and keen-eyed, is a man who looks like time carved him from the same stone. He's older, broader, and gray at the temples. This must be his father.

My breath stutters and the pain in my ankle flares again, this time cutting deep enough to steal my balance. I break formation, stepping back slightly and lowering my arms. Yvonne doesn't budge, her chin lifting a notch higher as she catches the same view in the mirror I just did.

I wipe my brows with the back of my hand and straighten, heat rising from my chest all the way to my hairline. Greyson, who'd been off to the side adjusting the speaker levels, turns and follows my line of sight.

"Ah," he mutters under his breath. "Guess the cavalry's arrived."

Mateo still hasn't moved. His expression is unreadable, but his presence burns like wildfire under my skin. I tear my eyes away, lifting a brow to Greyson, who immediately walks over to greet the man beside Mateo.

Yvonne finally lowers her arms, but not before leaning in just enough to whisper, "Didn't he tell you his father was coming today?"

I blink at her, stunned, and then I realize what she's trying to do. She saw the look on my face and knew Mateo didn't tell me shit, which means he and I aren't speaking. She has him now. My silence is enough of an answer as Yvonne smiles arrogantly, like a cat who's been lapping up the cream.

I turn away from her, bracing myself to meet the man who now holds the power to unravel everything we've been working hard for. Wiping my palms on the sides of my leggings, I cross the studio floor as my heart beats steadily but too loudly in my ears. Mateo stands beside his father like he's waiting for a verdict he already expects to go badly, his expression stoic but his eyes flickering with worry.

I stop in front of them and extend my hand. "Mr. Sanchez," I say evenly, "I'm Vaeda Lewis. Co-owner and lead instructor here at Fusion Core."

He takes my hand in his own, the grip firm but not overly so. "Emilio Sanchez. Thank you for taking the time."

"Of course," I reply. "Would you like to speak in my office?"

He nods, releasing my hand, and I gesture toward the side hallway. I glance at Mateo briefly. His eyes meet mine for a fraction of a second before dropping to the floor. He doesn't follow as Emilio steps ahead and I walk beside him, painfully aware of every echoing footfall as we move down the corridor. Once we reach the door, I push it open and allow him to step in first.

He does a quick survey of the space, and I internally thank Greyson for his cleanliness. It's neat, the walls lined with competition photos and event posters. The desk between us feels too big, too official for what's coming, but I motion for him to sit. He does, and I follow.

There's a pause, heavy and awkward, then he begins, "My son nearly died over a year ago."

I blink but remain composed. "I know," I say gently. "Mateo mentioned it to us. He's been very open about the fact he's in recovery."

Emilio's brows lift slightly. "Has he also told you that the lifestyle he lived, the one that almost killed him, was enabled by people in your world?" I still, the words hitting like cold water. "He was young and extremely gifted. There were people who saw potential and used it. Coaches, competitors, older dancers, and so-called friends." His jaw clenches. "They fed him pills to calm his nerves, gave him drinks to 'loosen up.'

When his performance slipped, they blamed him. When he overdosed, they vanished."

I nod slowly, heart sinking as I picture Mateo in that world alone, spinning and needing approval so badly he drowned in it. "I'm sorry," I murmur. "Truly. That should never happen to anyone, especially not someone so young."

"I didn't come here to make you feel guilty, Ms. Lewis," he continues, his voice slightly softer now. "But I needed to know where he was. I need to know if this place is part of his healing or if it's one more place full of people who'll look the other way."

My spine straightens. "Fusion Core doesn't look the other way." He watches me carefully. "I'm not naïve," I go on. "The industry has dark corners, but Greyson and I built this studio to be different. We don't tolerate substances. We don't tolerate abuse, pressure, or favoritism. If Mateo is here, it's because he chooses to be, and while he's here, he's safe."

Emilio's fingers drum once against his knee. "Is he happy?"

The question catches me off guard, but my answer comes without thought. "Yes."

Emilio's expression softens just slightly at that, like he's been holding his breath and doesn't quite know how to let it out. "He doesn't smile much anymore. He was a bright kid, always dancing, always in motion. After what happened… it's like the light got knocked out of him."

I nod, unsure if I can speak around the tightness in my throat. "He's worked hard," I reveal finally. "Mateo has earned his place here. He's talented, yes, but more than that, he's resilient. I think… I think dancing makes him feel whole again."

Emilio leans back in the chair, taking a slow breath. "I appreciate your honesty. I needed to look the people responsible for him in the eyes. I'm not trying to control him, Ms. Lewis. I'm just trying to keep him alive."

I meet his gaze, steady and calm. "We want the same thing."

A moment of silence passes between us, and I feel its weight settle into something mutual. Respect. Maybe even understanding. When we stand, he offers his hand again, and this time, the grip feels less formal. More human.

"Thank you," he says.

I walk him back to the studio floor, the sound of music rising again as Greyson cues up the next routine. Mateo looks up the second we appear, and searches his father's face, his eyes flicking to me with question.

I give him a small nod.

Chapter Twenty-Two

Varela

Mateo and his father left over an hour ago, and though the speakers still vibrate with music and the floor still echoes with steps from the remaining dancers, the absence of his energy is deafening. The space always feels a little off without him, like a beat is missing from the rhythm we're all supposed to be moving to, and it isn't just today. It's been happening since he's been putting distance between us.

Missed rehearsals. Empty stretches in class where he should be. I tell myself it's fine, that he's just under a lot of pressure. He has school, recovery, and family, but Paris is less than three weeks away, and this routine isn't going to perfect itself.

I crouch to zip my bag, heart heavy and aching with worry. Mateo is good, brilliant even, but brilliance means nothing if he's not showing up, and worse, I don't know if it's because he's slipping away from the studio… or from me.

Footsteps approach from behind. Light, purposeful. I don't have to look up to know it's Yvonne. She steps beside me, radiating sunshine, but it's only surface-level because I can see her dark intentions underneath. Her hair's pulled back into a tight bun, wisps escaping around her temples. I zip the last tooth of my bag and stand.

"Don't worry," she says lightly, tone smooth as satin. "I'll practice with him what we learned today." I glance over at her. She's already watching me with too-bright eyes and that saccharine smile. "I'm having him and his father over for dinner."

The words land like broken glass at my feet, the shards cutting deep into my flesh. I arch a brow. "Dinner?"

She nods, lips twitching. "Just something casual. My roommate's out tonight, so it'll be quiet."

I know what she's doing. I know exactly what this is. She's baiting me, and the worst part is it's working. My blood is already warming, my fists already aching to clench, but I won't give her the satisfaction.

So I smile politely, my expression empty. A perfect mask. "That's thoughtful of you," I reply coolly. "He could use the extra practice."

Her lashes flutter with exaggerated kindness. "Anything to help the team."

I sling my bag over my shoulder and meet her gaze squarely. "Of course."

She offers one last glittering smile before turning and walking away, her hips swaying just a little more than necessary. The door clicks softly behind her, and I stay where I am, unmoving, until the silence swells again. Then I let out a long, slow breath and sit back on the edge of the bench.

If I'm being honest, I don't know what worries me more, that she's winning his time... or that I was never supposed to want it in the first place.

I should go home.

The sky outside the studio windows has dimmed to dusk, making pink shadows dance across the floorboards. The overhead lights flicker, but the space feels hollow, like it's holding its breath. I stand at the edge of the floor, bag still slung over one shoulder, watching the mirrored wall in front of me like it might give me an answer.

I don't want to go back to my empty penthouse. I don't want to sit on the couch with my legs tucked under me and silence thick, pretending I'm not wondering if Mateo is laughing at Yvonne's table, sipping something warm and letting someone else see him unguarded.

So I stay and drop my bag gently onto the bench, then walk toward the speaker, my fingers hovering over the dial. I need to move and sweat, and the sting of exhaustion to distract me, but before I can cue the music, my phone vibrates against the bench behind me.

I glance at the screen, and guilt punches me straight through the chest when I see Gerardo's face looking back at me. I stare at his name for a beat too long, my stomach tightening. I haven't called him in days. Just hurried texts and check-ins. My excuses range from rehearsal chaos to fatigue, but the truth is simpler and far more damning. I haven't wanted to.

With a sigh, I bend down and pick up the phone, answering on the third ring and forcing warmth into my voice. "Hey."

"Vaeda, amor," Gerardo says, his voice crackling slightly with the international connection. "It's been a few days. Are you alright?"

"Yeah," I reply, but it's too quick. I glance at my reflection, the lie shimmering there like a veil. "Just… busy. The Paris competition's coming fast, and we've been living in the studio."

"I figured," he mutters. "I just miss you."

The words land softly, familiar and filled with love, and yet… they don't settle where they used to. "I miss you too," I whisper, though the words taste like ash on my tongue.

He updates me on his mother's condition. She's stable but tired. He might need to extend his stay. I nod along, even though he can't see me, as guilt threads through me like barbed wire. When did the space between us become so vast?

I turn away from the mirror, phone tucked to my ear, heart beginning to thud with unease, and then I hear it. The soft creak of the studio door behind me. My gaze flicks back to the mirror, and my breath stops in my throat.

Mateo steps inside quietly, the door easing shut behind him. He's still in street clothes, dark jeans and a fitted shirt that hugs his frame, sleeves shoved up to his elbows. His hair is a little messy, and his eyes are locked on me. I turn slowly, heartbeat kicking into a gallop.

"Amor?" Gerardo's voice crackles again in my ear. "Are you still there?"

I swallow, forcing my voice to be calm. "Yes. I'm here."

But my eyes are still on Mateo, who's walking toward me now, each step more certain than the last. He doesn't say a word, just watches me with a blank expression, but his eyes betray him. They burn like he's walking into the fiery depths of hell carrying a burden he doesn't know what to do with.

I shift the phone slightly, voice hushed. "Gerardo… can I call you back? Someone just came into the studio."

There's a pause, then, "Of course. I love you."

I close my eyes as a fresh wave of guilt crashes over me. "I love you too." Then I hang up.

When I open my eyes again, Mateo is only a few feet away, and suddenly, the silence between us feels louder than the music ever could.

MATEO

She's still holding the phone when I step into the studio, her back to me, her silhouette prominent in the mirror's dim reflection. Her voice is soft, too low to hear clearly, but when I catch the hushed, *I love you too*, it slams into my chest like a fist.

It's her husband. Of course.

Even after everything, he still lives inside those quiet words. I swallow hard, forcing the bile down, shoving the jealousy into the same box where I've been keeping every inappropriate thought about her since the moment we danced together. I'm not here to cause damage or make things worse, but one look at her smooth skin, hair in disarray, and her body caught between tension and exhaustion, has every rational reason for being here dissolving.

I came to thank her. That's what I tell myself.

My father spoke to her, and something shifted after that. He's more open now. He even mentioned looking forward to Paris, and that's because of her. I should just say it. Just thank her and walk away, but I can't. There's something about her standing here, vulnerable and alone in this room we've both filled with so many sins and silences, that makes it impossible to leave.

She lowers the phone, breathes, and I move. Before she can even turn fully, I close the distance and slide my hand to her waist, turning her gently but firmly until she's facing me. Her eyes widen as I bring my mouth to hers.

The kiss isn't gentle. It's not soft or patient or anything close to restraint. It's a war breaking inside both of us, all teeth and desperation, the kind of kiss you regret even as you're still inside it.

She gasps, lips parting just enough to let me in, her

fingers fisting the front of my shirt like she wants to pull me closer or push me away. Maybe both.

I crowd her backward until her spine brushes the mirror, and the reflection of us nearly steals my breath. We look reckless. Utterly ruined with her face tilted up to mine, her mouth swollen from my desperate kisses. My hands are already shaking with the need to touch more. To have more.

"Mateo," she whispers against my lips, breaking the kiss just enough to speak, but her breath is ragged and her eyes betray her. There's no hesitation in them. Only ache.

"Tell me to go," I rasp, voice gravelly, thick with want.

She doesn't. Instead, she pulls me back to her, her mouth crashing against mine with the fury of a storm that's been brewing for so long. Our bodies fit together like fate as my hands slide beneath her shirt, skin to skin, the moment nearly tipping into something irreversible. Until she pushes me away.

Her palms press against my chest with enough force to halt everything. I freeze, letting her create the distance she needs, though every part of me screams to pull her back. Our breathing fills the silence, harsh and uneven, then slowly, she gives a small shake of her head, and that single gesture breaks me all over again.

I take a step back, dragging a hand through my hair. I don't say I'm sorry, because I'm not, but I am wrecked.

"I didn't come here to make things worse," I manage. "I came to thank you. For what you said to my father. He's… different now. He's giving me space. Forgiveness even."

Her gaze flickers, but her arms remain tightly crossed. The guard is back up. "Still doesn't mean you should've kissed me," she spits, her words like razors, sharp and wounding.

"No," I agree quietly. "But I wanted to."

She lets out a short, cruel laugh, and it cuts deeper than I expect. "Why didn't you ask Yvonne to thank me for you?" she sneers. "I'm sure you two had a lovely dinner."

I blink. "Dinner?"

Her brows rise. "Yes. The one at her place? With your father?"

I stare at her, bewildered. "I didn't go to any dinner. She didn't invite us."

The fire behind her eyes dims just slightly, and Vaeda looks at me for a long, quiet moment, as if reassessing everything. "She said—"

"She lied, or you misheard her," I interrupt. "I'm having dinner with him *alone* in a bit before he has to leave." She swallows hard, retreating a step. "Vaeda," I rasp, "don't push me toward someone else just because it's easier to pretend this doesn't mean anything."

She doesn't answer, and I don't push. Instead, I leave her there with the truth of her feelings echoing in the swell of her lips and flushed cheeks.

CHAPTER TWENTY-THREE

The lock clicks into place as I close the studio door behind me, the chill of the evening wrapping around my ankles like a balm over my injury. I pause on the sidewalk, my hand still on the handle, as if letting go means admitting what just happened inside. Mateo's kiss still lingers on my lips, the ghost of his touch a brand I can't scrub off with denial.

I should feel triumphant because I pushed him away, but all I feel is the insistent ache of not having something I want and no power to erase it.

My heels click against the concrete as I start walking, my mind still flashing with the warmth of Mateo's lips against mine. The sky above is ink-dark, clouds swallowing the last remnants of the day. I focus on the movement, on the cold air against my face, on the city sounds that press in like static to drown out the thunder of my thoughts.

I make it two blocks before my phone rings and Greyson's name blinks up at me. I nearly let it go to voicemail. I don't have the energy for lightness, and I know that's what he'll try to give me, but I'm desperate to hear any voice but my own right now.

"Hey," I answer, the single syllable barely audible.

There's a beat of silence on his end before he says, "You sound like hell."

"I feel worse," I admit, surprising even myself with the truth.

"You want to come over? I've got whiskey, and judging you is not on the menu."

A flicker of something close to gratitude warms my chest. "That sounds like exactly what I need."

"Then get your ass over here."

I smile, small and tight. "I'm on my way."

The next cab that passes, I flag down, and the moment I slide into the back seat, the weight inside my chest shifts just enough to breathe again.

Greyson's apartment is warm and dimly lit with a cocoon of soft jazz and flickering candles that scream curated calm. He opens the door dressed in sweatpants and a hoodie, and for a moment, I'm struck by how different he looks outside of the studio. Real and human, not my business partner or my voice of reason, but my lifelong friend.

He hands me a glass before I've even shed my coat. "I poured you the good stuff." He snickers. "I figured anything less would be an insult." I take a sip and let the burn settle under my ribs. "Want to talk about it?" he asks, nodding toward the couch.

"No."

"Want to drink until you do?"

"Maybe."

I sit, tucking my legs under me, the exhaustion creeping into my bones now that I've stopped moving. Greyson settles beside me, close but not too close, and waits.

"It's Mateo," I finally say.

He hums, unsurprised. "It usually is."

"I can't keep doing this, Grey. I push him away and then I let him back in. Over and over. It's like I'm watching myself ruin everything I've built and I can't seem to stop."

"Because you don't want to." I shoot him a look. "I mean it," he presses, gently but firmly. "You want him, and you're not used to wanting something that you think is bad for you. You're used to being the strong one. The structured one."

"I'm also married."

Greyson's expression softens. "You are, but you're also lonely. You've been lonely for a long time. You know how I feel about your marriage, so to me, this has been inevitable. Gerardo is a great man, but he's not meant for you." The truth hits hard. "Your reaction to Mateo is like gasoline on a fire. You burn so hot."

"Which is exactly why it's dangerous." We sit in silence for a long stretch, the whiskey warming me more than the soft blanket I eventually pull over my legs. "Yvonne's been hanging on him like a shadow," I mutter.

Greyson arches a brow. "Jealousy doesn't suit you."

I roll my eyes. "I'm not jealous."

"You are."

I sigh. "Fine. I am, but not because I want him to be mine. Not really. I just don't want him to be hers."

Greyson lets out a long exhale. "You need to figure out what part of that is your ego and what part is your heart, because if it's your heart… you need to be prepared to face your husband."

"I already know that."

He nods slowly. "And you're considering it." It's not a question, it's a statement.

Another sip. Another burn. "I wish I could rewind time back to before he showed up. Back to before I saw what was missing from my life."

"But you can't. You've seen it now and felt it."

I lean my head back, staring at the ceiling. "I don't want to be this woman, Grey. I don't want to be someone who waits for a man to show up just to fall apart."

"You're not," he reassures me, voice low. "You're a woman who's been holding herself together for so long that when someone finally cared enough to break through your armor, you didn't know what to do with it."

I look at him. "What do I do now?"

"Either walk away completely… or let yourself want him and accept what comes with that."

"Mateo's ten years my junior," I remind him as I gulp down the rest of my drink. "Not to mention, a divorce could get messy."

"Mateo has an old soul, and yes, he's much younger than you, but his experiences have aged him well beyond the years he's been on this Earth."

The quiet after his words is filled with a realization. I don't know which is more terrifying, losing Mateo or keeping him, but I do know one thing: I won't survive this much longer without deciding.

MATEO

The clink of cutlery and murmurs of conversation create a soft, polished kind of noise that fills the restaurant. My father sits across from me, impeccably dressed as always, his tie loosened but still pristine, and his posture so straight it makes my own feel adolescent.

The waiter had just cleared our plates and left us with coffee, his black and mine with enough sugar to mask the bitterness. I stir it absentmindedly, watching the swirl fade into stillness.

"So," he says, resting both forearms on the table. "Are you seeing anyone?"

My spoon stops. The question isn't harsh or suspicious. Just… casual. Almost fatherly, in a way that feels foreign coming from him.

"I…" I clear my throat, scrambling to answer. "There's my partner. She's interested in more than friendship, I think, but I've been focused on recovery and dancing."

He nods slowly, taking a sip of coffee. "That's good. Smart. Take one thing at a time."

I don't look up. I can't, because the words feel like a betrayal. Not of my recovery, but of the very woman I can't stop thinking about. The one I kissed with every broken part of me and then walked away from. Again.

"She's been supportive?" he asks, shifting the cup in his hands.

"She's… someone I trust," I answer finally, unsure if that's a lie or not. I trust Yvonne to be loyal, but she doesn't command my soul. My soul belongs to someone else, and I think she's beginning to figure that out.

"She's not the reason you're being so quiet, is she?" he

adds carefully.

I flinch slightly. "No. She's not."

He leans back in his chair, his expression unreadable. "You're not the same boy you were a year ago."

"I hope not."

A small smile curves along his mouth. Not wide and showy. Just the kind of smile that means something because it's rare. "I spoke with Grace," he reveals quietly.

My heart skips as I look up, stunned. "You what?"

"She called, actually," he corrects. "Today, before I spoke to your instructor."

I grip the edge of the table. "Is she okay?"

"She's… hesitant," he admits. "But she asked how you were and wanted to know how Paris was coming along. I told her about it before coming here." I blink fast, emotion crashing in behind my eyes. "She said she's willing to talk to you… when you're in Paris."

A strange sound leaves my throat, part breath and part disbelief. "I thought she hated me."

"She doesn't." He shakes his head. "She was angry and hurt. She's still scared."

"Grace saw me near death because of my own actions." My hand curls into a fist on the tabletop as shame washes over me.

"She's still your sister."

I press a hand to my chest, trying to slow the thundering in there. The idea of speaking to Grace again, of making amends, however small, feels like someone's cracked open a window in a room I thought I'd suffocate in.

I remember the last night we were together before

everything fell apart. She styled my hair for a ballroom showcase and told me I looked like someone famous. We laughed so hard we cried. She stayed up late waiting for me to get home from competitions, texting me good luck, calling me her favorite dancer, and then a month later, I overdosed.

She sat by my hospital bed, crying in the chair she didn't leave for two straight days, and then, somewhere in the days and weeks that followed, something broke inside her. Maybe forgiveness got lost in the fracture. Maybe she needed to hate me just to breathe again.

"She wants to see me?" I ask again, unable to shake the disbelief.

"She wants to talk, and that's something."

I nod, swallowing hard.

My father watches me like he wants to say more, but doesn't. Instead, he picks up his coffee and takes another slow sip, his shoulders relaxing just a bit.

"You've come a long way, Mateo. Don't let the past convince you that you're still there."

His words hold weight, more than I've ever heard. Maybe it's the way the candlelight dances in his eyes, or the way he's not lecturing for once. He's just here, sitting across from me like a man who's seen his son nearly die and somehow found the grace to keep showing up.

I look down, blinking against the pressure behind my eyes.

"Paris is a new beginning," he adds, softer now. "Not a clean slate, but a next chapter. Use it."

We sit in silence for a while, the kind that feels more like peace than discomfort. Around us, the restaurant fades into murmurs and movement. A waiter refills our waters, someone laughs at a nearby table, and I sit with my hands curled around my coffee cup and let it all sink in.

For the first time in a long time, I feel the faintest hope that things might come back around.

The terminal buzzes with late evening chaos, rolling suitcases, weary travelers, and flight announcements cutting through quiet conversations. My father stands beside me just outside the security gate, his carry-on slung over his shoulder and his hand wrapped around the handle with the kind of hesitation he rarely shows. Roger lingers behind us near the car, giving us space, as he always does.

"Paris will be exciting, Mateo," my father says, his tone clipped, like he's keeping a hundred emotions at bay. "But no matter how far you go, don't forget why you're going in the first place."

I absorb everything he's saying. "I won't."

"You're not invincible," he adds, quieter now. "And this industry, these people, they'll give you a standing ovation one day and forget your name the next. Don't chase their approval. Don't let it swallow you."

"I'm not the same person I was before," I vow, but even as I say it, there's a flicker of doubt under my skin. A ghost of the boy with pills and broken promises.

"No," he agrees. "You're stronger, but strength can be fragile too." I swallow hard. He looks down, shifts his bag, then finally meets my eyes. "Just finish your degree, Mateo. Even if you never use it. Just so you know that you have something to fall back on."

"I will."

"And your sobriety," he continues. His voice breaks a little there, just enough to gut me. "That's the most important thing. Everything else comes second."

"I know."

He looks like he wants to say more, maybe even hug me, but instead, he grips my shoulder, firm and lingering. "I'm proud of you. I'm also scared as hell, but I'm proud."

"Thank you," I manage.

We hold each other's gaze for one more second before he turns and walks into the tide of passengers, his form disappearing into the rhythm of travelers. I let out a breath and head back to the SUV. Roger starts the engine without a word, merging into traffic as the airport fades in the rearview mirror.

"He's trying," Roger murmurs after a long stretch of silence.

"Yeah. So am I."

Roger hums softly, a note of agreement.

"You think I can really do this?" I ask before I can stop myself.

"Dance?"

"Stay clean and compete. Not fall apart again."

Roger glances at me, then back to the road. "You already are. One day at a time, Mateo. You just have to keep choosing to live."

The drive is quiet after that. By the time we pull up to my building, the city is lit up against the dark sky. The rhythm of evening life beats around me; horns, pedestrians, and vendors closing up for the night, and then I notice Yvonne. She's sitting on the front steps of my building, arms wrapped around her knees, hair loose around her face.

I frown, stepping out of the SUV before Roger can even place it in park.

"Yvonne?"

Her head lifts, eyes red-rimmed. "Hey."

"What's going on?"

She stands quickly, brushing at her cheeks like that'll erase the vulnerability I already saw. "I, um… I had a fight with Rachel."

"Your roommate?"

She nods. "I didn't know where else to go. I tried calling you, but—" she hesitates. "I figured you turned your phone off."

I pull my phone from my pocket and sure enough, it's still powered down from dinner with my dad. A twinge of guilt spikes in my chest. "I'm sorry," I mutter. "I didn't mean to leave you hanging."

She shakes her head. "It's okay. I just… I didn't know where else to go."

Roger steps up behind me. "You good here?"

I swallow and smile at him. "Thanks for the ride."

He eyes Yvonne for a second, then gives me a subtle nod before heading back to the car. I unlock the door to my building and gesture for Yvonne to follow me inside. The lobby's warm, the usual doorman giving me a half-curious glance that I pointedly ignore.

Inside the elevator, the silence is thick. "You want to talk about it?" I finally ask, watching the numbers tick up.

"Not really," she says, voice tight.

The elevator dings and we step into the hallway. My apartment feels colder than usual when we walk in, and I adjust the temperature before taking her coat and hanging it beside mine on the rack.

Then I set her bag down by the door and glance back at her. "You can crash here tonight. Couch pulls out. Do you need anything?"

She shakes her head, arms still crossed tight, so I nod once, unsure of what else to say.

She offers a small, weary smile. "Thanks, Mateo."

"Yeah, of course."

As I head to my room to grab her a blanket and a pillow, I can't help but feel the walls shifting again. Pressing closer. The last twenty-four hours have been an emotional land mine, and I'm not sure I've made it out unscathed. Yvonne is here in my apartment, my father is trying, and Grace might be willing to speak to me.

And I'm still standing even though I feel like I'm falling.

One day at a time.

CHAPTER TWENTY-FOUR

It's been two weeks of training, sweating, counting beats, and rechoreographing sections that should've felt seamless by now. Two weeks of watching Yvonne and Mateo move in tandem across the studio floor, their rhythm syncing like they were built for this. For each other. And two weeks of feeling like my chest might cave in.

Greyson stands beside me, clipboard in hand, as he marks something on the notes we've compiled. The Paso Doble track is loud and insistent, an unrelenting rhythm that pulses through the room like a heartbeat. Mateo's form is strong, spine straight, and chest forward. He leads Yvonne across the floor with commanding steps, the drag of his foot against the polished surface sounding with confidence.

Yvonne follows without hesitation, head tossed back, the cape of her practice skirt swirling with every spin. She's lighter now. Glowing. She feeds off his energy like it belongs to her, and it makes me sick.

"They're clean," Greyson says, tilting his head as Mateo catches Yvonne's wrist, pulling her into the cross-body lunge.

"They're predictable," I snap.

Greyson glances at me.

I can feel the heat behind my eyes, the tightness in my jaw as I watch them dance. Their chemistry is real, and it's nothing like what Mateo and I felt in that hip-hop studio, pressed together, breathless and trembling. No, this is polished, rehearsed, and safe.

Two weeks ago, he kissed me like he couldn't breathe without it, like I was his next inhale, and since then? Not a glance. Not even a touch outside of perfunctory practices that feel like someone else's memory. It's as if that night was an accident he's spent every day trying to forget.

"Paso is meant to be visceral," I continue, stepping forward as the music reaches a peak. "This feels like a stage production, not a battle. Mateo, again. This time with more power in the shoulders. Yvonne, stop dancing like you're trying to impress him. This isn't prom night." She stiffens at that, but I don't care. "Let's go from the top!" I bark.

The music cues again, and Mateo doesn't look at me. His jaw is clenched, but he doesn't speak. He just nods to Yvonne before they fall back into place. They start the opening stance again, bold and theatrical. Mateo's left arm strikes out, then circles around her waist, pulling her into the bullfighter's march. It's tighter this time, cleaner, but still...

"You're faking the fire," I growl when the music ends. "I don't feel anything."

"Jesus, Vaeda," Greyson mutters, grabbing his water bottle. "Walk it off."

I shoot him a glare. "No."

"Yes." His tone leaves no room for arguments.

I turn on my heel, storming down the hallway as my blood buzzes with rage and something far worse. Envy.

The way Mateo's hands fit against Yvonne's body, how

she leaned into him during that final dip, and the smile that flickered across her lips when she thought no one was looking. She has him. Not completely, not like I did, but enough, and I've never been so damn envious in my entire life. Not only do I want Mateo, but I want to dance in that Paris ballroom. Enough to make me feel like I'm being hollowed out from the inside.

I find myself in the bathroom, gripping the edge of the sink as I splash cold water on my face before staring into the mirror. This isn't about the choreography. This is about him. It always has been, but I'm still his coach, still his judge, and still the woman standing behind the curtain, watching him become everything he was born to be. Yet I don't get to celebrate that with him.

I take a deep breath, force my spine to straighten, and walk back into the studio. They're both stretching now. Yvonne glances at me with a smugness that could be mistaken for triumph, but Mateo doesn't look up. Greyson says nothing, just flips the page on his clipboard and cues the music for the Mambo.

And we go again like none of it matters. Like I'm not breaking from the inside out.

The city continues beneath me as I unlock the door to my penthouse, the metallic click echoing too loudly in the silence. I step inside and drop my purse and phone on the table, then close the door behind me, leaning against the smooth wood for a moment. My body aches from the hours in the studio, but the ache inside my chest eclipses everything.

It's two weeks until Paris. Two weeks of watching the man I crave dance with the girl who gets to touch him in ways that don't alter her world. I sigh and toe off my shoes, padding barefoot into the living room. The sky outside the floor-to-ceiling windows bleeds lavender and gold as the sun sets, and the room is cast in that strange, perfect light where everything looks prettier than it really is.

My phone rings and I cross the room slowly, almost not wanting to answer, but when I see Gerardo's name on the screen, guilt tightens its claws around my rib cage.

"Hey," I say softly, pressing the phone to my ear.

"Hola, mi amor," he greets me, voice warm and filled with happiness. "I just spoke to the doctor again. My mother is improving. They think she'll be released from the hospital next week."

Relief floods my tone, even though my stomach twists. "That's wonderful news."

"I'm going to stay a little longer, help her get settled, but after that..." A pause. "I may be able to meet you in Paris." The words land like a bucket of cold water.

He means well, he always has, and I should be happy. This is my husband, the man who stood beside me through the highest and lowest moments of my career. The man who never once blamed me when my ankle shattered both our dreams, but I'm not happy.

I force a small laugh. "That would be beautiful. We haven't been to Paris together in years."

"Too long. Remember that night under the Eiffel Tower? We were so young, and we danced like we were invincible."

"We were," I whisper. But now? Now I'm not sure what we are.

He launches into memories, telling me he wants to recreate that moment. He says he'll bring the old playlist, the one we used to practice with. That he wants to hold me again like before, and I tell him yes. I let the fantasy unfold because it's easier than facing the truth. I want him to be happy.

"I'll pack a sexy lingerie," I tease lightly, my voice strained.

He chuckles. "Then I'll definitely find a flight."

We hang up soon after, and I lower the phone to the counter. The room is too quiet, and the truth is loud in my chest.

I don't want to think about Paris with Gerardo, or about kissing him beneath the Eiffel Tower, or curling up beside him in a hotel suite with silk sheets. I haven't imagined his hands on my body or his mouth on my skin in a long time, but I've imagined all of that with someone else, and that someone is off-limits in every way that matters.

I cross to the windows once more and watch the activity below. The sky has deepened, the lights of the city flickering to life like stars. I tell myself to focus. To pack. To be a good wife. But when I close my eyes, I don't see Gerardo.

I see Mateo.

MATEO

The heavy front door creaks shut behind me, muffling the last murmurs of tonight's NA meeting. The scent of burnt coffee and peppermint breath mints still lingers in my nose as I step into the cool night air. It's quiet and serene. The kind of stillness that makes you feel your heartbeat in your ears.

I spot Roger's SUV idling at the curb, headlights illuminating the sidewalk, and I pull open the passenger door to climb in.

"Hey, man," he greets, glancing at me as I buckle up. "You look a little less weighed down than usual. Meeting go okay?"

"Yeah," I answer, scrubbing a hand down my face. "It helped. They usually do."

He nods thoughtfully, pulling out onto the street. The soft vibration of the engine fills the silence until he clears his throat. "How's that friend of yours?"

I glance sideways at him. "Yvonne?"

"Yeah. You mentioned she crashed at your place a while ago. Everything okay with her?"

I sink a little into the seat, head tipping back against the rest. "Her roommate's a nightmare. Loud fights, petty arguments, slamming doors. Some nights she doesn't want to go home, so she crashes on the couch."

Roger raises an eyebrow, amused. "And that's all it is?"

"Yeah," I reply firmly, staring out at the passing blur of streetlights. "That's all it is."

He hums. "She's cute. Seems like she really cares about you."

"She does," I admit, my voice quieter now. "But it's not

like that. Yvonne's family is in New Jersey, and her other friends don't have space. I do and don't mind her being around."

Roger doesn't push, but I feel his curiosity like a pressure in the SUV. I know what he's thinking—that it would be good for me to be dating again. To connect and move on from the disaster I caused. Only, I don't want to move on with Yvonne.

I stare out the window, my reflection in the glass a pale imitation of the man I'm trying to become. It's been two weeks since I kissed Vaeda like she was my entire world, and it's been two weeks of silence.

I've kept my distance, not because I stopped wanting her—that would've been easier—but because she asked me to. Her boundaries were clear, even if her eyes begged me to stay that night. So I gave her the space, but it hasn't made me miss her any less. Hasn't made me stop thinking about how her voice drops when she's tired, or the exact way her fingers curl when she holds a clipboard. How she smells faintly of rose water and sweat after a long day of dancing. How her eyes can go from steel to silk in a single blink.

"Mateo?" Roger's voice draws me back.

"Yeah?"

"You okay?"

I nod. "Just tired."

"We're here." He gives me a sad, knowing smile as I straighten and look out the window. My building is there, the lights of people's homes illuminating the night sky.

"Damn."

He doesn't press for more. He just gives me a nod, and I'm grateful as I get out of the SUV, burying my hands in my jacket pockets.

Once I'm upstairs, I unlock my apartment door and

step inside, greeted by the familiar hush of solitude. The sounds of the city are muted by thick glass, and the weight of the day clings to my shoulders like a second skin. I toss my keys on the counter and head straight to the fridge, grabbing a water bottle. My phone buzzes on the kitchen island, and I smile when I see FaceTime from Mami.

I swipe to answer, and within seconds, my parents' faces fill the screen, side by side, glowing under the soft lighting of their California kitchen. My mother's expression is warm and searching, while my father's is stoic but observant.

"Mijo," Mami greets, her voice instantly soothing. "We caught you at home?"

"Just walked in," I say, collapsing onto the couch. "Had a meeting tonight."

Her face softens. "How did it go?"

"Good. I needed it."

My father nods once, his eyes lingering on me a moment longer before he speaks. "You look tired."

I manage a smile. "That's because I am."

"Practices?" he asks.

I nod, running a hand through my hair. "Gruelling, but worth it. We're perfecting the Jive, Mambo, and Paso Doble. Long days, sore everything."

"And school?"

"Midterms are coming up," I answer. "It's a lot, but I'm managing."

Mami's eyes crinkle with pride. "We're so proud of you. Just seeing you like this..."

I feel it in my chest, that bittersweet sting of being seen, really seen, by the people who feared I might not make it.

My father leans forward slightly. "Is it becoming too much?"

I blink. "No," I say, more quickly than I mean to, so I take a breath and soften my tone. "It's not too much. I promise. I've got a handle on it."

He studies me carefully. "Mateo..."

"I swear, Dad. I'm good. Paris is in two weeks. Once that's done, I'll take a break and focus on school. Slow things down."

His shoulders ease slightly, but his eyes are still full of worry. "You just don't have to prove anything to anyone anymore. Not even to us."

"I know," I murmur. But I do. Maybe not to them, but to myself? Every damn day.

"I'll let you both rest." I smile, hoping they don't see anything deeper than my surface-level exhaustion. "You look tired too."

"We're always here, Mateo," Mami promises. "Any time, day or night."

"I know."

"I love you."

"Love you both," I tell them. "Good night."

The call ends, and I set my phone down, leaning back against the couch cushions. Just two more weeks, and maybe the weight I carry will finally lift. Or maybe it will crush me first.

CHAPTER TWENTY-FIVE

Vaeda

"Again," I say, my voice sharp but breathless as the Paso Doble echoes through the studio. "From the chassé turn."

Mateo and Yvonne reset, their movements fluid, driven by the relentless rhythm. My heart pounds in time with the drums, adrenaline pushing me past the ache already burning in my ankle. I've been favoring it for days, hiding the pain beneath a layer of willpower and grit.

This dance needs to be perfect because Paris is just over a week away.

"More aggression," I call out, stepping forward, demonstrating the pivot I want with the snap of my shoulders. "You're not painting the story with your bodies. You're performing a pattern. There's a difference."

They move again. This time it's better. Stronger.

"That's it," I say, and before I can stop myself, I take a step forward to correct Mateo's posture. I don't even realize how hard I'm planting my foot until a hot, white surge of pain rips through me.

It happens in an instant. A sickening pop and my leg

gives out as I hit the ground.

"Vaeda!" Mateo and Greyson yell in unison. Mateo drops beside me, his hand hovering over my shoulder. I try to speak but only a strangled sound comes out as pain steals the breath from my lungs, tears springing to my eyes as I clutch my ankle.

"Don't touch it," Greyson barks, already pulling out his phone. "We need an ambulance. Now."

Mateo backs away, his face ghost white as Yvonne stands frozen, a hand over her mouth.

The sirens arrive faster than I expect, and soon I'm being lifted onto a stretcher, the ceiling of Fusion Core spinning above me as the EMTs secure my leg.

"Achilles' heel?" one of them asks me softly, recognizing the injury.

I manage a nod through gritted teeth. The last time I was wheeled out like this was six years ago when it ended my career. I can barely swallow the scream that wants to rip out of me.

At the hospital, everything is a blur of tests, questions, and ice packs. Then I'm transferred to an MRI. When the orthopedic specialist finally returns, her face is calm and professional.

"You didn't rupture the tendon," she explains, flipping the chart in her hands. "But it's a severe flare-up. A combination of tendinitis and strain. You're lucky. If you'd pushed further, it could've torn completely."

"Surgery?" I croak out the question, my throat tight with fear.

"Not necessary, but you need to stay off it. Crutches are a must. You'll need rest, ice, compression, and elevation. And then physical therapy." I close my eyes in relief. "We'll start you on a short course of pain management," she continues. "Hydrocodone-Acetaminophen. Twenty tablets. Use only if the pain becomes unbearable."

My stomach twists, but I nod. It's common with this sort of injury, but I hate taking them. They make me tired and out of it.

"When can I begin therapy?"

"After a week of rest. So when you get back from Paris, you'll begin but, Vaeda," she adds gently, "you cannot dance on this foot until then. Not even lightly."

I nod, swallowing the lump in my throat.

The elevator ride to my penthouse feels longer than usual, the sterile hospital scent still clinging to my clothes. I grip the crutches under my arms, my knuckles white with tension. Greyson stands at my side, silent but watchful, holding the hospital-issued tote with my X-rays and prescriptions tucked neatly inside.

The pain hasn't fully settled in yet, but I know it will. What scares me more is what comes after. What lingers. The depression will hit when I least expect it, and when Gerardo finds out, it'll only be another reminder of what killed our ambitions. I never wanted to relive this again.

We step into the soft glow of my apartment hallway after the elevator dings, and the moment I cross the threshold into my house, my phone vibrates again. It's already been going off the entire ride back, buried at the bottom of my purse. Greyson fishes it out and hands it to me. Ten missed calls from Gerardo. I sigh, my stomach twisting.

"I told him," Greyson says softly, guilt woven into the words. "He needed to know."

"I get it," I say, though my throat tightens. "I just… I didn't want him to panic."

Greyson watches me for a moment before setting my things down on the counter. "You should call him."

I nod, sinking onto the edge of the couch, carefully maneuvering the crutches to rest against the arm. My ankle is elevated on a stack of pillows, the swelling starting to throb beneath the compression wrap as I put the phone to my ear.

He answers on the first ring. "Vaeda? Dios mío, are you okay? Why haven't you called me?" His voice is strained, urgent.

"I'm okay," I say quickly. "I didn't want to worry you."

"Too late for that," he snaps, then softens. "Greyson said you were hurt. At practice?"

"Paso Doble. I pushed too hard. It's not a rupture, but it's serious. No weight-bearing for a week. Physical therapy after Paris."

"Paris?" His voice rises. "Vaeda, you shouldn't even be thinking about traveling right now. Do you need me to come home? I can be on a flight tomorrow."

My chest constricts, and I look over at Greyson, who's pretending not to listen as he walks into the kitchen.

"No," I whisper. "No, stay with your mother. She needs you more. I'll be fine. Greyson's here." I refuse to argue with him about Paris because he knows I'm going, no matter what.

"But he's not your husband," Gerardo murmurs, hurt and fear mingling in every syllable. "You shouldn't be alone like this."

"I won't be."

A silence falls between us.

"What did the doctors say? Is it going to affect you

long-term?"

"Not if I follow orders. Rest, therapy, and no dancing. I'm on crutches for now."

He groans. "This should never have happened."

"It was an accident, Ger."

There's another pause before he exhales. "I'll call again tomorrow. Let me know if anything changes. And Vaeda… please be careful."

"I will."

"I love you."

I end the call and set the phone aside, heart thudding like I just lied. This was the first time I haven't told my husband I love him back, and it feels like an umbilical cord has been severed.

Greyson walks back into the living room, eyes scanning me as if checking for fractures he can't see. "Are you sure you want to do this competition?"

I nod, even though I'm not sure of anything, because while the pain in my ankle is manageable, it's the pain in my chest that terrifies me the most.

MATEO

The buzz of the airport surrounds us as luggage wheels drag against tile, the echo of announcements sounds from overhead, and the intermittent laughter of travelers mingle in. I stand near our gate with my carry-on slung over my shoulder, watching as our team slowly gathers in the seating area.

Adam and Kari are already there, heads bowed together over something on Adam's phone, laughing softly like this is a vacation and not the single most important competition of our lives. Yvonne breezes in a few minutes later, her pink hoodie tucked under one arm, a coffee in the other. She beams when she sees me, looping an arm around mine.

"Ready for Paris?" she asks, her voice warm.

I nod, managing a smile I don't fully feel. "Been ready." But my eyes aren't on her.

They're scanning the terminal for the person who gives me life, who makes my heart swell and bleed at the same time. Then I see her. Vaeda moves through the sliding security doors with Greyson beside her, her face composed in that icy, unreadable way that's become her default lately. She's leaning heavily on the crutches, her face simmering with anger at needing any type of support. She's favoring the injured leg, but she walks with pride. She always does. Even hurt, she makes heads turn and commands the room.

It's been a week since I've really spoken to her. A week of radio silence. I texted. I called. I stopped by the studio more times than I should've just to catch her alone. She always had someone else in the room, always had her eyes on anyone but me. Greyson, Yvonne, the floor, or the goddamn mirrors, and I've played along. I've been polite and professional, just like she wanted, but it's been eating me alive. Now, here we are, preparing to board a flight to Paris, and I don't even know if she'll be my instructor after this.

Vaeda nods at everyone in greeting, her gaze flitting over me like I'm nothing more than another student in her lineup. Then she lowers herself carefully into a chair, propping her injured foot on her suitcase.

"How's it feeling?" Greyson asks, crouching beside her.

"Tight," she grinds out, "but manageable."

Manageable. Like pain is just a thing you carry without complaint. Like silence is strength.

Yvonne pulls out her earbuds and offers me one. I take it without thinking, even as my attention remains fixed on Vaeda. She avoids my stare, flipping open her passport and reviewing the boarding documents like she hasn't already memorized every step of this process.

She hasn't been the same with me since that night when I nearly made her mine and asked her to choose.

"I'm going to find a bathroom," I murmur to Yvonne, who nods and slides into my seat the second I get up.

I don't go far. Just enough to lean against a column and breathe. I watch her from a distance now, the way she shifts in her seat to adjust her leg, the furrow in her brows as Greyson says something that makes her nod slowly.

I wish she would just talk to me and tell me it meant nothing so I can truly move on, but she's choosing silence, and maybe that's her answer.

The flight is boarding in staggered groups, but our team was early enough that we all move on together. I hoist my bag into the overhead bin and glance over my shoulder just as Vaeda settles into her seat in a row next to me, beside Greyson.

She places her crutches carefully along the window wall, then slips her sunglasses down over her eyes like a shield.

I drop into the seat next to Yvonne and buckle my belt. "Paris." She grins, elbowing me. "Are you ready for this?"

"Ready as I'll ever be," I say, forcing my tone to be conversational. I lean back in my seat, stretch my legs out, and glance toward the aisle. Vaeda's not looking at me, so I decide to push. "You always get this excited when you're on a plane, or is it just 'cause you're sitting next to me?" I tease Yvonne, pitching my voice just loud enough.

Yvonne laughs, flipping her hair over her shoulder. "Oh, you know it's you. You're the reason I packed three different bras."

"Good," I rasp, letting a lazy grin stretch across my face. "Maybe I'll help you pick one." She giggles again, curling closer, her shoulder brushing mine as she shifts in her seat. I shouldn't be flirting with her, especially knowing her true feelings, but I need to put a crack in the armor Vaeda has herself locked into.

Out of the corner of my eye, I see Vaeda shift just a fraction, a subtle turn of her head. Good. I rest my hand casually on the armrest between me and Yvonne, fingers relaxed. Close, but not quite touching hers. I know exactly what I'm doing. I want Vaeda to feel even a fraction of the torment she's put me through this week.

"This is your first time in Paris?" I ask Yvonne.

"Mhmm. I've been dreaming about it since I was a kid. I mean, romance, fashion, croissants... all the good stuff."

"I'll make sure you don't miss any of it," I murmur. She beams, and I nod like it means something. Like I mean it, but all I can think about is Vaeda's mouth parting when I kissed her, her fingers curling in my shirt, and the breathy gasp she made when my hands slid beneath her sweater.

Then I think about the soft, sad tremble in her voice when she said she couldn't choose me, and she still hasn't, because maybe that reminder will make me stop waiting.

The cabin lights dim as the flight attendants prepare for takeoff, and Yvonne adjusts her neck pillow before resting her head lightly on my shoulder. I let her. I even tilt my head against hers, but I keep my eyes forward, and I hope to God Vaeda's are on me.

CHAPTER TWENTY-SIX

Vaela

Morning comes with the dull ache of pain and the slow rise of anxiety.

The hotel room is soaked in soft light, the Paris skyline a watercolor blur through the tall windowpanes. I shift under the crisp sheets, every movement a jolt to my ankle. The air is cool, perfumed faintly with lavender from the pillow spray provided on the nightstand, which is a little French luxury wrapped around this very complicated trip.

The pain is worse today. I sit up slowly, the sheets rustling against my legs, and reach for the small bottle on the desk across from the bed. The pills inside the container clink together, and for a moment, I hesitate. I just need one. My fingers twist the cap and I swallow a pill dry.

I force myself out of bed, stepping gingerly on my foot and hobbling toward the bathroom. It's Friday, the first official day of the competition, and my body is protesting as if we've been here for days already. I miss my own bed, my favorite coffee, and I miss dancing along the floor of my studio.

The bathroom mirror reflects a pale, tired woman back at me. I don't put on much makeup, just enough to blur the fatigue, then twist my hair into a low, sleek bun and pull on a black blazer over a fitted, navy blouse and slacks. Once I'm all put together, I give myself a quick perusal. I look commanding, stern, and classy. I may be limping through this trip, but no one else has to know just how badly I'm unraveling.

By the time I make it down to the hotel lobby, the world is fully awake. The hotel is a restored 19th-century palace in the 8th arrondissement, a stone's throw from the Seine and just off the Champs-Élysées. The floors are marble, veined and gleaming beneath gold chandeliers, and the scent of espresso from the hotel café winds through the air. The concierge gives me a polite nod as I slowly descend the final steps.

Greyson is already there, looking far too fresh for someone who went to bed nearly as late as I did. He holds two coffees, offering one to me without a word, and I accept it with a grateful smile.

"You slept?" he asks.

"Enough."

"You took something?" I nod once, eyes forward. "You really should be on both crutches." He nods to the single crutch I have tucked under my right arm. I shrug, and he sighs but says nothing more. He knows better than to press.

Moments later, Mateo and Yvonne appear from the elevators. Mateo's hair is tousled in that effortless way that makes women turn their heads, and Yvonne is draped in a cream trench, laughing at something he just whispered. My stomach clenches, but he doesn't even look at me.

"Ready to head over?" Greyson asks, motioning for them to follow.

"Absolutely," Yvonne says, slipping her arm through Mateo's as if it belongs there.

I glance away, teeth grinding softly, then adjust my posture and fall into step beside Greyson as we exit the hotel and climb into the waiting van.

The drive is less than ten minutes to the Palais des Congrès de Paris, the host venue for the French Open Dance Sport Championships. The building is modern and sprawling with steel and glass framing, the event banner stretched across the entrance. Dancers are already filing in, some stretching on the stairs, others wheeling in garment bags like precious cargo.

Inside, the space opens into a grand atrium flooded with natural light from the skylights above. The ballroom is massive, lined with gold-trimmed balconies and tiered seating. The floor is being polished by staff in matching uniforms, and the scent of lemon cleaner clings faintly to the air. The energy is electric.

We're here. We made it, and if Mateo and I weren't so deeply buried in whatever hell we've created between us, I might even let myself feel something like joy. Instead, I focus on the logistics. Floor time has been arranged for early practice slots. Greyson confirms with the event coordinator while I take a seat near the floor, clipboard balanced on my knee.

Yvonne and Mateo change quickly and emerge from the dressing room in practice wear. She's in a sleek black leotard and a red skirt, and he's in a fitted black tee and pants. They look professional and polished. They don't look like they're carrying the weight of our studio's future as they smile brightly and gaze into each other's eyes.

As they begin their warm-up, I sip the last of my coffee and force my eyes to stay on their footwork. They look smooth, and thankfully, they appear as though they've been dancing together for years. It's a testament to incredible chemistry. My eyes flick from them to the others dancing around them. Sure, there are technical slips, or too sharp of a turn, but everyone looks great, and it only makes me shift in my seat with worry.

We need this win.

Greyson takes a seat beside me, his clipboard angled precariously on his left knee. "They look good, Vae. Real good."

I nod in agreement as I rotate my ankle, letting the pain center me instead of allowing my mind to focus on Mateo's hand low on Yvonne's back, or the way she brushes her fingers along his neck.

The two seats on my right remain empty because I gave Kari and Adam the morning to sightsee. They'll be joining us in the afternoon. For now, it's just us. Just them. Just me watching what I let slip away.

I brace my hand against the marble wall of the Palais des Congrès, waiting for the sharp flare of pain in my ankle to dull before I push open the heavy door. The venue is beautiful, palatial, and buzzing with quiet preparation. Dancers check into dressing rooms, and event coordinators flit through hallways with clipboards. The air is thick with excitement.

While Mateo and Yvonne continue to warm up before floor time, Greyson is already waiting near the registration table, coordinating badges and floor access bands. He lifts a brow as I limp toward him, though I do my best to hide it.

"You sure you're good?" he asks under his breath.

"Fine," I say. The painkiller I took this morning is already losing its grip, but I straighten my spine. I'm not letting this ruin the moment.

Yvonne and Mateo are laughing about something as they step off the practice dance floor. Their excitement is palpable, a kind of electricity humming around them. Mateo catches my eye, his grin softening into something more private, but I don't let it hold. I look away, motioning for them to follow us toward the grand ballroom.

The room is even more striking than I remember. A vast parquet floor beneath vaulted ceilings, crystal lights glinting off mirrors and velvet drapes. Music plays softly from a speaker in the corner as dancers test the floor, checking for slide and grip.

Greyson claps his hands. "Alright, team Fusion. Let's stretch and get started. Floor time is tight today. This is where you will be dancing, so get used to the polish on the floor, and check for divots or bumps."

Yvonne is already pulling her skirt from her bag and tying it at her waist. Mateo slips his fingers through his hair, the black dance tee he wears hugging his form like a second skin. He's focused today, but I can tell by the way his eyes flit to me that he's waiting for acknowledgment. A nod, a glance, or a sign of whatever we were before we buried it. He won't get it.

I lean against the back wall, clipboard in hand, and try to tune out the throb in my ankle. They move well together, especially here, where the energy of the competition elevates every step. Mateo's lead is fluid, and Yvonne matches it with an eagerness that almost looks like love.

Greyson joins me, arms crossed. "They got this. I can feel it."

"I hope so," I murmur, eyes still on Mateo. "Let's just hope they stay this clean tomorrow."

After about thirty minutes, I step away to find a quieter spot, telling Greyson I need a moment, and he nods. In the hallway, I pull out my phone and scroll through my contacts. My finger hovers before I tap the name I saved last night: **Grace Sanchez.**

Emilio called me the night before, thanking me again for my guidance, but also asking me to keep an eye on his son. *"If you ever see him unraveling, I need to know, Vaeda. He might not call me, but he'll tell you."* Then he gave me Grace's number, telling me she'd softened, and he hoped it was time to rebuild.

I hesitate only a second longer before typing:

Hi Grace,

This is Vaeda Lewis, Mateo's instructor. I know we haven't met, but your father said you were open to talking to your brother again. Mateo's in Paris for the French Open Dance Championship and doing really well. I thought you should know. We're having a team dinner tonight at 7:00 PM at Le Vieux Bistro near the Seine. I'd love for you to come. Here's the address if you're free.

Le Vieux Bistro 14 Rue du Clootre-Notre-Dame

I stare at the message for a beat before pressing send, and a rush of guilt follows because I feel like I'm doing something behind his back, but I didn't just reach out to be nice. I want someone else in his life to love him too.

When I return to the ballroom, Yvonne is laughing, a light ring of sweat glinting along her collarbone. Mateo is spinning her, then catching her back in a smooth lockstep. They hit the final beat and Yvonne throws her arms around his neck. His hands hover a moment before he lets them fall.

Greyson turns to me. "Are you ready to head out for a bite?" I nod, lips pressed into a thin line.

Just two days to the finals.

MATEO

The warm scent of garlic and roasted herbs greets me as I step into Le Vieux Bistro with Yvonne at my side. Outside, Paris is cloaked in soft golds and deep violets, the city humming with life, but in here, it's all candlelight and linen-draped tables, the kind of intimate charm only old-world places can carry.

Yvonne leans in as we step past the maître d'. "This place is gorgeous. It must be a Vaeda pick."

I force a smile, eyes already scanning for the table Greyson reserved. Adam and Kari are grinning, their eyes shining with pride. My chest tightens when I spot Greyson, because seated next to him is Vaeda. She's radiant, even in stillness. Her hair is swept up, and she's wearing a dark, wine-colored blouse that clings to her shoulders like something stolen from a painting. I feel that dangerous tug again, the one I've been trying to resist, but it isn't just the sight of her that stops me cold. There's a third figure.

My breath catches as she stands slowly, uncertain, with her hands clasped in front of her. Grace. *My sister*. My Grace.

Her eyes are glossy, wide with emotion, and she opens her mouth to say something, but nothing comes out. I haven't seen her in over a year. Not since the day she left the hospital, vowing to never speak to me again for what I put her through. I rush to her, forgetting Yvonne at my side and the others sitting at the table.

"Grace," I breathe out, my voice cracking like it's been trapped beneath rubble. Slowing down, I step toward her slowly, like approaching a startled animal, until I'm close enough to see the faint scar on her cheek, the one I used to tease her about. "I missed you," I say, and my throat closes.

She steps into me, her arms wrapping around my back, and I break, clutching her like I'm drowning. Like I'm eight and she's come to save me again from whatever monster I've pulled from my imagination. She shakes in my arms, and I realize she's crying too.

"You scared me so much," she whispers. "I didn't know how to forgive you."

"I didn't know how to forgive myself."

We stand there for what feels like a lifetime, just breathing each other in. The scent of her shampoo is the same and she still wears that stupid vanilla perfume.

When we part, her eyes are rimmed red but steady. "You look good." She sniffs and smiles tentatively.

I laugh through my tears. "You lie better than I remember."

She smacks my chest. "You smell like French soap and croissants."

Yvonne clears her throat behind me, and I remember I'm not alone. Vaeda hasn't moved, her eyes fixed on me as they dance with emotion.

"I— Uh, Grace, this is Yvonne, my dance partner," I manage. "And you probably already know everyone else." Grace offers polite nods, but her attention never strays far from me. "Thank you for coming," I say.

She shrugs, her lips trembling just a little. "Vaeda sent me a message. I didn't know if I would… but I… I wanted to see you."

I glance at Vaeda, but she's looking down at her water glass, swirling it slowly. Gratitude floods through me. We take our seats, and the conversation begins softly. The room seems quieter now, like the moment between us hushed the entire restaurant. Grace asks about school, about the competition, and about my sobriety. I tell her the truth, that it's hard. That I still go to meetings. That some days are better than others.

"But I'm trying," I promise. "Every day, I'm trying."

She reaches across the table and squeezes my hand. "That's all I ever wanted."

I don't realize I'm crying again until Yvonne places a napkin in my lap, and somehow, in this quiet bistro in Paris, I feel a piece of my life knitting back together. My eyes slip to Vaeda once more, and she's leaned in, listening to Greyson. I have her to thank for this.

The second day of competition dawns with a sky the color of tarnished silver. Light rain slicks the Paris streets as I stand at the window of my hotel room, watching droplets race each other down the glass. My nerves are already coiled tight, vibrating under my skin. Today, we're dancing Latin.

Yvonne and I meet in the lobby, dressed for our cha-cha. Her hair is sleek and high, her deep red dress glittering in the light like embers about to ignite. I'm in a black shirt, open at the collar and sleeves rolled to my forearms, with a black pair of slacks. The outfit feels like a second skin now, one I never thought I'd wear again.

We arrive at the Palais des Congrès and head backstage. The energy is electric. Dancers are everywhere, makeup artists fixing last-minute details, and coaches whispering into ears. The scent of hair spray and sweat clings to the air.

Our heat is called and we step onto the floor. The crowd is a blur of color and noise, but as the opening bars of the cha-cha start, my world narrows to rhythm and muscle memory. Yvonne is fierce tonight. Her eyes are locked on mine, her body sharp and expressive. We move in perfect sync—tight chassé steps, crisp Cuban breaks, hips snapping with every beat. I let the music pulse through me, pushing aside the pressure, the past, the panic.

I spot them as we turn on a syncopated lockstep: Greyson near the back with his arms crossed, and next to him is Grace.

She's standing between Greyson and Vaeda. Her hands are clasped at her waist, eyes wide with something like awe. Her presence steadies me, roots me in the moment. On the next turn, I glance at Vaeda. She doesn't blink as she watches us with a stern, concentrated expression. Every time I meet her eyes, something stirs inside me. Longing and regret. She holds my gaze longer than she should, then glances away, arms folded over her chest like a shield.

The routine builds, and we hit our spotlight moment, a check-and-slide into a rondé chassé. My hand grazes Yvonne's waist, her leg whipping past in a clean flick. The audience claps, and I hear the tail end of a whoop from the balcony, which sounds a lot like Kari. We finish with a staccato side-by-side Cuban motion, so clean, and then freeze in pose. Applause rises once more as the judges scribble.

Breathless, we exit the floor, and Yvonne grips my arm. "We nailed it. Did you feel that?"

I nod, adrenaline still flooding my veins. "Yeah. We did."

Greyson meets us with water bottles and a huge grin lighting up his face. "That was your cleanest cha-cha yet. Posture stayed strong and the connection looked solid."

Yvonne beams, but I'm watching Vaeda. She slowly walks over, her expression unreadable as she adjusts her crutch. Her gaze darts to Yvonne, then back to me.

"Good hip rhythm," she says, voice low. "Your frame was a little tight at the top, but otherwise… impressive." That almost sounds like a compliment coming from her.

Grace hugs me the moment Vaeda steps away. "Mateo, that was incredible!"

I lean into her warmth. "Thanks for coming again. You don't know what it means." She squeezes me tighter. Having someone here from my family keeps my mind grounded. It reminds me of where I've been and the people I hurt when I was chasing my own needs. I never want to be in that position again.

CHAPTER TWENTY-SEVEN

The ballroom feels different the next morning, more electric and tightly wound. Everyone is quieter and serious. Today, we begin the standard prelims, and our second dance is the Jive. It's not our strongest, but Yvonne and I have worked hard to polish the routine, to bring the right mixture of energy and technique.

The announcer calls our heat number, and we step out onto the floor alongside five other couples. The parquet beneath my shoes gleams under the overhead lights, and the buzz of the crowd becomes a distant hum. Every dancer is keyed up, legs bouncing with anticipation as we take our marks.

When the fast-paced rhythm kicks in, we launch into the Jive. The kicks and flicks, fast triples, the tight spring and bounce that makes this dance a test of stamina, and the style is on perfect display with some of the best dancers in the world. Yvonne is light on her feet, her skirt flaring with every spin, and her smile locked and ready. She's quickly becoming a great friend and one of the best dancers I have ever worked with.

My footwork is clean, honed by weeks of training, but about halfway through, as we switch into a series of underarm turns, my gaze flicks toward the judges' table. It's a reflex I didn't mean to follow. That's when I see him sitting in the third seat from the left. Victor Denier. A name I haven't thought about in over a year.

He's older now, a few more lines around his eyes, but unmistakable. He was one of the French adjudicators who used to rave about me when I competed with my former partner. He coached at a training camp in Lyon where we spent two summers prepping for internationals.

His eyes are on me, not just scanning, they're like lasers on my face. There's no recognition in his expression, but the scrutiny is there, and it presses into my chest like a thumb against a bruise. Does he know who I am? Has he heard the rumors?

I mess up the next roll off the arm turn. Not a full stumble, just a slight drag, but I feel it, and Yvonne shoots me a confused look as we recover.

"Focus," she hisses under her breath, lips barely moving.

I force a smile and dive into the next pattern. An American spin, link, and sharp kicks to the beat. The tempo drives us forward, making focus on anything else impossible. All that exists is rhythm and counts and the thunder of movement all around us.

The song ends in a blur of sweat and applause as we strike our final pose and hold it, Yvonne's breathing hard, her chest rising and falling. My heart is racing for different reasons. I messed up and it was a stupid mistake. We walk off the floor and toward the water station.

"You flinched," she says, panting. "What was that?"

I wipe my forehead with a towel. "One of the judges. I know him. From before."

She arches a brow. "Is that good or bad?"

"Could be either."

She says nothing, just hands me her bottle. I take a long drink, letting the cool water chase down the acid rising in my throat. Back across the floor, Victor Denier is still watching us. His pen moves across the score sheet, then stills as our eyes meet.

His gaze narrows slightly, then he nods, just once, and a chill snakes down my spine. I don't know if that nod is acknowledgement or warning. I don't know if he's heard about my reputation, the partying, and the disappearance from the circuit, or if he remembers the kid with clean footwork and ambition to burn.

This could mean a bias score if he has the same reaction to me as Vaeda did when she first found out who I was. It could mean everything I worked hard for toward my redemption could be for nothing as my past catches up with my present.

After callbacks are posted, the air in the Palais des Congrès thickens with tension. Dancers pace the hallways with clipped strides, brows furrowed, and their words are spoken in hushed tones. Everyone's holding their breath because now, the real pressure begins.

Quarterfinals–Adult Latin Division: Samba

Out of seventy original couples, thirty-six made the cut. Yvonne and I are sitting in the middle of the pack at number twenty. It's a place that neither satisfies nor comforts, and it gnaws at me.

Yvonne reads my face as we warm up on the practice floor. "We'll move up. Let's just get through this round."

Greyson shows up with the schedule in hand. "You're

dancing fifth, and it's Samba. Let's see that fire you two keep in your back pocket."

Then Vaeda appears, standing straighter than she should, one heel slightly raised to relieve the strain on her injured foot. Her expression is unreadable, her eyes blank as she looks from me to Yvonne. I wish I had her talent for disassociation.

"You underperformed today," she says without preamble. "Your hand changes weren't sharp enough, and you got ahead of the beat in the jive."

I hold her gaze, the tension between us vibrating like a wire. "We still made it."

"You barely made it." Her words are clipped and clinical. "Stop counting your steps. You should know them inside and out by now. It's time to command the floor and own it. Show them you belong out there." Then her gaze cuts to Yvonne. "And you need to match him. Don't just follow. Engage. There's no room for hesitation in Samba."

Yvonne nods, jaw tight.

Greyson's tone is lighter. "This is your strongest rhythm. Trust your training."

We leave them behind and disappear into the changing area. I pull on my deep green Samba shirt, the fabric cool against my skin, and adjust the tight cuffs at my wrists. The color pops under the lights, a visual spark to match what I plan to give them on the floor.

Yvonne is already warming up, shoulders rolled back, arms flicking into rhythm like a metronome when I step back to the floor. She doesn't speak, and I appreciate the silence. It's the calm before the storm.

When we're called to the floor, we step out into the chaos of dozens of couples flooding the parquet in a tide of sequins and rhythm. The Samba beat kicks in, bright and unrelenting. We find each other in the mess, and then we move. Voltas, whisk turns, bounce actions. My body sings with the tempo, grounded in the rhythm, riding the syncopation like a second pulse. Yvonne hits every movement with sharp energy, and her expression electric. The skirt of her costume fans out in quick bursts, like a flickering flame.

We circle, pivot, and lock into the final routine sequence. I flick my head and catch a glimpse of Victor Denier again. His eyes are on me, and I give a subtle nod back this time. The last eight counts pass in a blur of rhythm and sweat. We end in a sharp dip, my hand firm at her waist, and her breath hot against my neck.

Applause swells as we bow, and when we rise, I find Vaeda's face in the crowd. Her arms are crossed, her expression hard to read, but her eyes… her eyes are on me. Grace is beside her, clapping with exhilaration, her face red with excitement.

We walk off the floor in silence, heartbeats still thudding. We won't know the scores yet. The judges keep them sealed until the final tallies are posted after the semifinals. For now, it's all anticipation and waiting, but I know this much: we didn't just survive that round, we showed them we belong.

VAEDA

The air inside the ballroom feels thick, pulsing with music, heat, and the shimmer of sequins still caught in the air. Mateo and Yvonne bow out of their final pose to scattered applause, but all I can hear is the roar of my blood in my ears. They did well, better than I expected. Mateo moved like a storm unleashed, electric, fluid, and commanding. When his eyes lifted to meet mine in that final pose, I felt something inside me unravel.

Greyson claps beside me, his expression cautious. Grace leans in to speak, a smile locked on her face, but the pain in my ankle flares so violently it steals the breath from my lungs. I murmur to her and Greyson about needing a moment and slowly limp from the ballroom, past the swirl of dancers and officials, and into the quieter corridor.

The women's washroom is mercifully empty as I stagger in, clutching the sink as I brace my weight on one leg. My reflection looks pale, sweat curling at my temples, and my mouth set in a tight line. I reach into my clutch and pull out the small bottle of painkillers, unscrewing the lid with trembling fingers. Just one.

The pill hits the back of my throat and I chase it with a sip of water from the tap, then lean over the sink and press my palms to the porcelain, breathing in deep. My eyes lift once more to the mirror and the pain reflecting back at me isn't just physical. My heart is destroyed, every beat a protest against my ribs. I've never wanted someone so badly in one breath, and then wished I'd never met them in the next.

A groan of hinges cuts through the stillness as the bathroom door opens. I turn, startled when I see Mateo's form in the mirror. He steps in and closes the door behind him, turning the lock with a deliberate *click*. His chest rises and falls in rapid waves, sweat still clinging to his collarbones. There's a glint in his eyes that makes my stomach pitch, wild and hungry and unbearably raw.

"You shouldn't be in here," I whisper, even as my breath catches.

"I'm done with this fucking game we're playing," he snarls.

The distance between us shrinks as he stalks forward, his strong legs flexing beneath the fabric of his pants. My spine presses to the counter, my ankle flaring again as I straighten, but I can't think about pain right now. Not when his eyes are devouring me.

"You were unbelievable out there," I say, my voice tight.

He stops just in front of me, so close I can feel the heat radiating off him. His scent fills my senses, sweat and cologne and something purely him. "I danced like that because of you. I wanted you to see me. Really see me."

My pulse slams in my throat as he lifts a hand and brushes a lock of hair behind my ear, his knuckles grazing my cheek. I tremble, heat spreading through me in waves. "I see you, Mateo. I always have."

His mouth crashes against mine. It's not gentle. It's need and frustration and weeks of restrained desire set free. His hands cup my face, my waist, then slide around to my spine to pull me against him. I gasp, feeling every inch of him pressed against me, every sharp breath, every tremble.

I undo the top few buttons of his shirt, just to feel his skin as he kisses me deeper, harder. He groans when my nails skim his chest under the fabric of his shirt, then my hands find the hem, slipping beneath it to feel the hard lines of muscle beneath smooth skin.

He lifts me onto the counter, our bodies tangled, mouths desperate. I forget the ache in my ankle and the guilt curling in my chest, because right now, all I know is him. His hands, his mouth, and the way he says my name like it's the only word he's ever wanted to speak.

"Tell me to stop," he pants against my neck.

I can't, so I don't.

My fingers dig into his shoulders as I pull him closer, and we drown in the heat of it, in the fire we've been stoking for far too long. My hands move to undo his pants, his fingers sliding up beneath my shirt, skating across bare skin, the moment poised to tip into something we can never take back.

Then a sharp knock slices through the room.

"Hello? Is someone in there?" It's Yvonne.

Mateo and I jolt apart, breathless and stunned. I slide off the counter, biting down a cry as my weight lands on my bad ankle. I wave him urgently toward a stall, and he moves quickly, disappearing behind the door and lifting his feet just as I smooth my hair, adjust my shirt, and brace myself against the counter.

Another knock. "Vaeda?"

I unlock the door and open it a crack, letting my most composed expression slide into place. "Sorry. I needed a moment to myself."

Yvonne frowns, her eyes narrowing as she scans past me into the bathroom. "Have you seen Mateo? He disappeared after we got off the floor."

"No idea," I say smoothly, then offer her a smile that's all teeth and silk. "But he has a knack for wandering."

She doesn't look convinced as she lingers. Behind me, Mateo stays silent, unseen, the air between us still potent with what almost happened. Then she turns on her heel with a huff and disappears back toward the ballroom.

I wait until Yvonne's footsteps retreat down the corridor, the echo of her heels clicking like a countdown to the moment I'm about to regret. The door swings shut behind me with a hollow thud, and silence folds in around me again. I don't move as I stand in the center of the bathroom, eyes locked on the mirror above the sink, watching my chest rise and fall like I've run a marathon.

A breath, two, then behind me, the stall creaks open. Mateo steps out, rumpled and flushed, his shirt half-buttoned and his hair an unruly mess from my hands. His eyes find mine in the mirror and hold, but neither of us speaks.

It should feel like shame or guilt, but the only thing coursing through my veins is need. My pulse drums in my ears, fast and chaotic, sounding like an ominous warning.

"I thought she wasn't going to leave," he mutters, dragging a hand through his hair.

I turn to face him slowly, hands still braced behind me against the sink. "She's suspicious."

"I don't care."

"You should."

He walks toward me slowly, as if we're picking up exactly where we left off. "Do you?"

I open my mouth to answer but no words come. Do I care? I should. Every instinct is screaming at me to push him back again. Not because I don't want him, but because I want him too much.

Instead of answering, I push past him and grab my clutch off the counter, and he doesn't stop me. We step out of the washroom together, one after the other, carefully choreographed like the countless routines we've danced, except this one is lined with peril. His hand doesn't brush mine and his gaze doesn't search for me again until we reach the edge of the ballroom floor.

The space is a mess of sequins and energy and the slow dissolution of the evening's final rounds. Adam and Kari are laughing near the water station, and Grace is still seated with Greyson, a program folded neatly in her lap, her smile warming when she sees me, but mine doesn't in return.

Yvonne is standing beside Greyson now, her hand resting lightly on Mateo's garment bag. She turns when she sees us, expression unreadable, and I wonder what exactly she suspects. Mateo steps toward them, slipping seamlessly back into the rhythm of the team. I linger behind, throat tight, hating how badly I want to hold on to the weight of him. To bottle it. To revisit that moment of wild abandon, but I know better. I always have.

I make it halfway across the ballroom before Greyson stands and intercepts me, his brows furrowed as he glances at my ankle. "You're limping again."

"I'm fine."

"You're not," he snaps. "Where's your crutch?" I stiffen and nod toward the wall, the crutch lying abandoned against it. He sighs, lowering his voice. "Vaeda, you're making it worse."

"You don't get to lecture me."

"I'm not lecturing," he says gently. "I'm reminding you that you'll not only lose your career, but you may never dance again if you keep this up." I look away, jaw clenched. "You've been pushing yourself too hard."

"I'm trying to make it through this for the team and our studio."

He doesn't argue, and that's worse somehow. Instead, he just places a steadying hand on my arm, and it's the first time I realize I'm shaking. "Go back to the hotel and rest. I'll finish loading the team out."

I nod mutely because he's right. My future hangs precariously on an injury I am ignoring because I so desperately want to protect my image. All because I don't want to remind my industry peers of how I ended my career, my dream, and the need to keep my ego intact.

The hotel room is dim when I hobble in on my one crutch, the curtains drawn against the burnished light of Paris at night. My body is a mess of adrenaline and dull pain, and all I want is silence, but silence doesn't come easily.

Not when my mouth still tingles from the feel of his. Not when I can still feel the press of his hips against my thighs, the tremble in his hands, the rawness in his voice when he whispered, *"Tell me to stop."*

I sit down on the edge of the bed and pull off my shoes slowly, carefully. My ankle throbs, but it's nothing compared to the ache spreading through my chest. I've lied to everyone. To Greyson. To Gerardo. To me. I'm not in control anymore.

When I finally crawl into bed, I leave the pill bottle on the dresser, unopened, and stare at it for a long time before turning off the lamp and lying back against cool sheets. I don't dream of the Eiffel Tower or our team's routine. Instead, I dream of a bathroom tryst and locked doors. Of a man with trembling hands and eyes that look at me like I'm the only thing he craves.

Of a man I can never have.

Chapter Twenty-Eight

Saturday morning arrives far too early. The sky is barely lit, the streets of Paris painted in soft grays and pinks as the city slowly stirs awake. My ankle is stiff and sore, a throb pulsing deep in the joint as I stretch it from beneath the duvet. I shower slowly, letting the hot water work out some of the pain in my body, but it does little for the ache curling behind my ribs.

Today is the final day and the most crucial. It's the ballroom final, the last chance for Yvonne and Mateo to prove themselves, for all of us to prove that Fusion Core deserves to be here.

I dress in black slacks and a cropped, fitted blazer, my blouse silk and deep emerald. Understated but elegant. Although no amount of tailoring can pull me together completely. Not when I'm unraveling from the inside out.

When I arrive at the venue, the hair and makeup suite is already buzzing. Curling irons hiss, and hair spray clouds the air. Stylists move like dancers themselves, weaving around the competitors, sculpting sleek buns and smoky eyes.

I step further into the room and instantly wish I hadn't. Mateo and Yvonne are seated beside each other at the far end of the room. His eyes are crinkled at the corners, laughing at something she's just said. Her fingers reach up to adjust a curl at the base of his neck, lingering there longer than necessary, and my pulse stutters. I can't breathe. The air in the room feels thinner, laced with perfume and powder and jealousy.

I turn slowly, being careful with my ankle as my heel clicks against the marble floor. I went without the crutch today, as I spent most of the day yesterday without it. It's more of a hindrance than a help, and it would've made my escape cumbersome. Pushing out of the suite, my heart thundering inside my chest, I walk briskly into the corridor, head down, willing the sting behind my eyes to vanish. I can't let them see me like this. I can't let *him* see me like this.

But I don't make it far.

A hand grabs my wrist, spinning me fast. I gasp, barely catching my footing before I'm pressed to the cool plaster wall. Mateo's body cages mine in, his breath hot against my cheek, and his eyes burning.

"What the hell are you doing?" I hiss, but my voice is shaky.

He doesn't answer. He just crushes his mouth to mine, and I melt.

I try not to. I try to be strong, but the second his lips touch mine, it's like striking a match to gasoline. Heat floods every nerve, and my fingers fist the lapels of his jacket as he kisses me like he's been starving. Like he needs me more than oxygen.

When he finally pulls away, his breath is ragged, his voice low and wrecked. "I dreamed of you last night." My heart stutters. "And when we win this thing," he says, his forehead resting against mine. "I want to celebrate with you. Alone."

I don't answer. I can't. Not when the walls I've tried so hard to rebuild are falling again, one whisper at a time.

His hands slide down my arms before he lets go, retreating just enough to look at me. His gaze is saturated with a mixture of hope and hunger, or maybe it's just love in its most dangerous form. Then he's gone, footsteps echoing down the corridor, leaving me pressed to the wall, breathless and shaken.

I look up and down the corridor and release a breath. No one is here, and I'm lucky it's so early. We're becoming increasingly reckless, and there's going to come a point where we explode and incinerate everyone around us.

The ballroom is electric.

It thrums with anticipation, every seat filled, and every breath held. Camera flashes go off like strobe lights, illuminating the gleaming floor and the final number about to unfold. The grand finals. The showstopper. Our Paso Doble.

I stand just off to the side near Greyson and Grace, my arms folded, though not for warmth. My ankle is already screaming, yet my entire focus is on Mateo and Yvonne entering the floor. He wears a midnight black suit, open at the collar, his hair slicked back, eyes fierce and sharp as a blade. She's in crimson red, the kind of color that eats light and demands attention, but no matter how dazzling she looks, it's him I can't take my eyes off of.

He's no longer the hesitant student who first walked into my studio. He's a force. The music crashes into the room like a wave, and they begin. Their Paso is similar to a battle. Every movement is calculated, and every beat devoured. He drives forward. She yields, then strikes. They're fire and resistance, command and defiance. The crowd gasps when he drops her into a knee sweep and pulls her back up in one fluid motion, and I nearly forget to breathe.

They twist, charge, circle each other like predators, and when they hit that final pose with his hand gripping her wrist and her back arched in surrender, I feel every part of my body tighten.

For a moment, there's nothing but silence, then the ballroom erupts with applause like thunder. Judges stand as cheers ripple through the walls of the venue. Even Greyson whistles beside me, his face alight with pride.

I forget everything. The pain, the rules, and the distance I've tried so hard to keep.

I drop my weight onto my feet, the sharp lance of pain from my ankle ignored. My heart is doing double time as I move without thinking, slipping around the judges' table, ignoring Grace's gasp behind me. All I know is I need to reach him.

Mateo turns just as I break through the dancers and coaches gathered at the edge. Our eyes lock as I run the last steps and throw my arms around him. He catches me midair, laughing, arms wrapped tight as he lifts me clean off the ground and spins me once, twice.

"You were unreal," I whisper, my lips near his ear. "Absolutely, impossibly unreal."

He doesn't set me down right away. Instead, he breathes me in and pulls back to look at me. "We did it," he says, voice rough, eyes glittering. "I danced that for you."

I bury my face into his neck, the adrenaline, pride, and forbidden joy all crashing at once. People are watching and cameras are everywhere, but none of it matters. For this one moment, there's only us, and I don't care who sees.

MATEO

My pulse pounds in my ears, adrenaline and disbelief colliding as Vaeda's arms remain wrapped around my neck. She came willingly, her laughter ringing in my ears, and the bright sparkle of excitement shining in her eyes. For once, there's no hesitation between us, no careful restraint or guarded glances. Just Vaeda in my arms, joy illuminating her entire face.

The world around us fades into a blur of color and noise. All that exists is this moment, her heartbeat against my chest, her breath warm against my neck.

"You did it," she whispers, her voice thick with emotion, sending shivers racing down my spine.

"We did it," I correct her, smiling as I set her down gently, careful to steady her as she winces slightly from the pain in her ankle.

She smiles through it, eyes locking onto mine for a heartbeat longer than necessary. I wish I could capture that look, hold on to it forever.

Yvonne joins us, practically vibrating with excitement. Her eyes are alight with triumph and cheeks flushed from exertion. "That was incredible, Mateo!"

"You both were extraordinary," Vaeda says genuinely, nodding at Yvonne before her gaze drifts back to mine. Pride shines there, bright and pure. It feels like redemption, not just professionally, but personally.

Greyson approaches with Grace at his side. Both are grinning from ear to ear, and Grace's proud smile feels like forgiveness after a year of silence and pain. Her eyes are misty when she embraces me, murmuring into my ear, "I knew you'd find your way back."

The overhead speakers crackle softly, and we

instinctively quiet, anticipation gripping us.

"Ladies and gentlemen, dancers, please gather at the edge of the floor. The judges' final scores and placements for the International Ballroom and Latin Championship Adult Division will now be announced."

The murmur of excitement builds like an electric current throughout the ballroom. My heart speeds up, nerves tangling in my gut. Vaeda reaches out subtly, her fingertips brushing mine. A silent support. A secret strength.

Yvonne's hand grips mine tightly on the other side, her breath quick and uneven. "Whatever happens, I'm glad you are my partner," she rasps.

"Me too." My voice trembles, thick with sincerity.

The announcer begins calling the placements, starting from tenth place, slowly building up tension in the air. Every couple's name is met with cheers and applause, each step closer making my breath hitch.

"Third place… representing Académie de Pas Dorés from France… Antoine Leclerc and Elise Martin!"

My heart thuds painfully inside my chest as the French couple bows gracefully to thunderous applause.

"Second place… representing Studio Ritmo Ardente from Italy… Lorenzo Ricci and Sofia Conti!"

The roar of the crowd swells, deafening in my ears as the elegant couple steps forward, receiving their medals.

Yvonne squeezes my hand tightly, her knuckles white. Vaeda's eyes lock with mine again, her breath shallow, her pulse visibly racing in her throat.

"And first place, your champions for this year's International Ballroom and Latin Championship Adult Division, representing Fusion Core Dance Studio from New York, United States…"

Time seems to stop as blood pounds fiercely in my ears. My entire body is a taut wire, ready to snap.

"Mateo Sanchez and Yvonne Cardenas!"

The words explode through the ballroom, echoing like thunder. A roar erupts around us, the entire audience rising to their feet as confetti bursts overhead, glittering down around us in shimmering waves of silver and gold.

Yvonne screams in joy, leaping into my arms, tears streaming down her face. I spin her, laughter mingling with disbelief as applause crashes around us. Grace cheers loudly, tears streaking her face, and Greyson beams like a proud father, but it's Vaeda who draws my eye again, her gaze fixed on me, her lips parted slightly. Tears glisten along her lashes, pride and relief radiating from her in palpable waves.

This victory is ours. Ours as dancers, as survivors, as people pulled together by something greater than any of us.

The official approaches with medals gleaming, and my hands tremble as I bow my head, feeling the cool weight of gold drape around my neck. Yvonne receives hers, her joy infectious as photographers flash their cameras, capturing every euphoric moment.

I turn to Vaeda, heart hammering, and she moves toward me, stepping deliberately despite her pain. Her hands cup my cheeks, and she whispers softly, "I always believed in you."

My arms wrap around her once more, holding her close, drowning in the victory, in the moment, in the certainty that this feeling—this redemption, this joy—is everything I've fought for.

Everything I risked losing. Everything I refuse to let go of ever again.

The grand ballroom sparkles with an elegance reserved for winners, sunlight streaming through massive windows, gilded frames glistening, and chandeliers scattering fragments of light across the marble floor. Every moment feels surreal, wrapped in the undeniable sweetness of triumph. Laughter and voices hum warmly around me, punctuated by the rhythmic flash of cameras capturing memories that will last forever.

Grace squeezes my hand, her eyes shimmering with tears of pride as we step in front of the photographer. She leans into me, her arm comfortably wrapped around my waist, and for the first time in over a year, my heart feels whole.

"Smile!" the photographer calls, the bright flash illuminating the pure joy etched on our faces.

"I'm so proud of you," Grace murmurs, turning to hug me tightly once more. Her embrace holds forgiveness, understanding, and the hope of a healed bond.

Pulling out my phone, my fingers tremble slightly as I tap on my parents' contact. Within seconds, their smiling faces fill the screen, and my mother's tearful laughter brings warmth to my chest.

"You were incredible, Mateo!" she exclaims, her voice choked with emotion. My father, usually stoic and composed, grins widely, his eyes glistening suspiciously. "Greyson sent us all the videos."

"We're proud of you," my father says, clearing his throat, his voice roughened by unspoken emotion. "You did it."

My chest tightens at his words, feeling the weight of their forgiveness, their pride. "Thank you for believing in me again. I wouldn't have made it here without you."

"Of course you would," my father insists gently. "We just needed to learn how to believe again."

My mother touches the screen as if reaching for me. "Enjoy your day, Mateo. You deserve this moment."

"I love you both," I say softly, the truth of it profound and powerful. They smile warmly, sending kisses through the phone before ending the call, leaving me filled with deep contentment.

Turning, I find Greyson and Vaeda standing nearby, quietly sharing their own proud smiles. Stepping toward them, gratitude floods me. They are the reason I am here today. Their guidance, their patience, and their willingness to take a risk on me changed everything.

"Greyson," I start, emotion catching briefly in my throat. He meets my gaze, eyes crinkling at the corners with genuine warmth. "I can't thank you enough for believing in me. For fighting to give me a place when I had nowhere else to turn."

Greyson doesn't hesitate, stepping forward and pulling me into a firm, supportive hug. "You've earned every bit of this success, Mateo. Never doubt that."

When he steps back, Vaeda remains, eyes soft with unspoken emotion. Her posture is perfect and poised, but I can sense the vulnerability beneath her careful composure. My heart races as I step closer, our gazes locking.

"Vaeda," I rasp, my voice thick with sincerity. "None of this would have been possible without you. You didn't just teach me how to dance again, you reminded me how to live."

She inhales sharply, her cheeks coloring gently, eyes glistening as my words settle between us. Before she can respond, before propriety and rules can intervene, I lean down and press a gentle kiss to her cheek.

Her skin is warm beneath my lips, her breath hitching softly. When I pull away, her eyes are wide, vulnerable, and filled with a beautiful complexity I ache to unravel.

"Thank you," I whisper, holding her gaze a beat longer before stepping back.

The moment hangs delicately between us, filled with meaning and promise, before voices around us interrupt, drawing us back into the joyful chaos of celebration.

Chapter Twenty-Nine

The fading Parisian sun casts a soft glow through my hotel window. Outside, the city hums quietly, alive with the possibilities of twilight. Yet, within these walls, an unsettling quiet surrounds me, each heartbeat echoing with uncertainty.

I stand in front of the ornate full-length mirror, adjusting my dress, my fingers trembling slightly. The vibrant red fabric hugs my curves, reminding me of days when confidence wasn't something I had to feign. Today feels different, potent with both promise and regret. Beneath the dress, delicate lace whispers secrets only I know, the scarlet lingerie like a private declaration. A pledge to myself, a decision made.

The shrill ring of my phone breaks the tense silence, and my heart clenches at the familiar name glowing softly on the screen.

Taking a steadying breath, I pick up. "Hey," I answer softly, the forced warmth in my voice sounding foreign even to my ears.

"Mi amor," Gerardo's voice resonates gently, filled

with unmistakable excitement. "I've missed you terribly. My flight arrives early tomorrow morning."

Guilt pierces my chest, sharp and sudden, leaving me breathless. I swallow thickly, pressing fingertips to my forehead to ease the pounding ache forming there. "I'll meet you at the airport."

"Perfect," he replies, oblivious to the turmoil twisting within me. "We can have breakfast together at that small cafe, just like the first time we were in Paris. It'll be beautiful, Vaeda."

His hopefulness tightens my throat, tears threatening to blur my vision. The thought of breaking his heart seems impossible, yet necessary. The truth sits heavy on my tongue, waiting for release.

"Vaeda?" Gerardo asks gently, sensing the lingering pause. "Are you alright?"

"I'm just tired," I lie, the words sour but necessary. "I'll see you tomorrow, Gerardo. Have a safe flight."

"I love you, Vaeda."

My heart twists painfully. "I'll see you soon."

Ending the call feels final, like closing a chapter of my life I'm ready to leave behind completely. I take a shuddering breath, the weight of my decision settling fully upon me. My marriage had once been something precious, a bond forged through mutual ambition, friendship, and comfort, but comfort isn't passion. Comfort isn't love, not in the way my heart yearns for now.

Mateo's face flashes through my mind, his intensity, the fire that burns in his eyes, and the sincerity that vibrates in his every touch. I see him clearly, his quiet strength, the vulnerability beneath his resolve, the way his gaze lights a fire in my soul I thought had been extinguished forever.

Turning back toward my luggage, my fingers trace over

the satin and lace hidden beneath my dress. This isn't about seduction or temptation. It's a promise to myself, a willingness to embrace whatever the night holds without fear or regret. I refuse to push him away again, to deny the powerful current that has bound us so irrevocably.

I slip into delicate heels, their elegance disguising the ache still lingering in my ankle. Ignoring the dull throb as I straighten my shoulders, I take in my reflection with fresh determination. Tonight, I'm choosing the path my heart has already traveled. Tonight, I'm stepping fully into the unknown, unafraid, and ready to accept whatever consequences await.

With a final glance at my reflection, I gather my small clutch and step toward the door. Each step forward feels like liberation, like shedding the past to embrace a future uncertain yet thrilling.

Tonight, for better or worse, I'll let fate guide me. If that fate brings me into Mateo's arms, I will surrender fully, knowing that in his embrace lies the truth of my heart, the undeniable pull of destiny, and the fierce, all-consuming love I've been denying myself for far too long.

Stepping into the restaurant feels like entering a carefully painted dream. The warm glow of antique chandeliers cascades softly across marble floors polished to perfection, casting reflections that ripple like whispers beneath my steps. Tables are arranged artfully around the room, draped with pristine white linens and flickering candles nestled within crystal holders scattering gentle, golden light.

I move carefully, acutely aware of my aching ankle, the sharp stabs of pain intensifying with each measured step. I refuse to give in to it, gritting my teeth subtly to mask the discomfort. Tonight is about celebrating, and nothing, not even the throbbing reminder of my limitations, can detract from that.

At a table tucked in a semi-private alcove by expansive floor-to-ceiling windows, the rest of our group is already gathered. Greyson rises first, dressed impeccably in a tailored charcoal suit, his hair neatly styled, looking every inch the poised gentleman. His smile warms instantly when he spots me, filled with both welcome and quiet concern, ever the friend and protector.

"Vaeda, you look breathtaking," Greyson murmurs, giving my arm a gentle, reassuring squeeze.

"Thank you," I reply softly, grateful for his enduring friendship.

Adam and Kari sit side by side, their faces bright with the lingering excitement of the day's success. Adam's crisp white shirt and dark trousers pair effortlessly with Kari's emerald gown, the color vibrant against her glowing skin, her hair elegantly curled and cascading around her shoulders.

Yvonne sits across from them, her expression carefully neutral, though tension tightens her jaw slightly as she spots me. Her dress, a striking sapphire blue, clings to her figure with an elegance designed to command attention. Her makeup is flawless, enhancing her natural beauty, but her narrowed eyes betray the jealousy simmering beneath her composed exterior.

Then my eyes meet Mateo's, and the entire room fades into insignificance. He's seated near the head of the table, dressed in a perfectly tailored suit, the dark fabric contrasting beautifully against his tanned skin. His shirt is open slightly at the collar, revealing just a hint of the muscular chest beneath. His golden eyes drink me in slowly, deliberately, igniting a fire deep within my belly that burns away every ounce of uncertainty.

I feel exposed yet empowered under his scrutiny, the

silk of my dress whispering against my skin like a caress. My breath catches subtly when he stands, tall and impossibly graceful, his gaze never leaving mine as he pulls out the chair beside him.

"Vaeda," he says softly, his voice rich like velvet. "You look incredible."

Heat floods my cheeks, though I hold his gaze steadily. "Thank you."

I feel the eyes of the table shifting between us, curiosity and tension dancing in the air, but the only reaction that truly matters is Mateo's. The quiet intensity in his gaze, and the way his eyes linger on the subtle curve of my lips, my exposed collarbone, and my slender waist.

He reaches out a hand, steady and confident, guiding me gently into the chair beside him. His fingertips brush lightly against my bare shoulder, sending a jolt of awareness down my spine, then he leans slightly closer, his breath warm against my ear as he murmurs, "Are you alright?"

"I'm fine," I whisper back, the words barely audible as I hold on to composure with fragile determination.

Across the table, Yvonne's expression darkens perceptibly, her lips tightening into a thin line. Her jealousy is palpable, radiating in subtle waves that only heighten the charged atmosphere. I feel a pang of regret. She is young and hopeful, caught in the cross fire of something much larger than herself, but my heart refuses to yield to sympathy entirely, not when every nerve in my body is screaming in awareness of Mateo beside me.

The soft hum of conversation begins to pick up around us, the clinking of glasses and gentle laughter breaking the initial tension. Yet, the charged energy between Mateo and me remains undeniable and electric. His knee brushes gently against mine beneath the table, and my pulse quickens, the simple contact setting every nerve ending alight.

The evening progresses beautifully, filled with stories, laughter, and the subtle undercurrents of restrained desire. Every glance Mateo sends my way is a silent promise, an unspoken acknowledgment of what simmers so dangerously beneath our carefully maintained facades. My heart races each time our eyes meet as the room around us fades away until there's only him, his closeness, his warmth, and his quiet, powerful presence.

As dessert plates are cleared away and glasses refilled, Mateo leans close once more, his voice a velvet murmur intended only for me. "Later tonight, Vaeda… will you meet me?"

His words ripple through me, leaving warmth and anticipation in their wake. "Yes," I breathe out, the admission both frightening and thrilling in equal measure.

The weight of the decision settles deeply into my heart, mingling with guilt, excitement, and an intense longing. Mateo's gaze softens, satisfied yet yearning, his eyes holding promises I desperately want him to fulfill.

Tonight, boundaries will blur, consequences will be forgotten, and nothing else will matter except the man sitting beside me, the man whose eyes hold my future, my heart, and the key to everything I've been missing.

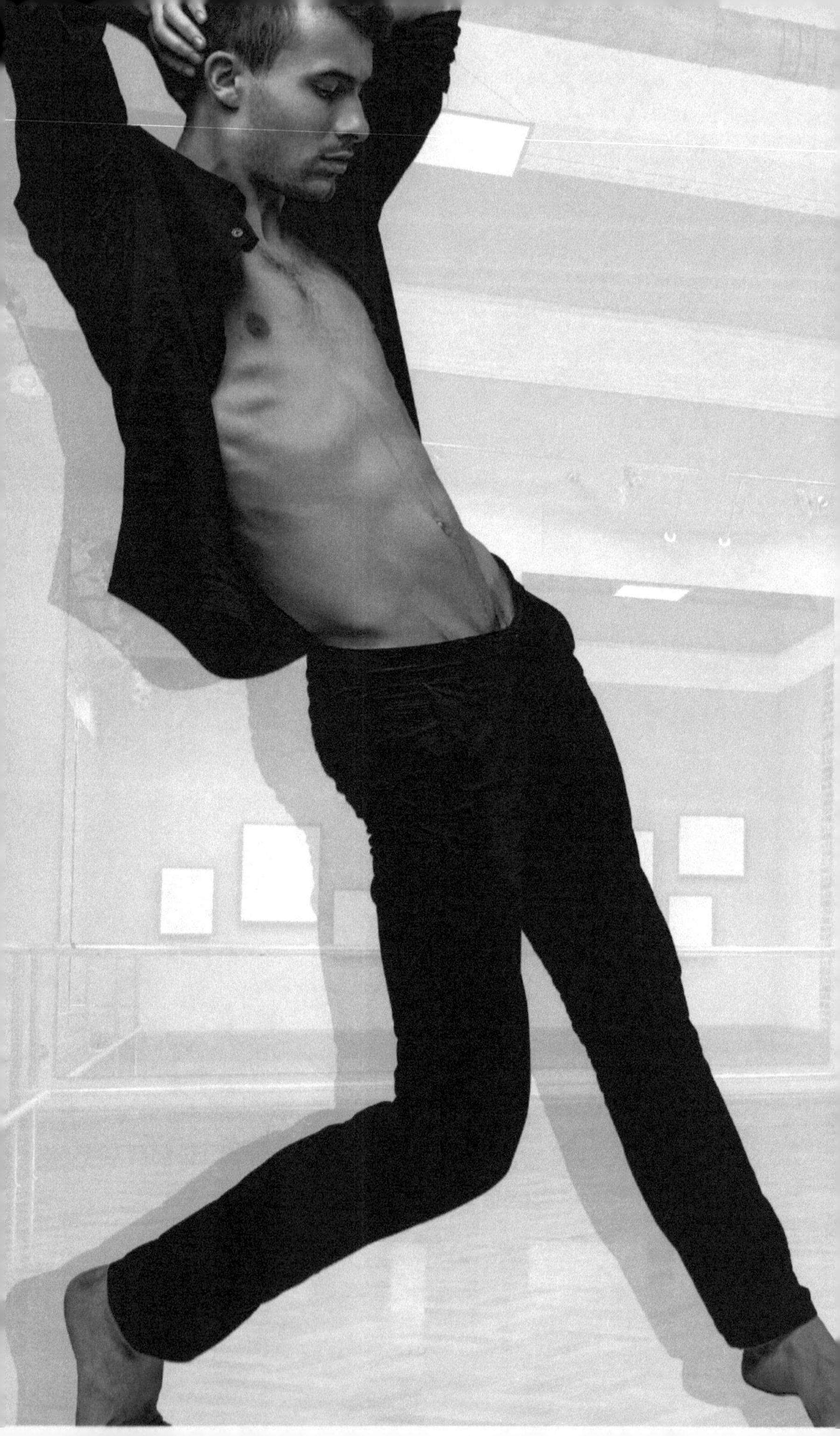

MATEO

The energy around our table surges, laughter bubbling over glasses clinking in celebration. Adam raises his drink, eyes gleaming with excitement. "We need to go dancing tonight! We deserve it after today."

Kari nods eagerly, her cheeks flushed from the exhilaration of the evening. "Yes! Let's go celebrate in style."

I turn to Vaeda instinctively, hope blooming inside my chest. Her eyes meet mine, the warmth in them softening, but beneath it lies hesitation.

"Vaeda," I say softly, almost privately amidst the joyful noise. "Come out with us?"

She pauses for a moment, her gaze flicking briefly downwards. A subtle shadow crosses her features, one I immediately recognize as pain. When she looks up again, her smile is gentle but apologetic. "I wish I could, but my ankle…" she trails off quietly, regret lingering in her voice.

Disappointment settles inside my chest, but I nod in understanding. Her injury remains an unspoken challenge, a stubborn reminder of the sacrifices she's made. Before the wave of frustration overtakes me completely, Vaeda leans in closer, her hand discreetly resting on mine beneath the table.

"But you can come to my room later," she whispers, her breath warm against my ear, sending shivers down my spine. She discreetly slips a key card into my palm, her room number clearly printed on it. My pulse quickens.

"Okay," I reply, my voice thick with anticipation. Her smile grows deeper, brighter, and I feel a rush of warmth radiate through my veins.

Yvonne's sharp eyes catch our brief exchange, suspicion flickering behind her polished expression, but she quickly masks it, lifting her glass to her lips with a forced nonchalance.

We all stand, laughter and conversation rising as we step outside into the Parisian night. The air is crisp, the city glowing under a canopy of stars, and the Eiffel Tower sparkles brilliantly in the distance, casting its iconic golden hue over the city.

Vaeda slips into a cab, her eyes filled with discomfort as she favors her injured ankle. Greyson leans in and says something to her, making her eyes light up with humor. Sometimes I watch them and their easy friendship and wish I could get those same reactions from her. For too long, we've hidden our true feelings away, and on the surface, we look nothing more than teacher and student. Hopefully, her decision to ask me to her room tonight means that's all changed. I pray it means she's choosing me now.

We arrive at Le Duplex, the lively rhythm of music already thrumming through its doors, vibrating beneath our feet as we approach. The club radiates energy, a beacon of neon lights and pulsing beats, welcoming us eagerly into its embrace.

Inside, the atmosphere is intoxicating. Laser lights sweep across the expansive dance floor, slicing through clouds of artificial mist. Bodies move in perfect synchrony to the deep bass as laughter and cheers mingle seamlessly with the vibrant rhythm. The DJ, positioned high above the throng, orchestrates the night's energy with ease, hands raised and head bobbing in sync with the music.

Adam pulls Kari into the crowd immediately, their laughter swallowed by the music. Greyson chuckles beside me, taking in the vibrant chaos, but eventually leans over, patting my shoulder affectionately.

"I think this old man is going to tap out!" he shouts above the noise, his eyes warm and amused. "I may have bitten off more than I can chew here. Enjoy yourself, Mateo. You've earned it."

I smile gratefully, watching him weave his way gracefully toward the exit, his suit jacket thrown casually over his shoulder.

Yvonne slides closer to me, her movements fluid, effortlessly matching the beat. Her eyes meet mine, filled with longing and hope. I smile warmly but keep a subtle distance, my thoughts inevitably drifting back to Vaeda waiting for me back at the hotel. Yet I allow myself to become part of the pulsing mass, the music carrying my body, offering a brief distraction.

We dance through song after song, the club becoming hotter, the energy more frenetic. I let the music seep into my bones, clearing away the lingering tension and nerves from the day's competition. Even amidst the neon haze and ecstatic beats, thoughts of Vaeda tug persistently at my heart. Her face, her smile, and her touch are never far from my mind.

Yvonne has been back and forth from the bar, and her movements are becoming sloppier, her breath saturated with the shots she's taking. I'm not one to judge, but I don't want to see her become blackout drunk and have something bad happen to her.

Eventually, Yvonne leans close, breathless and smiling, shouting over the thundering bass. "Glad we did this! We needed this."

"Me too," I admit, a genuine warmth in my smile. Yet a glance toward the exit, the anticipation of seeing Vaeda again, pulls at me powerfully. "Maybe you should take it easy with the shots?"

Her head tips back on a laugh as her hand slips into mine, pulling me toward the bar. "Let's get water." Her suggestion settles my concerns slightly as we weave in close to the bar.

She leans over the counter and brings her face close to the bartender's, telling him what she wants. I lean against the bar and look out at the crowd just as Adam and Kari approach us. Both are red-faced and sweating, their expressions filled with euphoria. For the first time, I wonder if they're a couple, and if they think Yvonne and I are seeing each other too.

"Mateo!" Yvonne grabs my arm and turns me around, grinning maniacally as she hands me a shot glass. "It's tequila!"

My stomach flips as my breath gets trapped inside my chest, and I try to swallow but my throat isn't working. Yvonne takes her shot and slams the glass on the counter, then looks at me expectantly. I can't believe this is happening, that she's disregarding my sobriety.

After a few more seconds, Adam grabs my shot and downs it, giving me a look of disappointment. "Dude, that was lame," he chastises. "I got the next round."

Adam shoves closer to the bar as Yvonne and Kari laugh together, both of them oblivious to my internal turmoil. Instead of yelling at Yvonne like she deserves, I turn on my heel and push through the crowd toward the exit.

I step out into the cooler night air and suck in a breath, hoping to calm my racing heart. Anger and embarrassment burn through me as I stand there, looking up at the clear sky. Soon, I begin to feel betrayed by Yvonne's actions. She was supposed to be my friend, the only one who knew about my sobriety tonight, and she let me down.

My thoughts turn to Vaeda, who has always been an advocate for my well-being, and my anger dissipates. I head toward the hotel as my heart races faster, anticipation blooming into eagerness. My footsteps quicken instinctively, drawn irresistibly toward Vaeda, toward the promise waiting in her eyes and her whispered words.

CHAPTER THIRTY

Mateo

The hotel hallway is dimly lit, the elegant sconces emanating soft, golden pools of light onto the plush carpet. My heart thuds erratically, matching the rapid rhythm of my footsteps as I step from the elevator, anticipation like a physical ache deep inside my chest. The sleek key card sits cool in my palm, the numbers etched upon it feeling like the gateway to a future I'm both desperate and afraid to embrace.

Every step toward her room quickens my pulse, excitement tangling with apprehension. The memory of the club, of Yvonne's betrayal, still simmers beneath my skin, but even that can't compete with the overwhelming pull toward Vaeda. She has become my magnetic north, and I'm helplessly drawn, unable to resist the allure of her presence any longer.

I pause in front of her door, number 1108 gleaming subtly under the muted hallway lights. My breath catches as I slide the card into the lock, the beep granting access like a whispered promise. The door clicks open, and I step inside, immediately enveloped in the soft, familiar scent of her perfume. It's a delicate mixture of vanilla and jasmine that wraps around me like a caress.

My eyes roam over her room, the neatly made bed with

its pristine white linens, and the small table beside it cluttered with Vaeda's belongings. My gaze catches on the prescription bottle, standing stark and ominous against the polished wood surface.

I approach hesitantly, my stomach tightening with unease as I pick it up, the cool plastic familiar and uncomfortable in my palm. My eyes skim over the label, my heart freezing as the words "Vaeda Lewis–Hydrocodone-Acetaminophen, take one tablet every six hours for pain" glare back at me. My throat tightens painfully, a wave of nausea rolling through my stomach.

Hydrocodone. My stomach tightens at the sight, an involuntary ache reminding me of darker days. I place the bottle down gently, heart racing slightly as concern for Vaeda mingles sharply with my own complicated past. I try to shake away the memories as I place the key card and my cell phone down, pulling me firmly back to the present.

Yet, amidst the churning dread, my heart stutters with empathy. Vaeda is in pain, physically and emotionally, and suddenly, my struggle feels mirrored by her own. I also know the dangerous path this medication can carve, and the thought of her caught in its relentless grip sends cold fear skittering down my spine.

The sound of running water from the bathroom registers in my awareness, halting my scattered thoughts. The soft rush abruptly cuts off, replaced by a silence that rings loudly in my ears. My pulse picks up, nervous excitement weaving seamlessly with concern.

A few moments later, the bathroom door creaks open slightly, steam drifting out into the dimly lit bedroom. My breath catches sharply, every nerve in my body hyper-aware of her proximity. Vaeda steps into view, wrapped in a plush white hotel towel, her wet hair cascading in dark waves around her shoulders. Her gaze meets mine instantly, eyes wide and uncertain.

"Mateo," she breathes out, surprise coloring her tone, her gaze flicking briefly toward the bedside table.

My heart thuds heavily against my ribs. "I hope it's okay that I let myself in."

She nods, biting her bottom lip slightly, the action sparking heat low in my belly despite the lingering worry. "Of course. I wanted you to come."

We stand frozen, silence stretching taut between us, loaded with desire, but something shadows her eyes, a flicker of vulnerability she tries to mask behind a soft, hesitant smile.

"Vaeda," I begin gently, stepping closer, the space between us shrinking with every heartbeat. "Are you okay?"

She swallows visibly, her eyes flickering away momentarily before returning to hold my gaze. "I'm fine. It's just… my ankle is still giving me trouble."

Her admission feels honest, yet incomplete. I reach out slowly, gently brushing damp strands of hair from her cheek, my thumb softly grazing her jawline. Her breath hitches, the subtle reaction igniting a fire within me that battles fiercely against my concern.

"You're in pain," I murmur softly, my eyes searching hers deeply. "I saw the prescription."

Vaeda's eyes widen briefly in panic before she quickly composes herself, offering a reassuring smile. "I'm only taking it if the pain becomes too much. I promise."

Her assurance does little to calm the anxious churn in my gut, but I push aside my fears for the moment. I shouldn't project my faults onto her. Just because I could never handle taking just one, doesn't mean she can't. Tonight is about us and finally giving in to the pull she's fought desperately against, the undeniable connection that pulses between us.

"Come here," she whispers, stepping into my embrace, her slender arms slipping around my neck. The feel of her body pressed close is electrifying, dissolving any lingering doubts. Her lips find mine, soft, warm, and insistent. I lose myself in her, in the taste of her kiss, the heat of her body, and the gentle tremors that ripple beneath my hands.

"Vaeda..." Her name falls from my lips like a prayer, filled with reverence and longing.

Her kiss is tender, yet hesitant, as if she's afraid to break the fragile spell enveloping us. My hand slides down, fingers tracing along her neck and over her shoulder, before settling at her waist. The towel shifts slightly, causing my breath to hitch at the bare softness of her skin beneath my touch.

Our kiss deepens as passion slowly builds like embers igniting into flames. Her arms tighten around my neck, pulling me impossibly closer, her body molding perfectly against mine. I lift her effortlessly, carrying her toward the bed, our mouths never separating as I lay her down gently.

"I want you," she whispers against my mouth, her words fueling a fire that threatens to consume us both. Her eyes search mine, vulnerable yet fiercely certain.

"You have me," I answer softly, sincerity saturating every word. "All of me, Vaeda."

I slowly pull away the towel, my breath catching at the perfection of her body beneath me. My fingertips trail over her curves, mapping her skin like sacred terrain, memorizing every inch. Her hands reach for me, gently guiding my clothes away, discarding layers until there's nothing separating us.

Her breath quickens, matching the rapid rhythm of my heart. I take my time, savoring every sigh, every gasp that escapes her lips, imprinting them into memory. We move together, our bodies blending seamlessly, each motion a silent vow. Our breaths mingle with whispers of affection and vulnerability filling the space between us.

"I need you," she murmurs, her fingers threading through my hair as she pulls me closer, deeper into her embrace.

Every touch is exquisite torture, every kiss a revelation. Our bodies become poetry, a dance choreographed by the deepest parts of our souls. The moment I sink inside of her, pleasure surges through us, intense and beautiful, shattering every wall we've built. And when we reach the edge together, tumbling over in perfect harmony, it feels as though I'm seeing clearly for the very first time. The world around us fades, leaving only Vaeda and the profound certainty that this is exactly where I'm meant to be.

We lie tangled together afterward, our breathing slowly evening out. Her head rests against my chest, her fingers tracing gentle patterns over my heart. My hand gently strokes her hair, my other arm wrapped protectively around her slender frame.

Turning her face gently up to mine, I brush the hair from her cheek, eyes locking onto hers. My heart pounds, vulnerability gripping me tightly, yet I know these words are unstoppable.

"I love you, Vaeda," I whisper, my voice filled with absolute certainty and raw emotion.

Her eyes widen slightly, a shadow flickering across them, but she says nothing. The silence between us stretches painfully, yet I hold her gaze, unwavering. Her silence echoes in my heart, a stark contrast to the truth I've just offered so openly.

Still, she remains quiet, her response lost somewhere behind her unreadable eyes.

VAEDA

The moment he says the words, I want so badly to say them back. I've made the decision to end my marriage, but Gerardo doesn't know that yet. I want to be able to tell him it's over, to have everything finalized before I say those words to Mateo.

Most of all, I want to mean them.

I know my feelings run deep for the man who's looking into my eyes, searching for a reciprocation that's sealed inside my chest. There's no right or wrong way to end a marriage and start a relationship with someone else. It's a different journey for everyone.

"I need just a little more time," I whisper as his eyes widen and his expression grows slack with surprise.

"What?" His voice is hoarse as he sits up, letting the blanket fall away from his body. "You're choosing him again."

"No." I reach out to touch his arm, but he pulls away from me, his face a mask of agony. "That's not it. I have some things to work out with Gerardo tomorrow—"

"What?" he yells as he scrambles out of the bed, his devastation evident in the heaving of his chest with every breath. "He's coming here? Did you invite him here? You wanted to have your fun with me first, right?"

His words are ripping a hole inside my chest with how hurt he sounds, and I begin to tremble as he haphazardly pulls on his clothes.

"He always knew about the competition, and he decided to come here before I decided this—"

"Before you decided to fuck me and shred my heart into tiny pieces!" he bellows as tears run down his cheeks.

"No!" I throw off the blankets and get out of bed, approaching him with my hands out. "No, that's not it."

"You keep pulling me in, and the moment I become putty in your hands, you shove me away. You act like you feel sorry for your husband, that you want to be with me, but all you want is to have your cake and eat it too." He swipes his cell phone off the table as I grab the sheet off the bed to wrap around my body.

"Please," I beg him. "Just hear me out."

"I'm done!" he exclaims as I turn around, unable to look at him and the hatred brimming in his eyes for me. A sob escapes my throat as a bitter laugh sounds behind me.

"You had your fun with a young man, now you can continue your boring life with your old husband." His words are filled with vitriol, and when I turn to yell at him to listen to me, he's already halfway out my door.

"Mateo!" I call out to him, but he ignores me, letting the door shut behind him.

I sit on the edge of the bed as tears cloud my eyes, and I try to figure out how we got here. Saying how I feel has never come easy, and I've been spoiled by a husband like Gerardo who doesn't force me to be vulnerable, but I've been neglecting myself by sealing my heart off in this impenetrable vault.

Standing from the bed, I walk into the bathroom, my ankle protesting now that my adrenaline is waning. I turn on the faucet and stare at the running water as I begin to self-reflect on my behavior tonight. I'm going to be breaking my husband's heart tomorrow. Is it too much to want to wait until I've broken it off? Just to give the situation some dignity?

I chew my bottom lip as I cup my hands under the cool water and splash it over my heated face. It's doing nothing to soothe the shame coursing through my chest, but I ignore it as

I splash some more. I grew up in a cold household, with two people who became parents when they were barely out of high school. It meant I was raised in school, and during after-school activities is where I learned I loved dance.

I loved it so much that I made sure I was as close to perfect with it as I could be so I could escape my small town and my small-minded, incompetent parents. I know that's why I'm frigid, why whenever I'm on the verge of being vulnerable, I harden my walls.

Mateo doesn't deserve that though, and I need to go tell him that.

I dry my face off and shut off the water, the pain in my ankle slowly spreading up my calf. I've been trying to avoid taking another painkiller, but if I plan on facing the man who owns my heart, I'd rather do it without limping.

After getting dressed in a pair of leggings and an oversized sweater, I look to my bedside table for my pills. Only they're not there. I do a quick circle in the center of my room, looking for that orange bottle, but it's nowhere to be found. My heart begins to pound because I know I left it on the bedside table, the same side Mateo had placed his phone.

"Oh, no," I moan as I grab my cell phone from the desk and dial his number. When I get his voicemail, I forget about the pain in my ankle and run out of my room, my heart up in my throat.

Mateo took my pills.

I run barefoot, limping, and heart splitting open in real time. The corridor outside my room stretches like a tunnel, the carpet muffling the frantic slap of my footsteps. I barely feel the pain in my ankle now, the adrenaline drowning it beneath the tide of terror surging through me.

Mateo took my pills.

The realization rings in my head with every pound of

blood in my ears.

I jab at the elevator button a dozen times, my breath ragged, the walls pressing in around me. When it doesn't come fast enough, I throw open the stairwell door and start climbing, my legs burning, my injured foot screaming with each ascending step. I push past it though because there's no other option.

When I reach his floor, I stagger into the hallway, gripping the wall for balance, barely able to breathe. My fingers shake as I dial the front desk.

"Concierge," a man answers smoothly.

"I need you to unlock room 1414. Now," I gasp. "It's an emergency."

There's a pause. "Ma'am, I'm not authorized to—"

"It's Mateo Sanchez's room," I cry, choking on my words. "He might be overdosing. Please, I'm his emergency contact. I don't have time to argue!"

The urgency in my voice must land because the man responds quickly, "We're sending someone up immediately. Stay on the line."

I don't. I hang up and bang on the door with the side of my fist. "Mateo! Open the door!"

No answer. Just the cruel, sterile silence of a hotel hallway where people sleep peacefully in their rooms, oblivious to the world collapsing just feet away.

About five minutes later, a security guard rounds the corner with a key card in hand. "Miss, please step aside."

He unlocks the door and I bolt inside, breathless. The room is dim, the bedside lamp casting a soft, amber glow over a meticulously made bed. Empty. The silence rings loud in my ears.

"Mateo?" My voice is raw, trembling.

Then I see it. The bathroom door is ajar and the light is on. I push it open and the world ends.

Mateo is on the floor, his body curled awkwardly, shirt half on, and lips tinged blue. The pill bottle I searched for—my pill bottle—lies on its side by his outstretched fingers, every last tablet gone.

"No... no, no, no," I whisper, dropping to my knees beside him. "Mateo!"

I shake him, my hands gripping his face, his chest, anywhere I can touch him, as if I can will him awake. His skin is clammy, breath shallow, eyelids fluttering like he's stuck somewhere between here and gone.

"Come on, Mateo," I sob, cradling his head in my lap. "You stupid, beautiful boy, don't you dare do this. Not to me. Not after everything."

My fingers fumble for my phone as I scream over my shoulder. "Call an ambulance! Please, someone call an ambulance!"

The security guard is already on his radio. I can hear it, but it feels far away and distant, like I'm submerged underwater, watching this horror unfold through glass. The guard kneels beside me, checking for a pulse, and when he finds it, it's faint.

"Stay with me," I whisper, brushing hair from Mateo's damp forehead. "You don't get to leave. You hear me? You don't get to leave me."

The tears won't stop. They stream down my face, falling onto his chest, my hands trembling as I hold on to him like he's already slipping away. The paramedics arrive seconds later, though it feels like a lifetime. They pull me back gently, lifting him onto a stretcher, spraying something into his nose, and then covering his mouth with an oxygen mask.

"We need to go," one of them says urgently.

I follow them out of the room, my sweater soaked with sweat and tears, my legs numb beneath me. I don't remember taking the stairs and I don't remember speaking to anyone. I only remember the sight of his lifeless body on that cold tile floor and the unbearable thought that I might never hear his voice again.

That I might have waited too long.

That I might have cost him everything.

My hands still shake as I climb into the ambulance beside him, gripping his hand tightly.

"Don't you dare give up on me," I whisper, leaning down to press my forehead to his. "I love you. God, I love you. Please, please fight."

But he doesn't respond, and for the first time since I met him, Mateo Sanchez is completely and devastatingly lifeless.

EPILOGUE

Mateo

It begins as though I'm falling.

Not the kind where you trip and stumble. No, this is heavier, slower, like slipping beneath dark water, deeper and deeper until the light above is nothing more than a faded blur.

My chest burns and my throat is tight. My limbs are weightless and useless, twitching with delayed commands. I can hear something, a voice? No, sobbing. A familiar woman. It's Vaeda.

I try to move. I try to breathe, but everything hurts.

Regret swells in my gut like a tide I can't stop. I didn't want this. I just wanted the pain to go away, for the ache inside my chest and the storm in my mind to quiet long enough for me to think. To sleep. To not feel like I was splintering apart, molecule by molecule.

I should have stayed with her. Should've waited. Should've heard her out for what she was trying to tell me. Instead, I acted like the broken boy I swore I'd stopped being. I thought I was past that darkness. Past needing something to numb the chaos.

I wasn't.

My vision swims, and I catch flashes of bright lights and movement. The scream of a siren somewhere distant and sharp. Pain slices through my belly and ribs. I try to cry out, but nothing comes. My mouth is dry, and my tongue feels swollen and heavy.

"Come on, Mateo." Vaeda.

She's really here. She came. I want to open my eyes and tell her I'm sorry, that I didn't mean it, that I don't want to die. That I wanted her to love me, not to bury me.

I feel her fingers threading through my hair, her lips against my forehead. She's shaking, or maybe I am.

"Stay with me," she whispers. "You don't get to leave. You hear me? You don't get to leave me."

I see her for a moment, or maybe it's a memory. Her in the hallway, the first time she really smiled at me, her in the rehearsal studio, cheeks flushed from dancing with her hands on her hips, and her whispering my name like a prayer. I want to speak. I want to tell her she's everything, but I'm fading.

My heart, which once beat to the rhythm of music and her laughter, stutters, then slows.

There's more shouting. Male voices now. Firm, clipped commands. Something about vitals, Narcan, oxygen. Yet none of it touches me.

The world narrows as her hand finds mine, her tears dripping against my skin, and her voice breaking.

"I love you."

I try to squeeze her hand, but I can't. I try to hold on, but I'm slipping under. Darkness curls around me like a wave.

And then...

Nothing.

For all book updates and social platforms, check out my website

C.A. Rene lives in Toronto, Canada with her family, where most of the year varies from chilly to frigid. Most days you'll find her wrapped in her many blankets in bed while reading or writing her next dark, twisted story.

Her stories boast of inclusivity and refusal to be conformed in any small box. Writing across genres is a hobby and drinking wine is a must… Or coffee … with a splash of Baileys.

For all book updates and social platforms, check out my website

Also by C.A. Rene

The Whitsborough Chronicles
Through the Pain

Into Darkness

Finding the Light

To Redemption

The Whitsborough Progenies
Ivy's Venom

Carmelo's Malice

Saxon's Distortion

Gabriel's Deception

Desecrated Duet
Desecrated Flesh

Desecrated Essence

The Reaped Series
The Reaper Incarnate

Hunting the Reaper

Claiming the Reaper

Hail Mary Duet

Blue 42

Red Zone

Steel Dragons MC

Dragon Slayer

Dragon Strife

Dragon Scorch

Hell's March MC Duet

Hell's Viper

TBA

Fusion Core Duet

Tension

Release

Second Chance Standalones

Fighting the Tide

www.ingramcontent.com/pod-product-compliance
Lightning Source LLC
Chambersburg PA
CBHW021335310726
48971CB00001B/136